BLESSED BY A HIGHLAND CURSE

THE ORIGIN STORY

A MACKAY CLAN LEGEND - A SCOTTISH FANTASY ROMANCE
BOOK 1

MAEVE GREYSON

This is a work of fiction. Names, characters, places, and incidents either are the product of the author's imagination or are used fictitiously, and any resemblance to actual persons living or dead, business establishments, events, or locales, is entirely coincidental.

Blessed by a Highland Curse

COPYRIGHT © 2024 by Maeve Greyson

All rights reserved. No part of this book may be used or reproduced in any manner whatsoever without written permission of the author or Author Maeve Greyson LLC except in the case of brief quotations embodied in critical articles or reviews.

NO AI TRAINING: Without in any way limiting the author's [and publisher's] exclusive rights under copyright, any use of this publication to "train" generative artificial intelligence (AI) technologies to generate text is expressly prohibited. The author reserves all rights to license uses of this work for generative AI training and development of machine learning language models.

Contact Information: maeve@maevegreyson.com

Author Maeve Greyson LLC

55 W. 14th Street

Suite 101

Helena, MT 59601

https://maevegreyson.com/

Published in the United States of America

To the believers of the unexplainable...

CHAPTER 1

MacKay Keep
Scottish Highlands
Year of our Lord 1379

Hopeful, yet guarding his heart against yet another disappointment, Laird Caelan MacKay shifted in his chair. From his position on the dais at the head of the great hall, he kept his focus locked on the wide archway at the far end of the room, waiting for the lass they had found to be led in from the courtyard.

The MacKay banners of vibrant blue and green hanging on either side of the entrance gently shifted against the stone walls, as though just as eager to meet this latest possibility. Hushed conversations took place close by, like a nest of hissing adders, distracting him from the subject at hand. His advisors needed to cease their whispering like gossipy old hens and stand firm in this latest choice. Their uneasiness in this noble task he had assigned them did little to assure him they had finally gotten it right.

"Surely, she's the one, aye?" Fergus MacKay, Clan MacKay's war chief, said while sidling closer to Emrys, the druid advisor to the laird and keeper of the ancient magick.

Caelan tightened his grip on the carved arms of the chair, straining to hear old Emrys's reply even though he no longer needed it. The timid lass, escorted by her father, the mighty Cormac of Glen Marren, was not the one. He allowed himself a heavy sigh but held his tongue, studying her closer, and praying he was wrong. Perhaps once he saw her eyes, the curse would change its mind, and his heart would recognize her.

Emrys gave a quiet snorting groan. "A sign should have come from him by now," he told Fergus, then threw up a hand and turned aside. "I thought surely she would be the one."

The shy maiden eased her way down the center aisle between the long trestle tables and benches that filled the cavernous gathering room designed not only for feeding and celebrating the clan but hearing their grievances. Her hesitant steps barely stirred the fresh rushes spread across the flagstones. She stole a nervous glance back at her father who had halted at the entrance and sent her onward alone.

Her sire gave her a stern nod, silently ordering her to continue.

She turned back toward the dais once more but kept her head bowed as, once again, she took up the path toward Caelan.

He narrowed his eyes and reached out with all of his senses, wishing his instincts were somehow mistaken. Teeth clenched, he admitted defeat and slumped back in his chair. No. He was not mistaken. This woman was not the one. With a curt shake of his head, he let Emrys and Fergus know that once again, they had failed in their assigned quest.

Emrys caught hold of Fergus's arm and shoved him forward. "Return the lass to her father. No sense in the poor child suffering the clan's stares any longer."

Fergus rolled his eyes heavenward, then intercepted the young woman and gently led her back to her sire.

Caelan hefted himself up from his seat and waited for the low murmuring of the clansmen gathered at the tables to fade. Once silence filled the vast hall, he inclined his head toward the girl's father. "Thank ye, Cormac, for bringing your daughter before us. Her grace and beauty will win many suitors for her hand, I am sure."

The old chief tightened his mouth at the gracious dismissal. Gone were the hopes of a match with the Laird of Clan MacKay. He turned and left the room, leaving his daughter to scurry after him.

With a summoning jerk of his head at Emrys, Caelan waited for the old one to shuffle to his side. "We are finished here," he said, biting out the words, not at all pleased with the outcome.

Frustration soured in his gut as he strode from the room and climbed the stairs to the curtain wall. Of late, he had taken to pacing the path atop the ancient stone barrier while staring across his land and fighting against the ache of loneliness and despair the dreams continued to bring. Deep breaths of the sea air and the sting of the harsh wind against his flesh as he walked the walls were the only things that brought him the least bit of comfort and helped him keep somewhat of a grip on his sanity.

With Fergus close behind, Emrys fell in step beside Caelan, squinting against the briny gusts thundering in off the sea to eat away at the ancient stones of the castle perched high upon the cliff. "We thought the Cormac's daughter was the one of your dreams. Comely looks. Dark hair. Flashing eyes. Did she not meet your description? The curse nay gave ye the slightest twinge about her?"

"Nothing." Caelan halted and propped his hands atop the cold rough blocks of limestone forming the merlins and crenels of the protective wall. The rhythm of the waves crashing far below mimicked the churning within him. "Nothing about that meek lass compares to the fiery woman in my dreams every night."

"There was nothing wrong with her," Fergus growled, shoving his way up beside them. "Did ye even look at her close? I am a warrior, Caelan. Not a feckin' matchmaker and I grow weary of this task." His ruddy face shifted to a darker shade as he worried a hand through his wild russet hair streaked with gray. "She would have made ye a fine enough match. Her dowry of lands and a good measure of fat cattle would not have gone amiss around here, either."

"Then you wed her." Caelan shoved off the wall and continued his pacing. They didn't understand. The curse forbade him from even considering anyone other than the woman the powers chose for him before he was even born.

Fergus dropped his chin to his chest. "I mean no disrespect. Ye ken ye are the brother I never had. But we have searched for months. Brought women to ye from all over Scotland. Did ye ever wonder if she truly exists? Perhaps the curse is merely toying with ye." He clenched his fists until his knuckles popped one by one. "Other matters need our attention—your attention. Your clan. Your people. Pick a wife, man. It canna be that hard to choose the mother of your future sons."

"I need my heart's mate!" Caelan roared in Fergus's face. He clapped hold of the man's chest and shook him. "The dreams are sheer torment. She beckons me. Taunts me to find her. Catch her. Claim her for my own. She has ruined me for all others."

Emrys grabbed Fergus by the shoulder and gave the man a sharp jerk of his head to prevent him from saying anything more. "Every laird of Clan MacKay has endured this curse, Fergus. They can have no other than the one who appears in their dreams." He jabbed a crooked finger at Caelan. "And if he goes against the curse and takes another, she would die within seven moons of their joining."

Fergus threw up his hands, turned, and headed for the stairs, his cloak billowing out behind him. "I am done with this madness. Summon me when ye need me to serve as something other than a matchmaker."

While Caelan did not appreciate his war chief's fit of temper, he understood the man's sentiments and couldn't ask for a better warrior to ensure the clan's safety. He shifted his glare to Emrys. "So, my fine advisor, what say ye now?"

Scratching his yellowed nails through his snowy white beard, Emrys once again squinted into the wind and stared out at the sea. "I believe it time to consult the mirrors, my laird. Use the elements to find the lass. By your leave, it is time for some magick."

Time for magick. The very idea made Caelan tense, as though

charging into battle. But if it would end the dreams, end the feckin' madness of seeing her but not knowing how to find her, then it would be well worth the risk. He rolled his shoulders and gave a curt nod. "Do whatever it takes."

HER BUBBLING LAUGHTER *floated on the breeze as she tossed her head and glanced back at him over her shoulder. Playfully bunching up her skirts, she scampered just out of his reach across the hillside painted purple with blooming heather.*

The sight of her shapely legs stirred him. He itched to tickle his fingers up their silky lengths to what he knew would be her welcoming heat.

Her dark hair floated and bounced in the air behind her, the raven curls tumbling down her back as her ribbons came untied and fluttered away. The thrill of the chase flushed her cheeks with a becoming pinkness. Her amethyst eyes danced with laughter.

She teased him with a smile while shaking a finger with a fake warning to stay away. The curve of her full breasts swelled above the neckline of her gown. Their supple bounciness as she ran made him groan. He longed to embrace her, possess her, ached to bury his face between those wondrous mounds.

"You'll never catch me!" As graceful as a red deer, she stayed just beyond his reach, effortlessly bounding across the hillside.

"Aye, my love. I shall have ye this verra day!" With a playful growl, he leapt around an outcropping of rocks, but his footing failed. Stones broke free, tumbling away and sending him over the cliff's edge. Horror filled him as the ground disappeared out from under him.

Caelan woke with a start. The coverings from his bed tangled around his legs as he hit the floor. "Feckin' hell!"

He beat the flagstones with both fists, pounding the cold rough surface that assured him once again he had been torn from his dream just as he was about to die.

"Emrys!" he bellowed while thrashing in the tangle of sheets to get himself to a sitting position and lean back against the bed. He scrubbed his face, trying to calm himself enough to reason. How many times had he chased that beauty? Why was it always the same? Where was the violet-eyed temptress who haunted him each night and always stayed just beyond his reach, leaving him aching with the need for her when he abruptly awakened?

"Again?" The white-haired man stood in the doorway, yawning and scratching his belly through his threadbare robes.

"Of course, *again*. Why else would I summon ye this time of night?" Caelan pushed himself up from the floor and yanked the bedclothes from around his body. "Either cast a spell to destroy the curse or find the damn woman before I go mad!"

He dragged his hands through his blonde hair, then swiped at the cold sheen of moisture across his chest. His vision hazed at the memory of the repetitive dream, making him swallow hard and absently rub his throbbing member. Another painful reminder he had failed yet again to catch her.

With stiff, hitching steps, Emrys made his way deeper into the room, still scratching his middle. "The curse is full upon ye and canna be destroyed with the magick I possess. There is naught I can do. Ye must find her and claim her."

"Tell me where she is, and I will!" Caelan fixed a baleful glare on the old man. If the supposed all-knowing druid insisted on spouting such useless wisdom, he could haul his arse back to his room. "Well?"

"Ye are well aware of our efforts. We have talked with more clans than yourself and I have fingers. Searched across the Highlands and Lowlands. Even sent runners to the surrounding isles. Not a single maiden we brought here suited ye." The ancient advisor hitched with a jaw-popping yawn, then raked his knobby fingers through his tufts of unruly white hair until the wild shocks stood even higher.

Caelan strode across the room, snatched his plaid from the chair at the hearth, and wrapped it around his waist. "Ye are supposed to be the most powerful in the old ways. More powerful than any among the clans. An all-knowing, all-seeing advisor to your laird. Why have ye failed me?"

The elder dragged out a chair from the small table in the corner and lowered himself into it. With his elbow propped on the table, he set his chin in his hand and fixed a narrow-eyed glare on Caelan.

"What?" Caelan couldn't bear the look in the old man's eyes. It made his gut clench. Emrys had a way of peering into a man and picking his soul to pieces.

"I searched through the Mirrors of Time. Did what needed to be done as ye bade me."

"And?" He braced himself. An ominous sense of dread squeezed him, making it difficult to breathe. Whatever the old seer was about to say—it could not be good. "Finish your feckin' thought, Emrys. I would know the worst of it."

"I may have located the lass, but I dinna think ye will find it a comfort." The druid shifted in the chair and groaned with another great yawn as he switched hands and propped his chin in the other one.

"If ye dinna cease making me drag the words out of ye, it will be a cold day in hell before ye find any comfort ever again!" Caelan slammed his fist on the table, rattling the candles in their stands and sending the melted tallow flying. Damn the old man. "Does it give ye pleasure to taunt your laird?"

With a heavy sigh, Emrys gathered his robes closer around his thin body. "The lass of your dreams does exist, but it pains me to tell ye that she nay dwells in this land or time."

Caelan steadied himself against the table as he sank into the other chair beside it. "I dinna ken what ye are saying. She nay dwells in Scotland *or* this time? What the devil does that mean?"

Stroking his scraggly beard, Emrys tipped his head to one side and tightened his clear blue eyes into a thoughtful squint. "Near as I can tell, the woman dwells far into the future, and in another land that as yet is not even known to us."

"That canna be so," Caelan said. "If ye are trying to buy more time to solve this quest, ye best cease that foolishness, old man." He leaned toward him, growling through teeth clenched so tightly that his jaws ached. "Dinna think to toy with me, ye ken?"

"I can show ye the truth of it in the mirrors. How many years have

I faithfully advised ye?" Emrys threw out his narrow chest and glared back at him. "In all my days as the seer to the clans, never have I been so insulted and over a mere woman, no less!"

Caelan rose from his chair, strode across the room, and nearly ripped the heavy oak door from its hinges. "After you, wise one. Let us make for your chambers so ye can prove ye speak the truth."

THE ROOM SMELLED OF NOXIOUS, pungent herbs and something else Caelan preferred not to know about. He wrinkled his nose and eyed the shadowy walls. While he considered himself a fearless warrior and respected laird, he left the mysteries of magick and mysticism to the druids and wise cailleachs of the clans. Unlike some superstitious cowards who would see them driven out or murdered for their ancient beliefs, he left them to their ways as long as they acted for the good of others and tended to the needs of the land and the people.

He followed Emrys through the eerie room, the sputtering candles and torches doing little to dispel the shadows dancing across the cluttered corners. Bowls filled with murky liquids lined the shelves dressed in cobwebs and dust. Some containers held things he was determined to forget he had ever seen.

They made their way to the farthest corner where an arched doorway led them into the chamber containing Emrys's most prized and private tools of the old ways. The mysterious Mirrors of Time leaned against the far wall, staring back at them like the great dark eyes of some primitive beast. The stones supporting the ancient mirrors were blackened as though charred by blasts of extreme heat. As tall as Caelan, each of the three shimmering windows into the unknown mists was as wide as his arms could span. Their wooden frames, dark with age, held strange symbols, intricately carved knots, and whorls, their meaning only known to those deemed worthy of their powers.

But unlike a polished shield that reflected whatever passed in front of it, the surfaces of these mirrors were undulating pools of blackest obsidian not reflecting a single light, shadow, or shape that might stand before them.

Caelan planted his feet in a defensive stance and tightened his fists, eyeing the mirrors with a leeriness that made his gut clench. "What must ye do to make them show ye what ye seek?" he asked in a hushed tone.

"Patience, my laird." Emrys fetched his staff from the corner. His thin, decrepit form seemed to grow and strengthen as he returned to his place in front of the mirrors. Whenever the old one held his staff, it was as though the years fell away from him as the elemental energy pulsed through his veins. He touched the crystal of his staff to the mirror farthest to the right. "Reveal the one of the amethyst eyes, she who our chieftain needs. Let us hear her, show us her time and place, reveal the one we seek."

The mirror's surface came alive with a burst of energy. The ebony plate changed into a roiling surface of stormy clouds. Lightning flashed in the peaks and valleys of the shapes as blurred images spun and danced, gaining momentum on the surface of the looking glass. After a bit, the gray shapeless forms cleared, revealing a small white house at the edge of a thick forest of pines. A thin stream of smoke rose from the crooked chimney, hugging the side of the tiny dwelling.

Heart pounding at the strangeness of it all, unable to breathe or form words, Caelan leaned closer, mesmerized by the vision.

The door to the house opened, and there she was. Dressed in a pair of the snuggest blue trews Caelan had ever seen and a wee white léine that clung to her shapely curves, the maiden of his dreams skipped down the steps of the house. Pulling her raven curls back from her face, she threaded her shining locks through the back of a strange hat that fit close to her skull as she pulled it on her head. Its brim was shaped like the bill of a duck and had tattered symbols scrawled across the front of it. The thing didn't even cover her ears.

Caelan frowned. What good would such a hat be when the winter winds blew? He blinked away the thought and stepped closer still, watching the lass of his dreams. She scrubbed her arms against the chill of the cool morning as she hurried to the woodpile stacked against the side of the house. After selecting a few good-sized chunks, she strode back to the door while glancing around the frosty clearing.

"Sam! Maizy! Time for breakfast!" Her musical voice carried across the vision as her violet-eyed gaze scanned an area Caelan couldn't see. At the sound of her call, a wee black and brown dog no bigger than a good-sized rat and a large, lumbering golden one emerged from the trees close to a tall, worn structure that must be her stable. They bounced to her side, tussling for her attention as they scampered up the steps and disappeared into the house with her.

As the scene faded, the surface of the mirror returned to a liquid pool of black. Then the glass shimmered with a smoky, silvery sheen, as though the mirror sought more information. Its surface stilled and returned to ebony, then spelled out in stark white script: Kentucky 2007.

"What is *Kentucky 2007*?" Caelan took a step back and turned to Emrys while scrubbing his knuckles up and down his breastbone to rid himself of the chilling eeriness of the room.

Emrys returned his staff to its place in the corner. "From what I have gathered from my path working, Kentucky is a place across the seas—or will be." Turning a pained glare on Caelan, he folded his hands in front of his middle. "And 2007 is the year in which your soul mate lives."

Caelan rubbed the back of his neck and rolled his shoulders, unable to shake the unnerving tingle plaguing his flesh. "2007? How can I dream of a maiden from across the seas in the year 2007 when this is Scotland, and the year is 1379?" He raked his hands through his hair, knotted his fingers in the strands, and yanked in irritation as he closed his eyes in disbelief. Pain, he understood. Being matched with a woman of the future? By Amergin's beard, what strange cruelty was this?

"The MacKays have always sought their soulmates. They canna settle for joining with anyone but their one true match for all time." Emrys crossed the room and gently opened a heavy book resting on one end of his worktable. He touched the timeworn pages with reverence. "Why do ye think your line nearly disappeared several times? If not for the benevolent hand of fate to bring the soulmates together, the MacKay line would have died out long ago. The stubborn males refuse to plant their seed with anyone other than the one woman who appears to them in their dreams." Emrys shook his head and pursed his wrinkled mouth. "Course, it didn't help when an occasional laird took a woman for her dowry rather than love, and she always died within seven moons of the marriage." He twitched a shrug. "That part of the curse convinced the others to avoid that path."

"And my heartmate lies in the future. Out of my reach forever," Caelan said. "Am I to live out my life alone, then? No wife? No heirs?" He wished he had never looked into those damn mirrors. At least if he had remained ignorant of the truth, he could have nurtured a bit of hope to keep him warm the rest of his days. "Do the fates hope to torment me into taking a woman of this century just so I can watch her die? I canna even look at another woman without thinking of those purple eyes that pierce my heart and soul!"

With a slow shake of his head, Emrys turned from the table. He held an ancient book open in his arms, staring down at it, and running a finger back and forth across the script on the pages. Without looking up, he advised, "Dinna speak disrespectfully of the Fates, my laird. In what we are about to do, ye will need more help from them than ye ever have before." He licked his thumb and turned a page, then ran his crooked finger along the faded lines again.

Caelan snorted and shook his head, then jabbed a finger at the wicked mirrors but could not speak through the turmoil pounding through him. He couldn't force the memory of her out of his mind and those clothes—bloody hell! That fine round arse of hers in those strange trews. His cock surged to a painful hardness at the memory. The way her breasts perked round and full beneath the tight white cloth of her wee tunic. He wiped the sweat from his upper lip with a groan.

"How are the Fates to help me?" he finally growled, cradling his pounding head and pressing the heels of his hands hard against his temples.

"Well..." Emrys tapped another page with a yellowed fingernail. "When traveling to the future, ye usually need all the help ye can get."

CHAPTER 2

Rural Kentucky
Spring 2007

RACHEL HAWKINS LAUGHED as she lifted the lid to the dog food bin, then danced around both bouncing dogs to fill their bowls. "Take it easy, you two. There's enough for everybody. If you eat all this, I'll give you more." She loved Sam and Maizy so much. Their happily wagging butts made her smile as they dove into the food as if they hadn't eaten for a month of Sundays.

After adding a bit more food to their bowls, she crossed the small area for a refill of coffee, then settled at her usual morning spot in front of the kitchen sink. She leaned against it and stared out the window while sipping her coffee, loving how the tall frosty grass covering the field sparkled in the sunlight like a child's art project decorated with glitter. "I'm going to enjoy these next couple of weeks off even if I have to disconnect the wall phone, stop the mail, and toss my cell phone into the pond. Then the only way the bill collectors can find me is if they fly over the house and drop notices."

Neither dog lifted their head nor stopped eating to acknowledge her. Their tails continued wagging to mark time with their rhythmic crunching.

She turned and leaned back against the sink, cradling the steaming cup between her hands. The past several months had been so hard, but, hopefully, things would level out now and start looking up. A determined sigh escaped her as she made up her mind. She would get through this. Always did. Always would. At least she was finally rid of her lying ex-husband, legally and physically. How she had missed all the warning signs still made her wonder if she had just ignored them to keep the peace. Of course, it was pretty hard to ignore when she walked in on him and his extremely loud girlfriend christening the expensive new sheets she'd splurged for and put on the bed that morning.

A disgruntled snort escaped her. She still couldn't decide which had made her angrier—the fact that her husband was screwing around on her or that he and his mistress had gotten their nastiness all over her precious sheets. She shuddered at the thought.

After another sip of coffee, she sagged down into the chair at the wobbly kitchen table. She never should've married David. Love really hadn't been a factor. He'd been more of an escape from college and the career that her emotionally abusive parents battered her over the head with for as far back as she could remember.

When she dropped out of university for marriage, they disowned her and told her they wouldn't speak to her or acknowledge her existence until she came to her senses and stopped embarrassing them with her inconsiderate behavior. As far as they were concerned, she was dead to them. Fine by her. She'd often wondered why they never put her up for adoption or abandoned her in an alley. It would have been more humane than the way they'd raised her.

A couple of years into what they always called her *ridiculously stupid* marriage, a car accident permanently silenced their cruel criticism and emotional abuse that had made up her childhood.

Now, three years later, newly divorced and teetering on financial ruin, she was determined to turn her life around without the love and acceptance she had always been denied by her parents—and eventually, by her husband. Only Granny had loved and understood her, and she had lost her when she was just seven. But things were going to change now, and she was going to find genuine happiness if it was the last thing she did. Nudged from her inner pep talk by a cold wet nose poking her in the ribs, she reached down and ruffled the velvety ears of the loyal lab. "I love you too, Maizy. You're my special girl, and you love me no matter what."

A high-pitched yip on her other side and a frantic digging at her legs let Rachel know in no uncertain terms that Sam also needed her attention.

"I love you too, Sam. After all, you're the only male I will ever trust again!"

The demanding little dog cocked his head to one side, his huge terrier ears perked as he intently took in every word.

Gently pushing them aside, she rose from her chair and went to the yellowed countertop beside the refrigerator. She pulled the ledger book from where she always stuffed it between the cookbooks, a crock of wooden spoons, and the knife block. She opened the book to the section marked with a paper clip.

"I have to figure a way to pay these bills and bring in more income, or we're going to find ourselves out of a place to live." She chewed on the corner of her lip while tapping the page. No matter how many times she added up the entries in the ledger, her pitiful savings account and upcoming paycheck ran out long before the numbers in the column were accounted for.

Her job at the steel mill barely kept her body and soul together and fed the dogs. The slump in the steel market had put a stop to any available overtime she might've volunteered for to bail herself out of some of this debt. Even though her marriage had lasted only a short four years, her conniving ex ensured he didn't walk away from the relationship empty-handed. Between lining up bed partners while she was on shift at the mill, he had methodically siphoned money out of their joint accounts into one bearing his name only and known only to him.

To keep the small acreage of land and the leaky roof of Granny's old house in her name, Rachel had been forced to take out a loan to buy out what the court had deemed was David's half in the divorce settlement. According to the laws, the lowlife was entitled to half of everything no matter how big of a horse's ass he was. Unfortunately, she'd not been able to afford the type of lawyer who was slick enough to convince the judge that her lying, thieving husband was a full-sized Clydesdale's ass.

The jerk had also been thoughtful enough to max out all their credit cards. Even topping out a few she hadn't known he'd taken out in both their names. Her lawyer assured her David would be held responsible for part of the debt, but since he'd disappeared from the face of the earth, the creditors found it easier to harass her for what they were owed.

As an afterthought, she shoved the ledger back among the cookbooks, picked up the ancient kitchen wall phone, and punched in the number to work. She had to make this call before she attempted to put work out of her mind during the next two weeks.

"Joel? Hey, yeah, it's Rachel." Cradling the receiver between her cheek and shoulder, she stretched to open the junk drawer and fished out a pen. "Yes, I am on vacation, but I was calling to see if any overtime time at all might be available for the week I come back. Any scheduled vacations or leaves of absence that might need to be covered?"

She narrowed her eyes at yet another crack in the grout work surrounding the tile around the sink's backsplash, while half-heartedly listening to what she knew was going to be Joel's answer. "I know you have to go by seniority, but just keep me in mind. I'll take it if nobody else will, okay?" She blew out what she hoped was a silent sigh as she leaned forward and propped her elbows on the peeling linoleum of the countertop. "Yeah, I'll try to keep my mind off work and enjoy my time off. I know. Okay. See you when I get back." She placed the receiver of the ancient, goldenrod yellow wall phone back in its cradle.

As she combed her fingers through her tangled mass of curls, the two-story garage standing just behind the house caught her attention. She frowned at it, narrowing her eyes as she folded her arms across her chest. "Maybe I could rent out that old apartment over the garage. I could clean it up and make it livable. Probably couldn't get much rent, but something is always better than nothing."

She tried to remember what extra furniture remained in the attic, and what it would take to turn that space into a *rentable* apartment that might bring in at least a few hundred dollars a month.

"Come on, guys."

Grabbing her ratty ball cap off the peg by the door, she whistled for the dogs as she pulled her hair through the back of the cap. Sam and Maizy crowded around her, fighting to be the first out the door on this latest adventure.

"We have some work to do, babies, or we're going to be living out of the pickup truck." Armed with a notepad and pen from the junk drawer, she marched outside, determined to turn the garage into a meal ticket—or at least a way to keep the dogs fed.

"THE FUTURE IS SHEER MADNESS!" Caelan flung the strangely slick and colorful parchment made into a book onto the pile of more of the same littering the floor beside the hearth. Emrys had called the things *magazines*. As far as Caelan was concerned, they were fit for nothing but wiping his arse after he took a shite. To prepare for their journey into the future, the old druid had called forth the disturbing material from the year 2007 through the Mirrors of Time. Caelan scowled down at the pile. Still unable to believe the things he had seen and read.

It would take more than one dram of whisky to settle his mind after studying that heap that needed to be fed to the fire. A chill ran through him. He couldn't believe what the world would someday become. "Why in Brid's name would the woman even contemplate not coming back here with me? Her world is—terrifying! Surely, she will run into my arms and beg me to save her."

"Be that as it may…" Emrys lowered the large, shiny magazine he held open wide. "That world is the only chaos she has ever known. To her, it is as normal as this place and time is to yourself." He tossed the thing aside and snorted. "Burn that one. One of those pages reeks of rotting flowers." He rubbed the corners of his eyes. "Damned if my eyes dinna burn hot as embers. I've not studied this much since my initiation, and that was well over five hundred years ago."

"Ye said ye went to the future many times." Caelan gingerly selected another bit of reading material, cringing as he flipped through the pages filled with entirely too thin women and men who wouldn't be able to hold a proper sword or shield if their life depended on it. "Is there famine in 2007? These people need to be fed."

"I have been to the future many times but not that far forward," Emrys said. "And my trips were for brief forages of knowledge and lore to ensure the tapestry of time and space remain intact." He pinched the bridge of his nose and massaged the corners of his eyes. "I can read no more this evening. Weariness blinds me."

"And the continuum will only allow us to stay for seven moons?" Caelan wished he had longer to win the lass's trust as well as her heart, but as he'd said earlier, surely, she would beg him to save her. "The span of seven moon cycles is all the time I have to convince her she belongs with me?" He nudged the pile of papers and books with the toe of his boot, sorely tempted to kick all of them into the fire.

"Aye, ye have until midnight on the night of the seventh full moon to convince her the two of ye are meant to be one." Emrys rubbed his eyes again as he continued, "And she must choose to return with ye willingly. Ye canna kidnap her as ye would do here in the Highlands of this time." He twisted and stretched, making his bones crackle and pop like the wood burning in the hearth. "She must know the entire truth of it—the truth that she can never return to her era or she'll not be allowed to remain here, and your love will be lost."

"From what I have seen of her life, and the age in which she lives, we should be back here with our first child well on its way by the seventh moon!" Caelan allowed himself a smug grin. The thought of finally being with the lass of his heart swelled his chest with joy and anticipation.

"Mind your arrogance, my prideful laird. Ye saw how she was mistreated by her parents and that man she called her husband. She trusts verra few now and men are not among those with which she lets down her guard—ever. What makes ye so certain she will fall into your arms as soon as ye show at her door? Do ye not feel she will find it strange when we appear? Mayhap, even frightening?" Emrys hit him with a hard, scolding glare.

"Will she not sense our connection as soon as she sees me? How could she not know I am the other half of her soul?" Caelan ignored the old man and stared into the fire. He hated uncertainty. It roiled in his gut like a poorly digested meal. The thought that Rachel might reject him hadn't occurred to him. Not that he was vain. It was just that when all his ancestors before him found their heartmates, the women had immediately known it as well.

What if she didn't trust him? What if she wanted nothing to do with him? How was he going to explain to her he was her eternal match, traveling across time and space to join with her and return her to Scotland to be his own?

The fire popped, jerking him from his worries and reminding him Emrys had yet to answer. "Well, old man? Will she not feel our connection when she meets me?"

"That all depends on how sensitive she is to the old ways." The druid rose from his chair, massaging the small of his back as he ambled around the room. "The future has numbed people to the energies that flow through the universe. Legends and lore have been forgotten and replaced with mind-numbing rhetoric and science." Still rubbing his back, he rolled his shoulders and continued pacing. "Few can see through the mists of time any longer. Fewer still can sense the mysteries that lie just within their reach. It'll not be easy convincing your Rachel to believe the truth if she is as tainted to the ways as most of her time has become."

"But ye saw her with her dogs and with the other creatures of the woods. The lass seems sensitive to beasts. What about the scene with her grandmother ye called forward?" Caelan leaned back and stretched out his long legs and folded his hands behind his head. "And she lives out in the country. Seems to have an affinity with the land. Surely, that will help us in our cause."

"Before we cross through the portal into her time, we might try sending her a few wee *suggestions* into her dreams." Emrys narrowed his eyes and tugged on his beard, a sure sign he was plotting.

"And what about the Fates not allowing any trickery? The choice must be of the lass's own free will—remember?" Caelan leaned forward with interest, propping his elbows on his knees. If the old one knew of a way to get around the Fates, well then, who was he to argue?

"I said *suggestions*. Not trickery. We'll merely send ye into her dreams. We've already seen that she longs to visit Scotland. A night with ye would merely add a bit of *realness* to what she might have if she accepts your invitation."

Emrys nodded and stroked his beard even faster. "That way too, when ye show up on her doorstep, ye'll not be a complete stranger, and when the time comes to reveal the truth to her, ye'll have a bit of proof. Ye can tell her of your time in her dreams, and she'll be convinced because ye know of it."

"Ye can send me into her dream plane? I'll be there? Able to do anything?" Caelan sat straighter, eager to get on with the idea and make it so. His own dreams had become sheer torment, Rachel always dancing just out of his reach. If he could visit her dreams and hold her in his arms, he would ensure she'd remember him upon waking.

Emrys cleared his throat and peered down his long nose at Caelan. "Aye, I can send ye, but only the once. So ye'd best make it unforgettable."

Caelan couldn't resist a smile. "Send me, old man. I promise ye the lass will find the dream *unforgettable*."

~

HE APPEARED over the crest of the hill, striding forward with an alluring power that made her heart pound harder at the sight of him. She had finally found him. The warrior she needed for...for what? She shook her head, uncertain of the answer. But it didn't matter what she needed him for—she simply needed him. The surety of his smile made her smile back at him. He held out his hand and nodded.

She started to run to him but paused to soak in the sight of him, admiring this amazing man before her. He had to be well over six and a half feet tall and not an ounce of fat clung to his muscular build. Never had she seen shoulders so broad or abs so...so climbable. She swallowed hard and wet her lips. The vision of him was about to make her drool. And those eyes of his. A vibrant green more brilliant than any emerald. Hair the color of golden grass rippling in a fall breeze. All that marred his ruggedly handsome face was a small scar that passed through his left eyebrow. But she decided she liked that—it made him even more desirable.

Then somehow, he was right in front of her, and their clothes were gone. She reached out and touched his chest, going breathless at the hardness of his muscles. He eased her into his arms and gently lowered her to the mossy ground, nuzzling below her ear. She breathed him in. He smelled so good. Pine forests. Wildness. A man wanting to satisfy her.

She smoothed her hands down his muscular back, tracing the ripples of his muscles as he tightened his embrace. A quiet moan escaped her as his mouth traveled down her throat, across her collarbone, and then lower. He pulled her nipple into his mouth and gently sucked.

His powerful hands and skillful mouth and tongue knew every sweet spot she needed touched. She arched against him, aching for his impressive hardness to fill her. She had searched for him for so very long. "I need you," she whispered while wrapping her legs around him.

He claimed her mouth, probing with his tongue, and rocking against her, teasing her with what he would eventually give her.

She tightened her legs around him and arched again, trying to convince him to drive into her. She couldn't remember wanting so badly to be taken or feeling as though she was going to die if he didn't hurry and fill her.

"Not yet," he whispered as he barely lifted his head to trace a fiery line down her torso with his tongue.

She filled her fists with his hair, melting against him as he worked his way lower.

"I need you to take me. Please take me." She bucked against him, her whole being on fire, as volatile as molten lava ready to erupt. She gasped as he claimed her with his mouth, his tongue teasing as he slid his fingers inside her.

Pure, raw sensation took her over as he drove her past all reason. Pulling his head even harder against her, she screamed as he carried her to the edge of bliss and pushed her into an explosive orgasm, keeping her there until she thought she would die and didn't care if she did.

Then, ever so slowly, with nips and swirls of his teasing tongue, he licked his way back up her body and covered her mouth with his once more. Now he tasted of her, smelled of their excitement, and made her ache all over again. His thumbs teased her nipples back to yearning hardness as he slowly settled between her legs.

With his hands on either side of her face, he stared into her eyes as he slowly slid his full length inside her until there was no end to him or beginning to her. They were fully joined as one—completely forged together.

He slowly withdrew, then dove back in as deep as he could go. "Now ye are mine until time is forgotten. I claim ye forevermore."

She found herself unable to breathe. This was not just sex. This was a sacred binding that you read about in legends. She held his gaze with hers and matched his thrusts with her own. "I am forever yours," she answered, the words somehow drawn from her, spoken from the heart as if she had waited all her life to say them.

As he drove into her, she tangled her fingers in his hair and held on tight, trying to hold off her orgasm as long as possible.

"Nay, my love," he growled. "Give over and find your pleasure."

She came harder than she had ever come in her life. A scream tore from her throat.

Her warrior buried himself fully and roared, trembling as he emptied inside her.

Suspended in time, his tender kiss first touched her forehead, then brushed her temple. "Open your eyes, my dear one."

She forced open her heavy eyelids and smiled up at him. All she wanted to do was sleep in his arms.

"Dinna be afraid when I come for ye, Rachel. Our love is fated to be. Dinna be afraid when I come to your door."

Rachel awoke with a start and kicked the bedclothes off. She was hotter than a firecracker, and the sheets were wet with sweat. She sat up and scrubbed her face, breathless and heart pounding like a jackhammer. Never had she had such a dream. So real. So erotic. So—

"Breathe, Rachel, breathe." She fanned herself and stared up at the ceiling. "My self-imposed celibacy must be kicking me in the hormones to conjure up a man like that!"

She raked her damp hair back from her face and held it up off her neck. Wherever her mind had found that sexy Scot, he was better than any romance novel hero she'd fantasized about as she'd read through the pile of books on her dresser.

His handsomeness, his body, but most of all that deep voice with that lyrical Scot's burr that turned her insides to a gooey mess. The way he'd held her. The way he'd touched her—the orgasms. Her body still vibrated with the aftershocks. She hadn't known she was capable of exploding into that many shards of ecstasy.

"Heaven help me." She blew out an amazed huff as she swung her legs off the bed. "Time to shower to get that Highlander off my mind, or I'll get nothing done today."

As she stepped up to the bathroom sink, she frowned at herself in the mirror. Her lips were red and slightly swollen, as though they had been kissed and enjoyed—repeatedly. "You're imagining things," she informed her image. "You probably chewed on your lips while you were dreaming." She peeled her threadbare nightshirt off over her head. The reflections of her breasts halted her. Her nipples were tight and *extremely* rosy as though they'd been nipped in love play, and the skin of her breasts was still slightly reddened as though they'd been fondled and nuzzled by a lightly whiskered face.

"I am losing my mind," she informed her reflection. A shiver ran through her as she remembered lying in his arms. "I wish real life men were like that." After a heavy sigh, she turned on the shower, selecting the coldest temperature she could stand.

Grabbing her soap and sponge, she lathered up, scrubbing vigorously as the cold water pelted her skin. But no matter how hard she scrubbed or how cold the water was sluicing down her body, she still couldn't shake the image of the man in her dream.

He'd been perfection itself. His body had been hard and unrelenting, as they'd both taken and given from each other. His shoulder length hair had fallen forward as he'd loomed over her.

She could still feel the smooth rippling muscles of his back as she'd raked her fingers down to his buttocks to pull him harder into her. Another shiver stole across her at the memory of how he'd buried himself inside her, filling her as she'd never been filled before.

"This is so not working."

She clenched her teeth and turned the water to a colder setting, standing directly under the showerhead to douse the fire of her smoldering body. Finally, giving up as her teeth started chattering, she flipped off the water and reached for her towel. Side by side, patiently waiting for her to finish, Sam and Maizy sat on the rug staring up at her.

"I know it's time for breakfast, but trust me, I had to have a shower first." As she toweled dry, the dogs did their best to help by licking the water off her feet.

"Quit now that tickles!" Giggles took her over as she hopped from foot to foot, trying to dodge the helpfulness of her two friends.

With another towel wrapped tightly around her body, she hurried into the kitchen and filled their bowls with food.

A loud knock rattled the front door, making her jump. Both dogs lifted their heads from their bowls, then dashed to the door, bouncing against it and barking to let her know they were ready to defend her.

"I'll be right there!" she bellowed over the barking dogs, hoping it wasn't a bill collector. Because if it was, she had just been stupid enough to reveal she was home. She scurried back into the bedroom and grabbed the pair of jeans she'd tossed across the chair. Hopping up and down as she pulled them on her still slightly damp body, she cringed as another hard knock shook the front door again.

"Just a minute! I'm coming!"

She found a sweatshirt and jerked it on over her head, hoping it was thick enough since she wasn't taking the time to put on a bra. She ran barefoot across the hardwood floors, made her way down the hall, and crossed the living room to the front door.

After whipping her wet hair out of her face and shoving both dogs aside, she tiptoed to peek through the narrow window. A gasp escaped her, and she couldn't breathe as she fell back hard against the door.

"It can't be," she whispered. "That's not possible."

Outside on her doorstep was the very man with whom she had just had the most amazing sex with in her life.

CHAPTER 3

Rachel pressed her hands to her flaming cheeks while staring down at the dogs patiently waiting for her to open the door so they could check out the intruders on the porch.

"This cannot be happening," she whispered to them.

Both Sam and Maizy perked their ears and cocked their heads, then Sam scratched on the door and grumbled a hurry up and open it, "Woof!"

She tugged at her sweatshirt, smoothing it as much as possible as she pushed off the door and faced it. Hand trembling, she clutched the knob and silently cursed as she fumbled with the deadbolt and chain. She opened the door barely wide enough to speak through the crack.

Both dogs shoved around her, jostling with each other to get their noses into the small opening to catch the scent of the stranger. Immediately, Maizy thumped her thick tail in an excited wag against Rachel's leg, letting her mistress know she heartily approved of the visitor.

Sam bared his teeth and vibrated with a low, throaty growl. Much like Rachel, his trust was harder to win.

"Can I help you?" she said while trying to sound sure of herself to the enthralling man.

"Aye, mistress. We've come about the room ye placed in the paper? The one ye said ye had to let?" The handsome Scot shifted his weight from foot to foot as though uncomfortable about something—which made Rachel even more twitchy.

"Uhm...we?" She risked opening the door a little wider and barely caught Sam before he shot out onto the porch and attacked.

The Highlander pulled an older man out from behind him. "Aye, my...uncle and me. We need lodging and saw the ad about the room ye had to let over your garage."

"I see." She cleared her throat and peered into the clear keen eyes of the older man with a long beard and long white hair that made him look like he'd stepped straight out of a Tolkien novel or movie adaptation. He offered her a polite nod while standing slightly to one side of his nephew.

"Uhm...give me a minute, please," she said. "I'll get on some shoes and show you the place, so you can see if it'll suit you." Before she could close the door, the big burly Scot caught it with his hand and prevented her from shutting it.

"I am certain the place will be fine. Our needs are meager since we'll only be working in this area for a wee bit of time." His deep voice was made all the more powerful by his mesmerizing accent.

Hugging the growling Sam closer, she swallowed hard and stared at the man's large hand that kept the door open. She hated having to trust him, but he seemed all right. It wasn't his fault she had dreamed about him. After sucking in a deep breath as if she was about to jump headfirst into the pond, she stepped back and opened the door all the way. "Come in. You and your uncle can have a seat while I get my shoes, and then we can work out the details of the place."

His smile and something unreadable in those green eyes of his made her catch her breath. "That is most kind of ye, lass," he said in that voice that reminded her entirely too much about that dream.

The Scottish mountain ushered his uncle inside ahead of him, as if sensing she might not feel as threatened if the older man entered her first.

"I am Rachel Hawkins and you are?" she asked while offering her hand to the bent old man. Something told her he would do her no harm.

"Emrys, lass, Emrys Myrddin." He gave her another polite nod. "I'm verra pleased to make your acquaintance." He took her hand in his and cradled it while patting it with his other hand. "Ye can call me *Emrys*. My last name befuddles most. This here is my nephew, Caelan Foster MacKay."

"Pleased to meet you, Mr. MacKay."

"Nay, lass. Call me Caelan."

Her small hand disappeared inside Caelan's large one, and the heat of his touch sent a searing jolt of tingling energy through her. With her gaze locked in his, her breathing turned into shallow gasps she couldn't control.

"And the pleasure is all mine," he added with an endearingly lopsided smile. He lifted her hand to his mouth and pressed a gentle kiss to it while inhaling deeply as if pulling in her scent. The smug knowing that gleamed in his eyes threw her off. It was almost as if he knew about last night's dream.

She blinked to break free of his spell and pointed at the well-worn couch across the room. "Have a s-seat, won't you? I'll get some coffee started, then we can go over the details of renting the loft. You would like coffee—yes?" Could she possibly sound any more idiotic? *Pull it together, Hawkins*, she internally scolded.

"Aye, coffee," Emrys agreed. "That would be most kind, lass." He ambled over to the couch and lowered himself into the over-stuffed cushions.

Caelan resettled his stance and just stood there, smiling—and leveling a gaze on her that made her want to squirm.

Backing her way into the kitchen, she set Sam on the floor. "Behave," she whispered with a warning touch of his nose. "Just look at Maizy."

The yellow lab had already climbed up on the couch and planted her head in the old man's lap so he could scratch her ears. The dog trusting them gave Rachel a bit of comfort, but Sam being harder to win over made her watchful. Dogs always knew a person's actual intentions. Sam had always hated David. She should've listened to the little dog. It would've saved her a ton of money.

The rat terrier slowly circled Caelan as though sizing up his prey. His tiny hackles stood on end as he emitted a low-throated growl.

"Sam!" Rachel tried to hurry with the coffee while keeping one eye on the determined little dog. That's all she needed—to be sued by a couple of foreigners because Sam bit them.

"Come here, my wee warrior." Caelan stretched out his hand as he knelt in front of the fierce beastie.

Rachel's fearless guardian geared up his growl to a faster speed, and his little black and brown body bristled even further.

"I would never hurt your mistress, lad. Ye can trust me." The Highlander kept his hand outstretched, smiling as he waited for Sam to come closer.

The furry fury risked another step and touched his twitching black nose to the back of Caelan's outstretched hand. After thoroughly snuffling the man's fingers, he settled back on his haunches and cocked his little head. Sam studied the Scot as if unable to decide where this individual had come from.

"Well, that was fast—and unusual," Rachel said as she stepped back into the living room while trying to balance the coffee carafe and three empty cups on a warped tray that only made it more difficult. With her nerves still shot over the coincidence of the dream and the actual man standing in her living room, she tried to fill the cups and spilled coffee everywhere but in them.

She tried to gloss over her lack of gracefulness by babbling, "It usually takes Sam a long time to warm up to strangers. He's not a very trusting soul."

"Allow me to help ye, lass." Caelan took hold of the coffee pot just as she added to the growing puddle of coffee on the tray.

"Thanks—sorry. I'm not usually this big of a mess. I guess it's a little early for me to be an impressive hostess." She mopped up the spills with the towel from her back pocket, her cheeks heating even more. She had to be red as a beet by now, and these two potential renters were probably ready to run from her as fast as they could.

Caelan filled the cups, handed one to Emrys, then settled on the couch beside him. After taking a sip from the steaming mug, he gifted Rachel with another disarming smile. "Dinna fash yourself, lass. It is verra early in the day. We should have waited before we came to see ye. But we were afraid we'd miss the room if we came too late in the day. There does not appear to be many places for rent in this area so close to the lake."

That made sense and put her more at ease. It also enabled her to breathe again. She was being silly about that stupid dream. As she settled into the armchair with one foot tucked under her, she nodded. "This time of year, affordable places to rent are hard to find in this area. You mentioned you and your uncle won't be here long, and with your accents, you sound as though you're from Scotland. What exactly brings you to this area?" She sipped her coffee and took another deep breath; thankful her heart had finally slowed to a normal rhythm even though the arresting man from her dream sat smiling at her from the couch.

"Aye, we are from Scotland. Here on a work visa as consultants for the locking mechanism at the new lock and dam."

He took another drink from his cup but appeared to be clenching his jaws. She must have gotten it too strong for his liking. "I'm so sorry. Do you need milk or sugar? I forgot to ask. I promise I'm not always this rude." Some hostess she was. Poor man.

Caelan lifted his cup as though toasting her. "Nay, lass. Quite hardy just the way it is."

Emrys ignored her. The old man seemed intent on paying attention to the dog. She also noticed he hadn't even tasted his coffee.

"Mr. Emrys, would you prefer tea?" she asked, trying to remember where she had last seen the box of tea bags. She was sure she had some somewhere.

"Just Emrys, lass, and no. I am fine." He gave her a polite nod, then returned his attention to Maizy.

A stretch of uncomfortable silence settled across the room. Only broken by the ticking of the old clock on the shelf above the television.

"The room isn't much," Rachel said, squirming in the chair to swap the feet she had tucked under her. The one she had been sitting on had gone numb. "But it's clean," she continued. "Warm in the winter and air-conditioned for the summer. Depending on the length of your stay, it should do for as long as you're in town—as long as you don't need anything fancy, of course."

Both men nodded like a pair of bobblehead dolls. They seemed perfectly content to sit with their coffee and stare at her, and she had the eeriest impression that they'd do so as long as she allowed it. It made her feel like the prize pig at the fair.

Unable to endure their scrutiny any longer, she jumped up and edged her way to the hallway. "My shoes. I need to get my shoes, and then I'll show you to the loft. We can talk money there, and you can decide if you still want to give it a go."

"I dinna care if it takes every gold coin in my castle. It shall be worth it," Caelan muttered.

"Excuse me?" She paused at the door, uncertain about what he had said.

"I said I am sure it will be worth whatever ye are asking," he said, his strained smile making her wonder what he'd really said as she continued down the hallway to get her socks and shoes.

ADJUSTING the vicious seam of the tight jeans splitting his crotch, Caelan shifted and glared at Emrys. "How the hell do the men of this century not cripple themselves with these feckin' things? They nearly strangle your manhood and stop the blood from reaching your bollocks."

Emrys wiggled in his baggy overalls, his grin somewhat hidden by his long, white mustache. "The sight of ye needs to remind the lass of what the two of ye enjoyed in her dream. From the amount of coffee she spilled and the high color to her cheeks, I'd say ye did yourself proud, my laird."

They both went quiet as Rachel returned with her socks and shoes in hand. At the sight of her putting them on, Sam scrambled into her lap, whining and pawing at her hands.

"I am not leaving you, sweet little man. We're just going outside. You can come too." She hugged her cheek to his and rubbed his neck while murmuring to him as if he were a child.

Caelan couldn't help but revel in the tender sight even though he was slightly jealous of the little dog.

She glanced up and met his gaze. "He hates being left alone. Almost panics whenever I have to leave him." With the tiny beast still trembling in her lap, she reached around him and finished tying her shoes.

"I dinna blame him one bit," Caelan said soft and low, praying she would take it as the caress he meant it to be. He ached with the wanting of her, wishing to be done with this game and head straight back to Scotland with her in his arms. The way they had made love in her dreams only made him yearn for her all the more. Never would he get enough of her. He burned to join with her again and again.

He cleared his throat and smiled as she gave him a leery glance. Best mind his words, he reminded himself. Just as old Emrys had said. But patience had never been one of his virtues.

She set Sam on the floor and motioned for Maizy who was still snuggled against Emrys's leg. "Come on, you two. Let's show our guests the loft, and see if it meets with their approval."

Caelan rose and followed with the dogs while Emrys struggled to flounder out of the over-stuffed cushions. He held the door for Rachel, politely bowing his head as he towered above her. "I am sure the apartment will be perfect. As we said, we'll not be here but a short while." He gave her another charming smile, his face mere inches from hers.

Her breath seemed to catch in her throat, and her face flushed red, filling him with a sense of victory. Aye, she remembered the dream and struggled with him standing so near. Good. He wanted her to remember every second of their loving for all the rest of their days.

She ducked her head and whispered, "I'm going to need another cold shower."

"Beg pardon?" he asked, knowing full well what she had said, but wanting to hear it again. He struggled not to crow like the proudest of cocks. He had served his precious wee lass well.

"The apartment has a shower," she said, her cheeks flashing even redder. She scooted through the door. "This way. To the garage at the back of the house."

Rachel led the way across the yard, dodging the bouncing dogs as they raced around her. "You can park your vehicle..." A faint frown puckered her brow as she scanned the yard and driveway, apparently searching for a vehicle other than her dilapidated truck. "How did you get here?"

Caelan halted and stood there with his mouth ajar while trying to come up with a reasonable lie. Neither of them had anticipated that question—and after all their studying about everything from the year 2007. He turned so Rachel wouldn't see his face and arched both brows at the old druid.

"Our truck played out down the road a ways," Emrys said with a jerk of his thumb in that direction. "So, we walked here. A mere stretch of the legs, it was. We reckoned once we were settled, we'd go back and fix the contrary beast, but we nay wished to miss out on the apartment."

Caelan hurried to bob his head in agreement. "Aye, the truck is down the road a bit. That wicked thing is forever causing us grief."

Rachel gave them a polite smile, seeming to accept the lie with no issue. She turned back to the garage and pointed at a graveled area next to it. "Well, once you get it running, you can park it there. After you see the apartment, I can give you a ride to your truck, if you want. I've got tools you can use too. Keep them in my truck. There's no need for you to walk back to yours."

While Rachel had her back to them and was busy unlocking the garage door, Caelan and Emrys shared an uneasy glance. They were now going to have to come up with a truck that didn't currently exist.

Caelan tipped his head at Emrys while mouthing, *well?*

The old druid shrugged and threw up both hands.

"That's verra kind of ye," Caelan said, struggling to control his tone. "But walking is no trouble at all. It's such a fine day, and the countryside is pleasing to the eye." He jerked his chin at Emrys.

"Aye the lad is quite right," the old man said. "Fact is, that's the only way I keep me old bones working as well as they do." He bared his yellowed teeth at Caelan, as if to tell him to change the subject.

"Whatever works best for the both of you. Just thought I'd offer." Rachel put her shoulder against the door covered in peeling white paint, jiggled the key, then bumped it open with her hip. "Sometimes it sticks when the weather's been damp."

She led the way up the enclosed staircase. When she reached the top, she abruptly halted and held up a hand as though suddenly remembering something she meant to say. She turned and came nose to nose with Caelan. With a startled look and a dangerous sway to one side, she staggered to right herself.

Caelan caught her in his arms to keep her from tumbling down the stairs. Her wondrous breasts felt so perfect and right, and her rapid heartbeat tickled against his chest. "Careful, lass," he said in a slow, deep whisper. "Ye are about to take a tumble." He tightened his hold and pulled her closer, loving how her softness molded against his hardness.

With her hands resting on his shoulders, she moved her mouth, but no words came out. As the heat between them increased to a raging inferno, she tipped her head the slightest bit and touched her mouth to his.

She tasted as sweet as she had last night. Caelan couldn't help but respond, cradling her closer and deepening the kiss with an appreciative groan.

She yanked her head back. "Oh my gosh, I am so, so sorry. I do not...I did not mean to...It's just..." She pushed herself away from him and fumbled open the door to the apartment. Her fair skin flamed a deep red as she rushed across the kitchen, threw open the window, and gulped at the cool, spring breeze as though starved for air.

Bloody hell. He should never have groaned but damned if he could help it. He came up behind her and folded his arms across his chest, waiting.

She remained at the window with her back to him, her head bowed as if she was deep in prayer. Then she slowly lifted it and eased a look back at him, glancing over her shoulder.

He bit the inside of his cheek to keep from smiling but couldn't hold back a grin. "The place is verra nice and will suit us just fine. Do ye not think so, Emrys?"

Emrys nodded as he meandered around the room and was a little too obvious about avoiding looking at Rachel. He opened one of the closed doors off to the side and eyed the small area beyond. "Aye, it will serve us just fine, and even we should be able to keep that wee kitchen clean."

She stared at them with her lips slightly parted, her gaze dancing back and forth between them, obviously waiting for one of them to comment on the kiss.

Caelan smiled and remained silent. Emrys did the same.

After nervously scrubbing her hands on her lovely denim covered thighs as though trying to wipe them clean, she turned and opened one of the kitchen cabinets. "Breaker box. Right here. Sometimes, if the fridge cycles while the coffee pot is making coffee, the switch will throw, and you'll have to reset it. Rent is six hundred a month. No deposit and that includes all utilities. Talk amongst yourselves and let me know if you have any questions." She wet her lips and visibly swallowed hard. "I need to check on the dogs." Then she bolted.

When her harried thumping down the wooden steps was followed by the bang of a door, Caelan moved to the window overlooking the yard between the garage and the house. Rachel loped across the expanse, then dropped on the back steps, and held her head in her hands, slowly rocking while the dogs guarded either side of her.

He blew out a heavy sigh, wishing he could go to her. Hold her.

Explain everything so she would know they were meant to be, and she wasn't losing her mind. "I upset the lass by returning her sweet kiss."

"Nay, laird," Emrys said as he joined him at the window. "She upset herself but go easy with her as much as ye can. It will be worth it in the end." He clapped a hand on Caelan's shoulder. "Remember to weigh the consequences before ye say or do anything. If ye frighten her too badly, ye may not have time to woo her back."

"I did not come this far to return to Scotland empty-handed." Caelan narrowed his eyes and kept his focus locked on his lady love. "She is my heartmate, and I will have her."

CHAPTER 4

Back at the window overlooking Rachel's house, Caelan blew across the top of the scalding bitter black water this place and time appeared to prefer instead of ale, fresh spring water, or mulled wine as a drink to start their day. His fine lass paced back and forth across the back porch of her house, her wee phone clutched to her ear. From the look on her face, whoever she was talking to didn't appear to be cooperating.

Her free hand chopped the air, matching the rhythm of her words—and her fair cheeks had gone scarlet again. She arched her dark eyebrows nearly to her hairline while shaking her head, her face filled with pleading.

Rather than blow out a heavy sigh, Caelan rumbled a low growl. Damn the soul of whoever it was on that phone. He hoped they went straight to the devil for making his dear one so unhappy.

She shoved her phone into her pocket and dropped to sit on the edge of the porch. With her knees pulled up to her chest, she buried her face in her arms.

"What is she doing now?" Emrys joined him at the window.

Caelan huffed with another low-throated growl. "I canna tell. Weeping probably. Whoever was on that phone of hers must have been an arse." He turned to the druid. "Can ye find them with a spell?" He flexed his fists. "I'd like a wee word with them."

Emrys narrowed his eyes. "Ye ken well enough that I canna do that."

Caelan tucked his shirttail into his jeans as he nodded at the window. "I'm going to go talk to the lass. Mayhap there is some way I can help with whatever troubles her."

"Go carefully, Caelan. Ye have seen her past in the mirrors. She will be slow to trust ye, but ye must be patient. Handle her gently."

Emrys crossed the room to the small kitchen, rattled a cup free of its hook, and filled it. "And remember, if she speaks of anything from this time that ye dinna quite understand, ye must quickly change the subject. It is entirely too soon to be introducing her to the many mysteries."

"I am not so daft as ye might think." Caelan headed toward the door.

"Ye're dafter than ye ken, my laird. Ye are a man in love with a woman." Emrys shook his head and dragged a stool over to the window. He settled himself comfortably on his perch and sipped his coffee as he eyed the scene outside.

"So, ye mean to sit there and watch as though we are an amusement?" Caelan stood with his hand on the doorknob.

Emrys smiled and lifted his cup in a silent toast.

Caelan shook his head, thundered down the stairs, and stepped outside. He noticed that when he slammed the sticking door to get it to stay shut, Rachel hurried to swipe her hands across her cheeks. Aye and for sure. The lass had been crying. Damn, that bastard on the phone.

She scrambled up from her spot on the porch and forced a calm demeanor he didn't believe for a second.

"Good morning to ye, Miss Hawkins." He nodded and offered her one of his most enticing smiles.

"It's Rachel. You can call me Rachel. All right?" She cleared her throat and glanced around in every direction possible to avoid looking him in the eyes.

"I am glad ye allow me to use your Christian name. Sometimes, it's hard for a foreigner to find a friend in a strange land." He shoved his hands in his pockets and ambled closer. What could he do to put her at ease?

She twitched with a nervous shuffle and tucked her hair behind one ear. "I'm sure you'll make lots of friends. Most of the people around here are open and easy to get to know."

Ye are the only one I wish to know. But he didn't say it aloud. Not the way she was fidgeting, as though barely able to stand in front of him. This was not going as planned.

"Is there something you need? Is everything in the apartment working like it's supposed to?" She backed toward the door, looking like a trapped animal trying to work up the courage to escape.

"Everything is fine, lass, but I wondered if there were ways Emrys and I might be more of a help to ye around here? Something other than paying our rent on time." He eased another step closer, praying she wouldn't flee and would somehow find the courage to trust him.

She narrowed her eyes and hiked her chin to a defiant angle. "Rent is all I need from you. I appreciate the offer, but I can take care of this place all by myself. Always have. I don't need anyone." What she truly meant came across clear as day and stung like a slap in the face.

Lifting both hands, he backed up half a step and gave her a bit more space. "I meant no insult to your abilities, lass. I can see by the look of the place that ye love it and care for it well. 'Tis only the nature of a good Scot to offer a hand and find out if there is aught he can do to help a lady."

She caught her bottom lip between her teeth and bowed her head. After an uncomfortable moment or two, she lifted it and met his gaze. "I'm sorry. I didn't mean to be rude. It's been a rough morning, and I've had a lot of people tell me I'll never be able to manage because I'm a woman living alone. Assholes." She flinched. "Sorry again. The *asshole* part wasn't directed at you."

Her face crumpled, and she angrily swiped her hands across her eyes and tried to stop the tears before they hit her cheeks. "Damn!

Damn! Damn!" she cursed softly, her voice breaking. "Look—I've had a terrible morning. The bank is hounding me to sell my land. My lawyer is nagging me to sell my land, and I'm getting tired of every male I come into contact with telling me what would be best for me to do!" Her purple eyes flashed like a raging storm, and her lovely bottom lip trembled. "And I realize the last thing you need is a crazy woman unloading all her problems on you when you don't even know her."

She wiped her face on her sleeve and sniffed. "I promise I'm not crazy, and I have a plan." Another sniff hitched from her. "And I won't do this to you again—I swear. All I need from you is rent. Nothing more. Nothing less, and trust me—you'd be doing yourself one hell of a favor by staying as far from me as you can get before the shittiness that is me and my life rubs off on you." Whirling in place, she yanked open the screen door, stomped inside, and slammed it shut behind her.

Caelan pulled in a deep breath, widened his stance, and waited. She reminded him of an abused animal that needed patience, understanding, and love. He had plenty of everything except the patience part, and he could damn sure work on that.

She reappeared in the doorway just as he'd sensed she would. "Look I'm sorry. Again. If you're brave enough to come inside for a cup of coffee, I'll attempt to be civilized rather than ranting like some sort of loon."

He slowly walked toward the door, allowing himself to offer her a sympathetic grin. "I believe ye will find I'm a verra fine listener, and I shall try my best not to tell ye what ye should do."

"Yeah well, that'll be a refreshing change for me. A man who's not going to tell me what's best." She gave him a real smile this time while holding open the battered screen door.

He hurried to step through before she changed her mind. "Of course, I'd have to know ye much better before I could tell ye what's best for ye," he teased. "But I'd be sure to tell ye in such a way that ye understood I was speaking from my heart and not trying to hurt ye."

He couldn't resist pressing the advantage, since he'd actually made it inside the house and was now sitting at the kitchen table.

Pulling two cups out of the cupboard, Rachel rolled her eyes at him, then filled them both. "You seem to be a very nice man, Caelan." A heavy sigh shuddered free of her. "I'm sorry I went nuts on you. Things are just a little tough around here right now, and the dogs are usually the only ones around to listen to my ranting."

She set his coffee in front of him, then eased down into a chair, and propped her chin in her hand. "You didn't have to work today? Are you on an odd shift or something?"

He smiled down at the mug of dark, steamy liquid he cupped between his hands. "Since we just arrived a few days ago, Emrys and I are taking a bit of time off to become acclimated to the area and to this time."

"To this time?" Rachel frowned as she appeared to muddle over his choice of words. "Oh, you mean jet lag? I understand, or I guess I do. I've never traveled enough to experience it myself."

"Aye. Jet lag." He nodded and sipped his coffee, having absolutely no idea what the woman meant by *jet lag*. He'd have to ask Emrys as soon as he got back to their room.

Remembering the old druid's advice, he switched to a safer subject. After a glance around the kitchen, he settled more comfortably in the chair. "Your home is welcoming and warm. Have ye lived on this land all your life?"

She let her gaze flit to the cracked countertop, the worn baseboards, and the water-stained ceiling, before giving him a dreamy smile. "This was my grandmother's house. She left it to my parents in the hopes they'd raise me here." Her smile turned sad, and she seemed to swallow hard as she ran a finger across a deep scratch in the tabletop. "They didn't like it here. They preferred town, but, for whatever reason, they never sold the property, and it became mine when they died."

Caelan cocked his head to one side and leaned in to prop his elbows on the table's edge. "Ye were close to your grandmother?" he asked softly, already knowing the answer. He and Emrys had seen the loving bond the two had shared.

Rachel brightened, and her dreamy smile returned. "I guess you could say she understood me better than anyone. She always had time for me and always believed in me. She loved me no matter what."

"It sounds as though she was your sanctuary." Now, Caelan swallowed hard, longing for Rachel to be his safe port in any storm.

She scooted her chair away from the table, hurried to push herself to her feet, and put her cup in the sink. "She was my sanctuary," she said, while staring out the window. The light spring breeze fluttered the faded curtains framing the small opening and lifted the dark curls around her face. She blinked hard and fast, swiped at her cheeks again, then cleared her throat. "Enough about me. Tell me how two men from Scotland ended up in Kentucky, just to work on a dam."

Caelan tensed. It was his turn to clear his throat. He and Emrys had worked out the basics of their story but hadn't bothered to research any intricate details as to their supposed form of earning a living while they attempted to coax Rachel into the past. "Well, I guess ye could say we are the best at what we do. The dam builders found us, made an offer, and we accepted."

With everything in him, he hoped he had said it right. He rose and moved to stand beside her. As he leaned back against the counter, triumph washed across him when he noted that she didn't scoot away and seemed to believe him.

Rachel opened her mouth to say something else just as the phone rang. She glanced at the display, recognized the number, and started shaking her head. She stared at the thing as though wishing she could throw it as it peeled off three more rings.

"Are ye not going to answer it?" he asked, unable to remain quiet any longer.

"No. I already know what they're going to say, and I don't want to hear it." She walked to the door and stared outside. The phone eventually quieted. She turned and grimaced in disgust as the light that was labeled *messages* on a black box started blinking red.

She blew out a heavy sigh and raked a hand back through her hair. "Caelan, I've enjoyed our visit. But I have some errands to run, and then I have to get busy if I'm going to get everything done before my vacation is over. She pushed open the door and tipped her head toward the porch while dismissing him with a smile.

With a defeated nod, he stepped out onto the porch but paused just as he passed through the door. "I realize we've just met. But if ye need anything, I hope ye trust with all your heart that ye can call on me. I will help ye any way I can."

"That's very kind. Thank you." She caught her bottom lip between her teeth again and bobbed her head with a stiff nod.

He gave her a sad smile and stepped off the porch. Emrys was right. This would not be easy. The lass had been betrayed so many times that she wasn't about to trust anyone. He glanced back just as she melted deeper into the house and closed the solid wooden door that sealed off the screen door to the kitchen. He didn't know which was worse, watching her mistreatment in the Mirrors of Time or seeing the aftereffects of so many bitter moments in her past.

"It nay matters," he swore softly. "The lass will learn to trust me." He rolled his shoulders, then stood taller as he strode across the yard, determined to show her he meant her no harm.

RACHEL BLEW a stray curl out of her eyes while ratcheting the log chain tighter around the base of the stump. This task had become a quest. A matter of honor and stubbornness. The huge, sprawling stump blocked the entrance to the field she intended to lease to her neighbor. If she allowed the man to grow his soybeans on her little bit of acreage, what he paid her in rent would be enough to at least cover the taxes and insurance for the house and land—and with any luck, maybe even more, depending on his harvest. In her current state of financial desperation, she wasn't about to let a stump stand in the way of having at least two good-sized bills taken care of for the next year.

She stepped back and cocked her head to one side, critically eyeing her handiwork. "Think it'll hold?"

Sam and Maizy stared at the stump and Rachel with equal interest. This wasn't the first time the dogs had watched her play tug of war with the stubborn mass of wood. Both of them yawned. Apparently, her current tactic to conquer the thing was less interesting than when she'd hacked at it with an ax, dug around it, or tried dislodging it with pry bars. She didn't want to try burning it out. The thing would smolder forever.

"This is going to work," she assured them. "You wait and see."

After a determined nod, she tightened the leather pulls on her gloves and hoisted herself up into the seat of the ancient tractor. After a deep breath and a glance at the heavens for Granny to bring her luck, she turned the key and coaxed the wheezing piece of farm machinery to life.

She twisted in the seat and watched the chain, easing the tractor forward until the slack came out of it. It held fast around the stump just as she had planned. This would work. The smell of victory charged her full of adrenaline. She gunned the tractor for the winning lunge, and the engine sputtered and died. "Aw, come on, Bessie, really? Now? Where's your hunger to win?"

She hopped to the ground and pulled her screwdriver out of the tool pouch strapped around her waist. "I'm serious, Bessie," shel told the tractor. "Now is not the time to be a stubborn piece of shit!"

"Such a mouth on a woman!" Caelan rumbled with a deep laugh that both infuriated and excited her.

She whirled to face him, lost her footing in the tangle of long grass, and ended up sprawled on her backside. Teeth clenched to keep from hammering him with some even choicer words. She glared up into his amused, green eyes. "Don't you know it's dangerous to sneak up on someone when they're around loud machinery? Especially me!" She thought about throwing the screwdriver at him but needed it to adjust the carburetor.

"Your wee bit of loud machinery appears a mite quiet about now." He flashed a crooked grin at her.

"Well, it won't be long!"

Teeth still clenched, she waved away his hand and scrambled to her feet without his help. The way his mere presence made her heart pound, she'd probably have a stroke if she actually touched him—especially after the kiss on the stairway. Not to mention that dream. After shooting him a frosty glare he'd do well to pay attention to, she made a few adjustments, then tucked the screwdriver back in the pouch. "Now, if you would be so kind as to step back a few feet, I'll get on with what I was doing."

A shiver of longing rippled through her as she brushed too close when she passed him. The mere scent of him, the way his warmth almost seemed to reach out and caress her, shook through her, pulled at her like a magnet to steel. Never had any man ever affected her this way. She coughed and rolled her shoulders to dispel the feeling as she climbed back up onto the tractor. She didn't have time for men, especially not after what the last one had cost her.

With the steering wheel clenched between her gloved hands, she focused on the stump and tried to ignore the tempting Scot standing a few feet away.

Caelan narrowed his eyes while cocking his head much like the dogs had done. "Are ye certain ye should use that chain for this task? Looks to be nothing but pure rust in spots." He aimed a frown at the strand wrapped around the stump. "Some of those links are stretched and look a mite weak to be pulling on something as sturdy as the base of an oak."

"I know what I'm doing." Besides, it was the only chain she had, and she couldn't afford to buy another. Rachel silently wished he'd either go to work or, even better, go back to Scotland. A disgusted huff escaped her. No. She needed him to stay. That rent money was badly needed. She settled more comfortably in the seat and gripped the steering wheel tighter. "This'll work. That stump's been there long enough that the roots should be rotten. I'm going to pop it off, then smooth out what's left with the front blade. Bessie, here, will make a fine path to that field."

Caelan shook his head as he nudged the chain with the toe of his boot, then squatted down to inspect it closer. "Nay, lass. This bit of metal will never hold. Snap into pieces, it will, and go flying. Let me fetch another chain or I could work on the stump for ye with an ax."

"I know what I'm doing—just get out of the way and watch." Rachel started the tractor and revved it while glaring at him. "Stand back!" she shouted over the roaring rattle of the old diesel engine. She released the clutch with a pop, then twisted in the seat to bare her teeth at the stubborn stump.

"One more time," she said, then down shifted the engine until it hummed and groaned under the strain of the pull. Her adrenaline spiked again. She'd show Caelan. She faced the front, held tight to the steering wheel, and stood to get better leverage on the tractor's old gas pedal, which tended to stick. With a hard shove, she stomped it to the floor and held on tight as the front of the tractor bounced into the air. "Come on, Bessie," she shouted, holding fast. A thrill rushed through her as the load shifted, the front wheels hit the ground, and the machine inched forward. "Yes!"

"Rachel! Stop!" Horror filled Caelan as the chain snapped just as he had feared it would.

It shot out from around the stump and struck Rachel right between her shoulder blades. Her head snapped back and her entire body arched into the air from the force of the hit. She pitched sideways and tumbled away from the wheezing tractor.

He caught her before she hit the ground, then lunged and rolled with her wrapped in his arms to keep the churning back tires of the machine from grinding over them.

"Emrys!" he bellowed over the chugging and belching of that noisy piece of destruction that needed to be replaced by a good horse. He eased Rachel down to the ground and stared at her.

"What have ye done?" Emrys shouted as he hobbled across the field, his hitching gait even worse with his struggling through the clumps of overgrown grass.

"She refused to heed me. The woman would not listen. Tell me my precious lass has not killed herself, I beg ye." He brushed her hair out of her face and almost choked at the pallor of her cheeks beneath her sooty lashes.

"The first thing I'll be doing is stopping that infernal racket!" With a narrow-eyed glare at the tractor, Emrys mumbled something unintelligible. The machine halted, and a black puff of smoke spewed from its rusty pipe as it gave one last grumbling gasp.

Gently running his fingers along her throat, Caelan searched for her heartbeat. "She lives, but it is verra weak. I can hardly feel the beating of her heart. Do something!"

Emrys gave a wheezing grunt as he knelt beside her and shooed Caelan's hands away. "*Haud yer wheesht!* Let me hear her and *not* yourself." He pressed an ear to her chest and frowned for what seemed like forever.

The old druid sat up, held his hands over her, and closed his eyes. Slowly tilting his face to the sky, he seemed to listen to some silent song heard only by him. "She is badly bruised but will heal. The energies are amazingly strong with this one."

He opened his eyes and smiled at Caelan, his blue eyes twinkling beneath his scraggly white brows. "It appears the Fates are protecting your lass. That snapping chain should have broken her back and stopped her heart. They must have noble plans in the works for the two of ye. I would go carefully, my fine laird." He offered a regal bow of his head, and his good humor melted, replaced by a sober expression. "It would seem ye have been chosen, and we all ken how difficult life can be for those who are chosen."

He grabbed Caelan's shoulder and tried to hoist himself up from the ground, his ancient knees popping in protest.

"Are ye going to fetch some herbs to help her heal?" Caelan helped the man stand, then struggled to remain calm as the ancient one turned to walk away. "Emrys! I command that ye answer me."

The old druid turned and once again tipped his head in a regal bow. "I am leaving ye with the lass. Prove to her ye can take care of her. Ye dinna need me here for that."

"But ye must heal her! Tend to her wounds. I know nothing about herbs."

Emrys shook his head, then lifted his hand in farewell as he hobbled back across the field and disappeared into the woods.

Caelan stared after him. Unable to believe that the old fool had left him here to either fail or prosper with this precious woman. He dropped back down on his knees, carefully picked her up, and cradled her to his chest. He couldn't believe how small and fragile she felt now that she was hurt. She reminded him of a newborn lamb he had once carried from a field. Watching her face for any sign of coming to, he slowly made his way back to the house.

Both dogs stayed at his heels. Silent. Their noses held high as they kept watch over the man carrying their beloved mistress. Even boisterous Sam remained quiet and subdued. The wee dog knew that his woman was not well.

After shouldering open the door, Caelan wandered through the house with Rachel in his arms, glancing into each room until he found what appeared to be her bedchamber. He eased her down onto the bed and regretfully withdrew his arms from around her.

Uncertainty, dread, and a helplessness he hated pounded through him, making him rake both hands through his hair as he stared down at her. A curse on Emrys for deserting him—for deserting Rachel in her time of need. Caelan knew how to love the lass, adore and protect her, but damned if he knew what to do to help her heal. Surely, she would be more comfortable if he loosened her clothes. Maybe that would ease her breathing.

With a nod to himself at the rightness of the decision, he started with her boots. Boots were safe, and if she awakened while he undid them, she would not be angry or affronted. At least, he hoped she wouldn't. He had told her what to do about the chain, and she'd nay liked it or listened to it. Instinct told him that as soon as she opened her eyes, he very well could be in for an arse chewing merely because he'd been right. He frowned at the ragged, knotted lacing lashed haphazardly through the holes of her footwear.

"Feck this." He pulled his dagger from his boot and cleanly sliced through all the laces. A grunt of satisfaction escaped him as he slid off her worn boots. As he peeled off her socks, he marveled at her tiny feet and smiled at her bright red toenails.

"There's that done then," he muttered, still eyeing her.

He leaned closer and watched her for any sign of waking. While her steady breathing eased his soul, her pallor and closed eyes tightened the knot of worry threatening to cut off his air. He whistled out a strained huff and allowed his gaze to travel across her clothing, soiled and covered in bits of grass and leaves. Surely, she would not wish for such a mess to soil her bedclothes.

He fumbled with the closure of her denim trews, clenching his teeth as he unzipped the wicked contraption he had painfully discovered could nip the feckin' hell out of you if you caught yourself in it. Once safely opened, he eased the bottoms down and out from around her lovely arse. He sucked in a sharp inhale as the back of his fingers grazed her silky thighs. The dainty black satin and lace sling encasing her womanly treasures nearly undid him.

"By Amergin's beard," he groaned under his breath. The hardness of his rising straining against the uncomfortable seam of his modern denims made him long for the comfort of his fourteenth century attire.

"Get a hold of yourself, man," he scolded through clenched teeth. He slid the bottoms down her legs and off her feet, gently arranging her on the sheets after brushing the soil out from under her. He eyed her shirt for a long moment before attacking the tiny white buttons that closed the soft blue fabric. Tempted to just rip the thing in two and slide it out from under her, he forced himself to stop and count to ten to gain some control. After unbuttoning the last wee fastener from its slot, he carefully worked her arms out of the sleeves.

"Merciful goddess and blessed Fates." Her ivory skin made him forget how to breathe. More of the flimsy black satin and lace shielded his view of her breasts, twin mounds of mouth-watering perfection. His hands trembled too much to undo the frustrating metal knotwork of the satin and lace binding. Out came his knife once more. He cut through it where it joined between her breasts.

Another groan left him as he worked the thing out from around her, leaving her completely revealed to his gaze. "This is pure madness," he whispered, closing his eyes. The sight of those dusky rose nipples, pert and waiting to be suckled, was permanently branded in his mind. The memory of their sweetness, when he had tasted them in the dream, tortured him even more. Jaw clenched, he reached to the foot of the bed and gently pulled the blanket up over her, tucking it up around her shoulders as he brushed a featherlight kiss to her forehead.

After adjusting the painful seam that was about to split his throbbing cock in two, he settled into the overstuffed but tattered armchair beside the bed. Here he would stay until she awakened, standing vigil and protecting her.

Faithful Sam jumped into his lap, circled widdershins three times, and then settled down with his nose pointed at his mistress. Maizy lay at his feet, her head on her paws, facing the bed. Together, the three of them would keep their beloved Rachel safe.

IT HURT TO BREATHE. It hurt to swallow. Heaven help her if she had to cough or sneezed. Not opening her eyes, Rachel remained as motionless as possible, sipping in shallow breaths and praying that neither of the dogs would choose to jump up onto the bed.

Not quite certain about what exactly had happened, the only thing she knew for sure was that she must not be dead. Or if she was, she had gone to hell, and this was her punishment. Bracing herself, she pulled in the deeper breath she so badly needed. A searing jolt knifed through her, daring her to be stupid enough to try that again.

"Shit," she hissed through clenched teeth.

"I am here, Rachel. Breathe as slow as ye can, lass. I ken ye are in pain, but ye are alive. That's what matters." A large, warm, callused hand touched her cheek with a gentleness she hadn't known since Granny got hauled off to the nursing home. Caelan's deep voice gave her a point of focus through the fog of torment.

She forced open her eyes and found him gazing down at her, so much caring in his green eyes she had to force herself not to think about it. "What happened?" She flinched and knotted her fists in the sheets. Talking increased the agony.

"The chain," he said quietly. "It snapped and hit ye."

"So you were right," she whispered, waiting for him to either crow about it or rub it in her face.

"None of that matters now," he said as he dabbed a cool, damp cloth across her forehead. "All that matters is that ye heal and return to being my precious firebrand, ready and able to kick me arse if I displease ye."

"If you keep being so nice, I'm going to cry, and then I'll sniff and cough and maybe even puke," she warned, closing her eyes again to avoid the terrifying kindness and caring in his expression. "Puking would not be a good thing for me to do right now. So, just stop it. Okay?" She risked another deeper breath and twisted the sheets to bear the pain. "How is it I'm not dead? Or am I dead, and this is hell?"

"Ye are not dead even though I am sure this seems like hell for ye. Emrys is somewhat of a healer. He said ye are badly bruised. Thankfully, nothing was broken. Ye just need to rest and mend. Soon, ye will be finer than frog hair split three ways."

"Stop stealing Kentucky sayings," she whispered even though his efforts to brighten her outlook made her heart twitch in favor of him —dangerously so.

"What can I do to help ye, lass? What can I fetch ye? Water? Chamber pot? I can do whatever ye need."

Chamber pot? Was he serious? Surely, he was still just trying to make her smile. "Pain pills," she whispered as she forced herself to endure the torment of lifting her hand and pointing at the bathroom. She had a leftover bottle of pain pills she'd been prescribed when she had all of her wisdom teeth surgically removed. The nasty pain medicine made her nose itch, so the bottle was still full. If he could find them in the medicine cabinet, at least they would knock her out for a while. She could tolerate an itchy nose a lot easier than this agony.

"Pain pills?" Caelan repeated, staring at her as if he had never heard of such a thing.

"In the bathroom cabinet over the sink. Brown bottle. White cap. I can't remember the name of them, but it should be the only medicine bottle in there. I don't even take vitamins." She managed a bitter smile. "I'm healthy when I haven't done something stupid to myself." She needed him to stop talking and just look. If it was even possible, she felt herself growing paler.

He left her side. She prayed he was headed to get the pills. From the sound of things bouncing off the sink and the tiled floor, he had to be plowing through everything in the medicine cabinet. He reappeared at the bedside, cursing under his breath while prying at the bottle's lid.

"You found them." She'd sigh in relief, but it would hurt too much.

"Aye, I found them, but I canna get the feckin' things open." He pulled a knife out of his boot, pried off the lid, and shook one of the tablets into his hand. "Lore a'mighty, lass. Hurting the way ye are, how will ye swallow this?"

She had forgotten the pills were huge. "I will swallow it because I have to have some relief." She opened her mouth and waited for him to place it on her tongue.

With a grim look, he dropped the tablet into her mouth, then supported her while holding a glass of water to her lips. As he eased her head back down onto the pillow, she panicked as it caught in her throat. Even before she could tell him, he lifted her back up and gave her enough water to wash it down. But after swallowing the tablet, she still coughed. It sent agonizing pain through her, as if someone had shoved their hands into her back and was trying to split her in two. She cried out at the torture, clutching her sides as her tears streamed.

Caelan slid into the bed and gathered her to his chest, holding her tight until the terrible spasms racking through her ceased. She knotted his shirt in her hands and buried her face against him, begging the pain to go away. "I can't stand this," she moaned. "Please make it stop."

"I would take it from ye if I could, my love," he rasped into her hair. He held her close, mumbling something under his breath in words she didn't understand.

"What are you saying?" she whispered, trying to latch onto anything to get her mind off the hurting.

"An old verse from my home," he said. "An oath, ye might say—in the old one's tongue."

"Tell me so I can understand it. Give me something to think of other than this pain." She wished the pain pill would hurry and take effect. If it didn't, she was going to vomit from this torture, and that would make it even worse.

"I give ye the strength of my heart, my love. I give ye the strength of my soul. I bind our fates and destinies. We two are now a whole. For the good of all and with harm to none, so let it be uttered, so let it be done. So mote it be."

"So mote it be," she whispered with a smile, remembering that Granny used to always say that exact phrase sometimes. The memory brought her comfort and a sense of peace she hadn't felt in a very long while. With a strange sense of floating on air, she found herself able to breathe a little easier. Thank goodness those pills hadn't expired, and they had kicked in amazingly fast. "Thank you for everything, Caelan," she said in a breathy whisper as her pain and tension melted away. "I don't know what I would have done without you."

"If I have my way about it, lass. Ye will never be without me again."

CHAPTER 5

Caelan stared up at the ceiling, his heart easier and his soul filled with more contentment than he ever thought possible. In Rachel's bed, with her tucked in close and sleeping in the crook of his arm, her head on his chest, he couldn't imagine heaven would be any better than this. Gently, so as not to disturb the rest granted her by the wee pills that magickly numbed her pain, he stroked her hair, running the silky strands through his fingers while breathing in her sweetness that made those flowery vines she had called honeysuckles pale in comparison.

When she moved her head, nestling like wee Sam trying to get more comfortable in the pillows, he went still, fearing he had disturbed her.

She pulled in a deep breath, eased it out with a breathy sigh, and then spoke in a sleepy whisper, "I must be having that dream again." She hugged her arm and leg across him, snuggling closer and torturing him with the fullness of her breasts pressed into his side.

Teeth clenched; he held his breath to keep from groaning.

"I wish he was naked too," she mumbled while curling her leg tighter around him. "Skin to skin would be so much better. Like the last dream."

Caelan bit the inside of his cheek until his mouth filled with the coppery tang of blood.

She wriggled her fingertips into the space between the buttons of his shirt and toyed with his thick chest hairs. A happy sigh came from her, so happy that he envisioned her smiling. "I love a man with a hairy chest," she sleepily purred.

Goddess help—she's feckin' killing me. With the greatest of care, he tried to untangle himself from her embrace and slide away, knowing if the pills were wearing off, and she fully awakened, she would not be happy to find him in her bed, and her naked.

"Take your clothes off," she said in a breathy voice that made him ache to do as she said. "I like the way your skin feels against mine." Moving surprisingly fast for one so dazed with those wee pills, she stretched and nipped at his throat.

He had to get away from her. She was in no condition for love play, no matter what her drugged mind thought, and if she awakened even more, he felt certain she would change her mind—and fly into a fury. She reached for him as he slipped out of the bed but only ended up as far as his pillow. With the fluffy barrier hugged tight in her arms, she smiled and relaxed, slipping back into a deeper level of sleep.

Teeth clenched so tight his jaws ached, he covered her with the soft white sheet. If she wasn't injured, he would like nothing better than to rub every inch of his skin against hers. But now was not the time.

"Sam," he quietly called, motioning for the little dog to come to him from his place at the foot of the bed. He picked the wee warrior up and placed him beside Rachel's head. "If she wakes, come get me. I know ye understand what I'm saying so, come and fetch me if she so much as squeaks, ye ken?"

With his little head cocked to one side and his pointed ears perked at attention, Sam gave a soft yip as though accepting the task assigned him. He turned three times in the tightest of circles, then firmly cushioned himself up against the top of Rachel's head. He stretched and barely licked her nose, then tucked his head between his paws and went to sleep.

Satisfied that the dog would do as he'd asked, Caelan hurried into the bathroom and splashed cold water on his face. This would have to do since there was no icy loch in which to dive, and he refused to leave her long enough to go jump into the pond to cool his painful yearning. Staring at his reflection in the cracked mirror above the pale pink sink, he frowned. Rachel's injury was going to complicate matters. He needed to be able to woo her, win her trust and her heart—and he had little time to do so. Seven moons was not that long.

Especially since he had to wait until the proper moment to tell her that on Samhain, they would travel over six hundred years back in time to start their life together. From what he'd observed so far, there was nothing here to keep the lass from wanting to travel back with him. The only things she might even think about missing were her faithful companions, Sam and Maizy. Surely, Emrys would come up with a spell to bring the dogs along.

Caelan narrowed his eyes at his reflection. Where was that seer, anyway? The old druid could add some of his healing powers to Rachel's wee pills. She seemed to be resting much easier this morning, but it would still be days before she was able to move without a great deal of pain.

He dried his face on the pink towel that matched the sink and tried to rub the knots out of the muscles in his neck. Only the lightest of sleep had come to him, mere dozing as he'd held Rachel while she slept. At her every twitch, he had gone fully awake and alert to do whatever she needed, but the night had thankfully passed without issue. And he'd held himself completely motionless, fearing the slightest movement might cause her distress. Hours of locked muscles now had him as sore as if he'd been beaten. But she was worth it, and he'd reveled in her precious warmth cradled in his arms.

"Ye've done well enough, I see." Emrys stood in the bedroom doorway, his spindly arms folded across his chest.

"She sleeps for now thanks to the wee pills she had in the bathroom." Caelan pointed for Emrys to join him in the kitchen. He raised a finger to his lips at Sam as the dog perked up and watched him walk past the bed. With the bedroom door pulled to but not closed entirely, he paused and listened for a moment before continuing down the hall.

As soon as he joined Emrys in the kitchen, he allowed himself a low growl, "Where the devil have ye been? Ye could have helped her if ye'd but laid hands upon her instead of leaving us there in that field. I've seen ye ease the pain of many a warrior as he lay groaning from his battle wounds."

"The Goddess protects the lass. How do ye think she survived such a blow to her back?" Emrys peered at the coffeepot, frowning as he held it up, and discovered nothing but dregs sloshing around its bottom. He returned it to the coffeemaker and glared at Caelan. "She fares much better than she should have, ye ken that as well as I. And from what I saw reflected off the waters of the pond, she should be up and around in but a few days' time."

He shuffled over to the refrigerator and pulled out a small bottle of orange juice. With his brow wrinkled even tighter in concentration, he finally worked the cap loose with his arthritic grasp.

"What do ye mean when ye say ye saw something reflected in the water? Have ye seen whether she returns with us to the past?" Caelan wasn't certain he wanted to hear the answer, but he needed to know the truth of it so he might prepare himself.

"I called up the reflection to see if I was to assist in her healing. To see if her life was threatened in any way." Emrys drained the bottle of juice, mopped his mustache with his sleeve, then tossed the empty container into the tall black trash bin.

"I did not look to see if she returns with us. Ye must go carefully with what ye ask and with what ye do with the knowledge once ye receive it. Every action causes a ripple, a consequence. I do ken well enough that ye must use this time to draw her closer to ye—win her heart. That is the only way to teach her it is safe to trust ye, and she nay has to fear being hurt again."

Hitching his way across the room to the back door, he paused with his hand on the knob. "And be patient with the lass. The two of ye have a few trials yet, but nothing ye canna overcome." After a sly wink, he was out the door with Maizy at his heels before Caelan could ask anything more.

Caelan snorted in exasperation. He should have known better than to try to get a straight answer out of the old druid. It seemed the concept of a simple yes or no completely escaped the ancient man.

Fetching the pot from the coffeemaker, he moved to the sink to fill it, trying to remember exactly what he'd read about making coffee. The old druid usually made it for them every morning. All the gadgets of this complicated time made Caelan's head feel as though it were about to burst. Nothing was as simple as building a fire or saddling a horse. Everything involved intricate steps that, if not followed precisely could end in disastrous results. He daren't risk revealing his ignorance of such things. At least, not until he was sure of her heart.

He lowered himself into a chair at the small kitchen table, eyeing the machine and waiting. A huff of relief left him as the coffee appeared to brew as he had seen it do when Rachel and Emrys made it. Thank the gods and goddesses. It looked like he'd done it correctly.

The slightest sound came from the bedroom. The sound of movement that should not be. He hurried down the hallway just as Sam came trotting out of the bedroom door. The dog sprang up and down in an excited bounce, then yipped and spun to return to the bedroom. Apparently, he'd been headed to fetch Caelan as he'd been instructed.

Rachel teetered on the edge of the bed, bleary-eyed and her knuckles white as she clutched the mattress to keep from falling.

"What the devil are ye doing!" Caelan rushed across the room and caught her up in his arms just as she was falling forward.

Her violet eyes flared wide with surprise. She squeaked and tried to cover herself with her arms. "What are you doing in here?"

As he eased her back onto the bed, she caught up the sheet and yanked it across her. With her arms tucked tight to her sides and clutching the covers to her chest, she glared at him. Fury and indignation flashed in her eyes. "Answer me! What are you doing in here?"

"I am here because ye are in no condition to stay by yourself! Ye need caring for, and I'm the one to do it." He sat on the edge of the bed and steadied her with an arm around her shoulders. "Do ye not remember what happened? How the chain nearly cleaved ye in two because ye refused to listen and heed my advice?"

Rachel narrowed her eyes and bared her teeth like a cornered animal. "Typical male. First thing you say is *I told you so*. Go away and leave me alone. I can take care of myself. Always have. Always will."

Before he could stop her, she floundered closer to the edge of the bed and slid her feet to the floor, biting her bottom lip as she stubbornly fought the pain.

"Rachel! Let me help ye."

"I do not need your help," she said through clenched teeth. She swayed and caught hold of the dresser for support, breathing heavily as though she had just run a race.

He stood beside her, shifting back and forth as he fought the temptation to sweep her back up in his arms. Why would she not let him help her? "What are ye trying to do, lass? Are ye hungry? Are ye wanting water? Coffee? What the feck is it? Tell me so I can help ye!"

His temper rising, he struggled to keep his tone below the level of an enraged roar. Never in all his life had he met such a stubborn woman. What the devil did they teach them in this century? What the feck was wrong with letting a man take care of them? He caught hold of her arm as she swayed to one side again.

"If you must know," she hissed, "I have to use the bathroom, and you are not going to help me!"

He scrubbed his face and sent up a prayer to the Goddess Brid for patience. Without another word, he calmly picked her up and cradled her gently to cause her as little discomfort as possible. He moved through the narrow bathroom door, stood her in front of the toilet, and tried to take the sheet from her.

"I can handle it!" She slapped at his hands, flinching with the movement but not surrendering without a fight. Her fire and stubbornness both angered and thrilled him. What passion this woman had—if only she had the good sense to go along with it.

"Go away," she growled.

"Stubborn woman," Caelan muttered as he turned and stood in the doorway with his back to her.

"You are not going to stand there while I try to pee!"

"I am, and there is nothing ye can do about it."

He didn't bother to turn his head and look at her, just jutted his chin higher and ground his teeth in determination. The lovely Miss Rachel Hawkins was not the only stubborn person in this wee house.

Something hit the back of his head, then thunked to the floor. He snorted. It would take more than a wee cake of soap to bring him down.

"Go away!" she growled again, then yelped. Apparently, the longer she was on her feet, the worse her pain became.

With a deep intake of air to hold his temper and his tongue, Caelan remained silent in the doorway. He stared up at the ceiling, narrowing his eyes as he promised himself to teach the lass a few lessons in wifely manners once they returned to his beloved keep in Scotland.

The toilet seat thunked. Thank the gods and goddesses. The woman had finally given up and sat her fine round arse on the porcelain chamber pot. He pulled in another deep breath and blew out a victorious snort.

"I hate you!"

But her tone said otherwise. She sounded weary, injured, and in sore need of love. He would give her that and anything else she needed no matter how many times she swore she hated him. A slow smile teased at the corner of his mouth. He shifted his weight and leaned against the doorjamb. Hate was a powerful emotion, as strong as love, and more often than not, there was a very fine line between the two. As the sound of tinkling water filled the air, he allowed himself to smile even broader.

The roll that held the paper for wiping rattled, then the toilet flushed. He would not turn until she told him she was ready, but he kept alert and slyly watched her out of the corner of his eyes to make sure she remained steady on her feet.

She pulled herself up by hanging on to the sink, washed her hands and face, and dried them. Her pallor concerned him, but he would give her the space she needed as long as he could.

He tried not to smile at her stolen glances to make sure he kept his back turned. Little did she realize that years of war and skirmishes with other clans had trained him to almost be able to see out the back of his head. She held tight to the sink as she sidled over to her robe hanging on the hook. Her grimace as she slipped her arms into the sleeves and wrapped it around her broke his heart and made him long to turn and hold her.

"Are you going to let me out of here or what?" she said hoarsely with her head bowed.

He turned, once more scooped her up into his arms, and carried her back to her bed. After settling her gently against the pillows, he helped her adjust her robe and covered her with the blanket. Then he perched on the side of the bed and took her chin in his hand to force her to look at him. "I am here to care for ye and to help ye heal. Nothing else. I am not one of those bastards from your past who mistreated ye so. I am a good man who intends to protect ye and keep ye safe with everything I have in me. Ye will allow me to do this. Ye will trust me, and ye will stop behaving as if ye are the only person in the world who knows what is best for ye. I did not come all this way to go back to Scotland empty handed, ye ken?" He pressed a tender kiss to her forehead, then handed her another pill and the glass of water from the bedside table.

"I'll be bringing ye some toast and a bit of coffee now," he continued in a firm tone she would do well to heed, "then ye can go back to sleep. Take your wee pill now so ye can get the sort of rest that will mend your body."

Her glare locked on him, she popped the tablet into her mouth and downed it with a swallow of water. Then she narrowed her eyes into a leery squint. "What do you mean by *go back to Scotland empty handed*?"

Shite. Well, he couldn't very well un-ring a bell, now, could he? But now was not the time to explain, so he ignored her and headed for the kitchen.

CHAPTER 6

Propped in a ridiculously enormous amount of pillows in the middle of the bed, Rachel sat with her hands folded in her lap, narrowing her eyes to better focus on her plotting. This had to stop. Immediately. All she remembered of the past three days were brief periods of frustrating consciousness between lengthy fogs of drug induced sleep.

When she wasn't awake and fighting for her independence, she was passed out cold thanks to the pain pills. Which was good since they had controlled the pain, but it was also bad because of the number of times she'd awakened to find herself protectively cradled in the arms of one very large enticing Highlander—and enjoying it a great deal more than she should. She would not get involved with that man. What was the point? He was returning to Scotland...eventually. She couldn't remember if he had ever said when. She wanted to say that the sooner he left, the better—but she'd be lying to herself, and she knew it. The stubborn Scot had already worked his way through her armor. She clenched her teeth tighter and shook her head. No. She would not...She closed her eyes and fought the four-letter words filling her mind and her heart. No. Absolutely not. No way would she allow herself to love him. With a determined nod and an oath to make it so, she decided there would be no more pain pills. Time to get over it the old-fashioned way of grinning and bearing it. In five days, she had to go back to work at the mill. Vacation time was almost up, and she couldn't afford a leave without pay.

Whether or not the chivalrous Caelan MacKay liked it, his days as her primary caregiver were at an end. She had to get stronger, and the only way she would accomplish that was to get out of bed and start moving. The longer she idled away under the critical eye of her self-ordained keeper, the weaker she became. There was no other choice. She had to get back to work.

Tilting her head toward the partially opened bedroom door, she listened. All appeared to be quiet in the house. And if she wasn't mistaken, the back door had closed with its usual squeaky thud after Caelan had pressed an entirely too tender kiss to her forehead while he thought she slept. A hard swallow did nothing to dislodge the lump of emotions that memory triggered. That mountain of a man was the most gentle and caring anomaly she had ever encountered, and he scared the living daylights out of her. She snorted away the whirl of insecurities churning through her. Now was her chance to start her more aggressive approach to her full recovery, not sit here thinking *what if...*

"No daydreaming," she ordered herself quietly.

As she eased out of bed, it pleased her to discover that her back and shoulders were loads less stiff and painful. Enough twinges remained to remind her of the failed battle with the stump, but she could at least move around now without clenching her teeth and probably even manage a sneeze without crying out in pain.

She crossed to the dresser, found a sweatshirt and jeans, and dressed as quickly as she possible. Dizzying weakness made her stop twice and lean against the bedside chair. "Too many days in bed," she groaned as she leaned over and pulled on her socks.

Her clogs would be easier than sneakers, so she slipped those on and made her way to the bathroom to brush her teeth and comb her hair. She rolled her eyes at the memory of her most recent battle with Caelan when he had insisted on standing in the doorway while she bathed. He was so stubborn. But his worry for her and his caring was eating away at the walls she'd built around her heart.

"Damn him," she muttered, rubbing her chest which had gone all warm and tingly at the thought of him.

She brushed her teeth, then attacked the tangles in her hair. Her attack softened as she remembered last night when he had taken the brush out of her hands and gently ran it through her long tresses until the curls shone and slipped through his fingers like ribbons of ebony silk—his words. Not hers.

She couldn't remember a time when a man had aggravated her so much and also possessed the power to make her tingle with yearning whenever he walked into the room. One *come hither* glance from those emerald eyes of his, and she felt the embers smoldering at her core. How could a man she had known for such a short time have the power to bring her to the point of bursting into a sexual bonfire by just smiling at her?

As she pulled her hair back into a neat ponytail, she huffed at her reflection in the bathroom mirror. "Don't even think about getting involved with *Mr. Scotland*. He told you he's only here for a short time. Remember?" Sad thing was, she feared it was too late. Already, she couldn't imagine a life around here without him.

Sensing a pair of beady little eyes boring into her back, she turned to find Sam sitting in the doorway. He cocked his head, watching her intently.

"And you! The only male I ever fully trusted! You totally betrayed me, Sam." She eased down into a squat and smiled as the wriggly pup balanced his front paws on her knees and covered her face with kisses. "I know. I know. He can be very persuasive. I don't blame you for doing what he asks."

She lifted her chin to dodge more fervent kisses and scratched behind his ears. "But now I'm better, and it's time you were back on my side. So, when you see him coming, you let me know before he gets here. Okay?" She pointed at the hallway, then couldn't help but smile as Sam trotted ahead of her like the grand marshal of a parade.

After a deep breath to brace herself against what part of her would probably hurt, she yanked open the solid back door that always stuck during this time of year. The blinding sunlight angling into the house made her squint, but a smile came easy as she filled her lungs with fresh spring air. Sam nudged the broken screen door open with his nose and bounded down the steps. Ears perked and tiny body trembling at attention, he stood guard like an immovable sentinel in the middle of the cracked sidewalk.

Rachel propped open the main door with a kitchen chair, enjoying the warm breeze sweeping into the kitchen through the screen door. "The wind is out of the south. Maybe I can get the window over the sink open too. That'll give us a much needed airing."

After fishing her toolbox out from under the kitchen sink, she selected her small pry bar and favorite hammer to convince the stubborn window to open. She wedged the pry bar under its edge and gently tapped and wiggled the lever until the sticking frame finally gave up and opened slightly. Once she slid the pane up the rest of the way, she propped it open with the stick of wood still in the sill from last summer. The faded curtains fluttered in the breeze as though the room inhaled a deep breath of the warm, refreshing air.

"What in the name of creation are ye doing now?" Caelan charged across the yard, heading toward the house.

Sam's warning bark came too late. She'd been discovered. Rachel groaned. "More warning next time, Sam? Okay?"

Caelan hit the porch with a thud and nearly tore the dilapidated screen door off the hinges to get inside.

With the hammer and pry bar still in her hands, she stifled the urge to hide them behind her back. No. This was her house, and she had every right to open the windows if she wanted. She jutted her chin higher and braced herself for battle. "I'm opening the windows to air out the house. It's a gorgeous day and warm enough to let in some fresh air."

"Give me those tools. What I meant was why are ye out of bed? And ye ken good and well that was what I was asking!" He snatched the implements out of her hands and set them on the top shelf of a cabinet well out of reach of her five foot two-inch frame.

Or so he thinks, she thought smugly. Had the man never heard of stepladders, stools, or chairs? "I'm much better, and it's time I got out of that bed. It's the only way I'm going to get stronger. I appreciate everything you've done, but I'm fine now and can take care of myself."

She fought to control the pitch of her voice as he stalked closer, towering over her with a face like thunder. "Besides, I have to go back to work on Monday. I don't have any more vacation time left this year. The quicker I get back to my old self, the easier it's going to be for me to return to work."

A step back bumped her against the cabinet. She swallowed hard at finding herself cornered between it and Caelan. She tipped a nonchalant shrug. "I'm sure you need to get back to work too. I don't w-want to be responsible for making you lose your job. Y-your rent money's going to be a b-big help to m-me."

Since when had she developed a freaking stutter? Teeth clenched; she glared up at him. Damn him for being so silent and making her stammer like some teenager caught out after curfew. "Will you please say something and stop looking at me like that?"

He narrowed one of his eyes to a critical squint, then nodded once as though coming to a final resolution of some internal struggle. He grabbed her by the shoulders, pulled her into his arms, and covered her mouth with his.

Caught off guard, she stood completely still, her hands resting on his chest. Mind reeling, the first coherent thought that made it through the wonderfully possessive storm overtaking her was that he had kissed her like this in her erotic dream.

After a long claiming kiss that threatened to make her knees give out from under her, he wrapped an arm around her waist and cradled the back of her head in his other hand. Tilting her back, he plundered her mouth even more, as if pouring his soul into her. He pulled her tighter against him, grunting in satisfaction as she reached up and tangled her fingers in his hair.

Desire and so much more flooded through her with a powerful energy unlike anything she'd ever experienced. It consumed her, surrounding her with fire and making her want—everything. With that one unbelievable kiss, he had filled her with the insatiable need to be taken right on the kitchen counter. Struggling for control, she pushed him back and pressed the back of her hand to her lips. Chest heaving, heart pounding, she gasped for breath and fought the urge to dive back for more.

"Ye will not dismiss me from your life," he said soft and low in the deep rasping voice from her dream. "I am here to claim ye, and I mean to succeed. Ye may think ye've had your fill of men, but that was before ye met me." He tipped her chin higher and narrowed his eyes, studying her with a fathomless gaze. "Ye will trust me. Ye will love me, and soon we two shall be one. I have matters I must attend to right now, but when I return, we will discuss this further. After I've prepared ye a nice bit of supper, we will relax and have the good long talk we've needed to have for some time now."

Before she gathered her wits enough to speak, his mouth closed over hers again. This time, the kiss was a brief, gentle reminder of what could be if only she chose to allow it. Then he turned and was out the screen door with traitor Sam at his heels.

AS HE MOVED DEEPER into the woods, Caelan tilted his head to better track the low murmuring chant carried to him on the wind. Emrys was up to something, and he meant to find out what. While he had immersed himself in Rachel's care and healing, the old druid had made himself scarce. It was never a good thing when the man could not be found or was too quiet for too long. It always meant the ancient one was meddling with something better left alone.

He crossed the mossy ground in silence, then raised a finger to his lips and motioned for Sam to sit. Emrys and the yellow lab sat at the edge of the pond. That could mean but one thing. The old druid was scrying into the mists again, attempting to discover...something. A thick cluster of young cedars sprouting around a mound of loose limestone shale provided ample cover as Caelan crept forward until he was on his stomach. He cocked his head to one side to catch every single one of the seer's words.

"Maizy, there be difficult times ahead." Emrys rocked back and forth the slightest bit as he stared down into the water and rubbed the lab's velvety ears. The dog watched him with an adoring gaze and thumped the ground with her tail.

"He is not a patient man," the old druid continued, "and he canna understand the women of this time. He thinks he can tell her how it will be, and then it will be done. The daft idiot nay realizes that his Rachel's beauty has not gone unnoticed."

Caelan slowly closed his hands into fists, digging into the mossy thin layer of dirt covering the limestone mound. He would kill any man who dared touch his Rachel. She was his soulmate, and he'd traveled through time to join with her heart, mind, and soul. He clenched his teeth, wondering what information Emrys had failed to share.

The druid barely stirred the water's surface with the tip of his staff. He snorted out a grunt as the reflection of a dark-haired man shimmered across the pond. "That one will be a problem and cause our Rachel a great deal of pain. Some things never change with the passing of the centuries. Powerful men can either be instruments of great good or weapons of cruelty and unhappiness."

Caelan stretched to see the image of the man appearing on the rippling pond. He committed to memory the cruel face, and the lies held in the cold blue eyes. He would remember that ruthless mouth and jutting chin with no problem. The next time he saw that man, he would stop the bastard before he ever got to Rachel and caused her harm.

RACHEL TRUDGED down the driveway in silence, her mind whirling into overdrive at all the jumbled thoughts and emotions churning through her. With her worries blinding her, she didn't even notice the family of raccoons scurrying across the road until she almost tripped over the last one that lagged back and stared up at her. Usually, completely in tune with nature, her latest confrontation with Caelan had pushed all else from her awareness.

She barely touched her lips, shivering as she remembered the taste of him, the insistent yet gentle demand of his mouth on hers. With a bewildered shake of her head, she shoved her hands back in her pockets and scuffed the toes of her shoes through the loose gravel.

Where had he come from? How could she dream about him, and then suddenly he was there? Granny never mentioned anything about summoning someone with dreams. Of course, she'd lost Granny at the age of seven. Much too young to discuss an erotic dream powerful enough to summon the lover to your doorstep the next day.

What had Caelan meant by saying she was going to love him? She pulled in a shaking breath and rubbed her knuckles up and down her breastbone. Did she love him? She barely knew him. A tiny voice inside laughed at that argument. Since when did love go by a standard timetable?

"I think I do love him," she whispered to the trees. But that wasn't the point here, now, was it? What had he meant when he said he wouldn't go back to Scotland empty handed, and the two of them would be one? Who talked like that other than the heroes in her romance novels?

He stirred feelings deep within her she'd never experienced before. Yes. She did love him. But was this actual love? How could she be sure? She'd never really thought she was capable of *genuine love* after her dysfunctional childhood and the disastrous marriage that had only been a way to piss off her parents and get out of college—kind of a two for one. She'd always thought of herself as broken when it came to love. After all, what kind of person married somebody just to spite their parents?

Lust was a major factor with Caelan. That was a given. But there was more here than just the physical urge to rip off his clothes and run her hands and mouth over every wonderful acre of him. She grudgingly admitted she looked forward to him walking into the room just so she could watch the play of his muscles as they flexed with his every move. The sound of his voice alone made her heart skip a beat with every lovely Scottish roll of his r's.

"David cost you a freaking mint and was more trouble than he ever came close to being worth." Of course, she had brought that on herself. Maybe that was her karma for pissing off her parents and hadn't she really used him before he used her? She hated it when her conscience made her look at the truth from every angle. A yank of her collar up around her face helped block the coolness of the evening breeze, but she didn't turn back, just kept trudging on, hugging herself against the mess she'd made of her life.

She was on the verge of bankruptcy and could even lose the two hundred acre farm her parents had resentfully left to her since she was their only child. So far, she'd kept the bank and creditors at bay, but who knew how much longer she'd be able to tap dance around them?

Especially since some out of town big wig named Christopher Larkin had set his sights on her land. A real estate developer, Larkin was ruthless in his never-ending search for more potential acreage. He was well known for ripping away every tree, plowing everything under, and running off all the wildlife.

His subdivisions with their cookie cutter houses filled up several thousand acres at this end of the state. Her banker had already approached her once, gently wheedling with her about perhaps selling off a hundred acres or so to Larkin to get back on her feet.

But Rachel had watched Larkin Construction's raping of the land for so long—too long, in fact. The bile rose in her throat at the suggestion of giving over even a single blade of grass to that man. Two hundred acres might be more than she could handle right now, but at least all the deer, fox, owls, and other woodland creatures would have a sanctuary against his machines for as long as she could hold out. She'd never met the avaricious Mr. Larkin, but she looked forward to spitting in his eye if she ever did.

As the sun sank lower behind the hills, a shiver raced through her, making her sore back twinge a little harder. She'd probably better turn back. She couldn't keep walking down the gravel road forever. The farther she ended up walking down the road, the farther she was going to have to walk back.

Weariness hit her hard and made her pause to take in the view. The land always made her feel better. The earth cradled her, and the trees whispered for her to not give up hope. Oranges and reds of the setting sun kissed the fresh spring growth, promising that once again, winter had failed to stop the rebirth. Everywhere she looked there were signs of new life, new beginnings with the promise of what was yet to come.

Taking in a deep breath and letting it ease out, she relaxed as Mother Nature kissed her cheek and sang to her through the budding branches of the trees. One way or another, everything would be all right. She wouldn't give up and consider otherwise.

CHAPTER 7

Caelan ran his finger along the line in the cookbook one more time to ensure he was preparing the baked chicken pie just right. He bent to the level of the kitchen countertop and inspected the piecrust from every angle. It looked like a disaster, but he'd followed the wee book word for word. Hopefully, the thing would be worth swallowing rather than spitting out.

What a feckin' complicated task it was to prepare even the simplest of dinners. He had never realized the work that went into a meal. Mistress Jennet and Mistress Florie back at the keep always bustled about when preparing meals that sometimes were called upon to feed the entire clan, but he had always assumed that was just their nature. The way they handed out duties to the kitchen lads and maids with firm commands and a shake of their fingers as though countering an attack—now he understood why.

The efficient women had always seemed to pull suckling pigs, loaves of bread, savory puddings, and baked pies out of thin air without so much as batting an eye. There had always been something wonderful bubbling in the kettle over the kitchen fires *just in case the laird would need a wee something to tide him over.*

When he got back, he was going to wrap his arms around both

the women and tell them how thankful he was for all the wonderful meals they had labored to make over the years.

Never again would he take them for granted, or bellow at them from the head table in the great hall. He would ensure they both understood how much they were appreciated just in case he had been guilty of taking them a wee bit for granted.

Breath held and teeth clenched to keep from ruining his handiwork, he eased the pie into the oven. The broken screen door banged behind him, making him smile and breathe easier. Even without turning, he knew Rachel was back. His senses spiked with joy at the feel of her in the room.

"Sit ye down at the table," he said without a glance her way, "and I'll pour ye a bit of the mulled wine I made. It'll run the chill right out of your bones."

Choosing a pair of heavy ceramic mugs yellowed with age, he filled them with the aromatic liquid from the pot on the back of the stove. He set her steaming mug in front of her, then settled himself at the table with her, sitting on the other side to give her the space he sensed she needed. After tonight, that would change, he promised himself. He tipped a nod at the cup in front of her. "That's a recipe my clan has known for so long we've forgotten where it came from. Many a warrior has sworn his heart to his maiden over such a mug of wine."

"You have a very unusual way with words. Do all Scotsmen talk the way you do?" Rachel fidgeted in the chair, staring down into the steaming mug while worrying her fingertips around its rim.

He eyed her over the edge of his mug as he stoked his intentions with a wee sip. "I dinna ken about *all* Scotsmen, but as a Highlander, I speak from my heart."

"I've always dreamed of going to Scotland," she said. "The pictures I've seen are beautiful." She hugged the cup between her hands and lifted it to her lips, pausing as if almost afraid to taste what was within. She gently blew across its surface, then swallowed hard before pulling in a wee sip.

Caelan forced himself not to smile while waiting for her reaction. It would not be mannerly to gloat.

She wrinkled her nose at him, like a child about to tease its playmate. "This is wonderful." She took a deeper drink, inhaling as she held it in her mouth.

"Aye, lass, it is wonderful." He relaxed back in his chair, his heart warming—as well as other parts of him. He loved the windblown mess of her hair. Her unruly tresses were so black that they almost shimmered with shades of blue when the light caught them just right. The chill from her walk and the first few sips of the sweet warm wine had set a lovely blush high upon her cheekbones. Her amethyst eyes had gone so dark they were nearly ebony. Even though she could be a fury when she wished, she struck him as tiny and fragile, like a wild fawn on its first forage away from its mother.

Her heartbeat pulsed beneath the ivory skin at the base of her throat, making him pull in a deeper breath. Beyond his control, his lips twitched, longing to kiss the spot and warm her blood with his caresses. The timer on the stove buzzed with a loud annoying chatter, rudely interrupting him from his reverie.

"What's for supper?" she asked, while stretching to see what he had in the oven. The tensed set of her shoulders had relaxed, and her smile came easier now. Mulled wine was the best medicine Caelan had ever found.

"Chicken pie," he said, while frowning at the lopsided crust and its holes bubbling with the golden gravy. "Your wee book said it would be done by this time, but do ye not think it should be more brown?"

"That stove is older than I am, and the oven has a mind of its own. Go more by what the food looks like than what the recipe says. If you want it darker put it back in for another five minutes. That should do the trick." She propped her chin in her hand and shifted with a telltale sigh while her gaze raked across him.

Caelan tried not to smile at the pure lust in her eyes, but he couldn't help himself. If not for the fear of driving her away, he would drape her across the kitchen table and feast on her rather than the chicken pie.

Her eyes flared wide as she seemed to realize he'd read her

thoughts. The blush on her cheeks flamed a brighter red. She ducked her head, cleared her throat, and took another sip of her wine.

He chuckled to himself as he slid the pie back into the oven and reset the timer. As a successful laird for the past fifteen years, he read people easier than books, but he would show her mercy *this time*. "Why have ye never traveled to Scotland?" he asked to give her something else to focus on, "since ye always dreamed of going there."

"Money." She rose from the table and placed her empty mug in the kitchen sink. "A trip to Scotland is a luxury I can't afford right now." Another wistful sigh escaped her. "But maybe one of these days...Never say never." She fixed a dreamy eyed look out the window and slowly swished her cup under the running water.

With the caution and ease he used with unsuspecting prey; Caelan folded the dishtowel as he studied Rachel at the sink. "Ye know..." He paused, choosing his words with the greatest of care. "Ye could always come back to Scotland with Emrys and myself when it's time for us to return. We've plenty of funds, and ye would nay have to fash yourself about paying for an inn. We've plenty of rooms in our keep. Stay with us as long as ye like."

She seemed to brace herself against the sink, and her shoulders returned to the tensed slant of earlier. After a deep breath and a loud, whooshing exhale, she turned and faced him, forcing a smile he knew she didn't mean. "Thank you for the kind offer. But when and if I ever go to Scotland, it will be because *I* paid my way."

He tossed the dishtowel to the table and closed the distance between them. With his hands planted on either side of her to hem her in, he leaned closer, forcing her to meet his gaze. "Have ye so quickly forgotten what I told ye earlier?"

He kept his voice to barely above a whisper but fueled his tone with the intensity of the longing she stirred within him. "I waited a verra long time to be with ye, lass, and ye ken well enough, that I am not a patient man. The love and the life I offer ye is not charity, and ye would do well to remember that."

Just as he was about to seal the oath with a fiery kiss, a loud knocking rattled the screen door that opened into the side yard.

Growling a Gaelic curse under his breath, he pushed himself away from her so she could answer the door.

She stared at him with her lips parted and a leeriness flashing in her eyes. It was almost as though she wished to say something, but either couldn't decide if it was the right time or couldn't find the words.

He stared at her, waiting, praying she would say what he wished to hear. She had to feel the same as he did. He saw the beginnings of it smoldering in her eyes.

Blinking hard and fast as though suddenly waking from a dream, she cleared her throat, smoothed down her shirt, and hurried to the side door.

"Can I help you?" she asked whoever stood outside.

Caelan couldn't see the visitor, but he would listen—and make sure Rachel was safe since both dogs had gone off exploring with Emrys.

"I hate to bother you," the deep voice said, "but I was wondering, would it be all right if I used your phone? My car stalled, and my cell phone can't seem to get a signal out here. My provider must not have any towers nearby."

Caelan moved closer, angling to get a look at the man. Rage exploded within him, and fury poured through his veins. It was the man whose image the pond had reflected as a danger.

The dark-haired devil leaned against the porch post with his arms crossed over his broad chest as though he had not a care in the world. His white teeth flashed like dangerous fangs against his tanned skin, and when he smiled, the cleft in his chin deepened to match the dimple in his right cheek. Aye, that was the bastard from the pond. The one Caelan needed to oust from Rachel's world.

"If you'd rather not let me in, I understand completely," the evil one said with the craftiness of an artful liar. "If you have a portable phone, simply pass it out here to me, or would you rather I write the number down for the car rental place for you to call? Either way, I'd really appreciate your help." The man's voice was like poisoned honey. He spoke as though trying to hypnotize Rachel, like a snake mesmerizing a bird.

Caelan longed to lunge forward, grab the bastard by the throat, and crush him. But he held back, knowing if he behaved as his instincts wished, it would terrify Rachel and break the fragile connection he felt growing between them. She was not of his world. She would not understand his bloodlust and need to protect her in whatever way necessary—even if that meant killing a man. Emrys had hammered that advice into him dozens of times before they traveled to this century. Caelan clenched his teeth, holding hard and fast to the old druid's wisdom.

She opened the screen door wider and waved the man inside. "It's okay. You can come in and use the phone. It's right over there."

The vile devil grinned and hurried inside. "By the way, my name is Jayden Smith, and you are?"

"Rachel Hawkins, and this is my friend Caelan MacKay." She backed away, eyeing the two men with a smugness that warned Caelan the minx was in the mood to see if he would lose his temper. Perhaps the lass wanted to see him battle for her heart after all.

Smith held out his hand to Caelan, his smile icing over to match the cold heartlessness in his eyes. "Jayden Smith, Mr. MacKay. Pleased to make your acquaintance."

Caelan glared at the man and allowed him to stand with his hand extended for what seemed like an eternity. The cruel reflection of the bastard's face in the pond kept running through his mind. But it was always wiser to keep an enemy close—where they could be watched. He caught hold of Smith's hand, squeezed it hard, and gave a curt nod. "Aye, Mr. Smith. So ye say ye're having a bit of car trouble?"

"Yes," Smith bit out as he pulled his hand away and flexed his fingers, frowning down at them with a pained grimace that gave Caelan no small amount of pleasure. "A rental. So, there's no telling what's wrong with it." He swept a gaze around the room, then he lifted his nose higher and sniffed. "Something smells great. I always enjoy my trips to the country for the food."

"I can't take credit for it," Rachel said with a sly twitch of a brow at

Caelan. She cracked the oven door and assumed an innocent expression that made him itch to turn her across his knee and smack her fine arse for her. A teasing minx, she was. "The chicken pie he prepared is huge. I'm sure there's enough for three. Would you like to stay for dinner?"

"I am certain Mr. Smith would prefer to be on his way as soon as his car can be seen about." Caelan narrowed his eyes at her, sending her a silent warning to behave.

"Actually, I would love to stay," the fiend said with a damning smile that made Caelan itch to throttle him. "The rental place will take forever to show up way out here." The bastard made himself comfortable in a chair at the table and stretched out his long legs in front of him. With a subtle nod at Caelan, he barely flexed his nearly blue-black eyes into cunning slits as though accepting the silent challenge. "So, where do you live Mr. MacKay since from your accent you don't sound as though you've been in this area very long?"

Teeth clenched so hard that his jaws ached, Caelan flexed his right hand, aching for the sword usually sheathed at his side. "Scotland is my home," he said with a low warning growl. "My uncle and I rent the apartment above the garage while we're here as consultants on the dam construction."

"Consultants? I see." Smith stroked his chin, keeping his tone condescending enough that Caelan contemplated tossing Emrys's advice to the wind and thrashing the fool. With a smug nod, Smith reached for the portable phone Rachel had set on the table, then excused himself as he dialed the number on the card he pulled from his pocket.

"Be nice," Rachel whispered, brushing against Caelan as they pulled dishes from the cupboards.

"Ye dinna ken anything about this man, lass," he said in a low voice for her ears only. "Dinna trust him." He stole a glance at the wicked wretch still talking on the phone.

"I don't know very much about you either, but I'm still nice to you." She went a bit sheepish and twitched a shrug. "Well...most of the time, I'm nice to you. Sort of." She nudged him out of the way to get into the silverware drawer.

"Negativity and evil surround that man. Can ye not sense it?" He struggled to choose his words with care, unsure just how deeply to delve into the world of mysticism with her. In his studies, before he had traveled forward in time, he'd discovered that some in this time still believed and followed the old ways, but he'd also seen a great turning away, and a dangerous mockery of anything to do with the energies and magick of the realms.

Rachel, her hands full of mismatched spoons and forks, stood there and eyed him as though trying to argue with what he'd said. However, she agreed with him. He saw it in her eyes. But he saw a reluctance there as well. She didn't wish to admit to anything she didn't understand or couldn't explain.

"I don't *sense* anything about that man," she said in a hissing whisper. "For heaven's sake, he just showed up here ten minutes ago. And as for you," she whispered while elbowing her way around him, "I haven't quite decided how I feel about you."

He wanted to call her a liar, but now was not the time. Instead, he grumbled more Gaelic profanity under his breath as he followed her to the table with the plates and bowls. At least, there was the fine view of her lovely backside as she leaned across the table to set the silverware in place.

"All set." Smith hung up the phone and tossed it onto the counter. "The rental company should be here in about an hour. That's just enough time to enjoy that dinner that smells so great, and get to know each other better."

"Speaking of which..." Rachel took the plates and bowls from Caelan and nudged him aside to finish setting the table. "What exactly brings you to this area? I take it that since you're in a rental, and you mentioned trips to the country before, you're not exactly from around here."

"Business brings me here. A client had some financial matters that required my attention." Smith accepted the glass of iced tea Rachel sat in front of him.

Caelan wished it contained a slow, painful poison.

"Personal attention?" she asked. "That makes you sound like some kind of hitman for the mob or something, though I have to admit you really don't look the part." She ladled out a generous portion of the steaming chicken pie onto the plate.

"Nothing nearly as exciting as that," he answered with a soft laugh. "More like corporate accounting stuff. Financial paperwork and such." The man narrowed his eyes as his gaze met Caelan's.

That's it, ye bastard, Caelan thought, stoking the rage consuming him. *Look into my eyes and see how I feel about ye.*

"Caelan, this is fantastic," Rachel said around the steaming bite she had just popped into her mouth. She waved a hand in front of her face and blew in and out. "It's hot like lava, though. I think I need to let it cool for a little while." She closed her eyes and beamed as she continued chewing. "You can cook for me any time you want."

He allowed himself a prideful smile. "As I've told ye, Rachel, I am a man of many talents. All ye have to do is allow me to show ye."

She choked, coughing and glaring at him as she grabbed her tea. After composing herself, she turned to Smith and cleared her throat. "So if it's business that's brought you to our area, where exactly is home base?"

"For now, Chicago," he said, shooting her a flirty wink as he scraped his plate clean. "I'm able to keep on top of everything pretty much from there. I rarely have to travel outside the city. When I do, it's usually because I've chosen to, not because I have to."

"And your company still pays for it? You're not afraid they'll shut off the funds when they find out you traveled when you really didn't have to?" She rose from the table and began gathering the dishes to stack them in the sink.

The man was lying through his teeth, and Caelan hoped Rachel saw it as clearly as he did. She trusted no one. Now was not the time to start, and that bastard was definitely not the one she needed to trust.

"I do a good job," Smith gloated with a shrug. "And because of my work, the company turns a hell of a profit. Shall we say we have somewhat of an understanding?" He rose to join Rachel at the sink, deftly sidestepping the chair Caelan kicked into his path.

"Hmm, I don't know about that," she countered. "I've seen employees who justify any type of behavior by saying the company owes them, or doesn't treat them right, or pay them enough. But I've always believed if the company doesn't treat you right or pay you enough, then go somewhere else. Don't use that as an excuse to steal from them or sink to their sleazy level."

Standing entirely too close to Rachel, Smith leaned back against the counter and folded his arms across his chest.

Caelan cursed under his breath, envisioning himself shoving the man through the tiny kitchen window over the sink.

From Smith's infuriating smile, the bastard knew exactly what he was thinking. "You are a company's dream come true," the devil told Rachel. "They don't make many employees like you. Where exactly do you work for a living or do you stay here and run the farm?"

"I work at the steel mill in town," she said as she filled the sink with hot, soapy water. "And I run this place." As she slid more plates into the suds, she continued, "I've been a crane operator for about five years now. I hate shift work, but it pays the bills."

Caelan cleared his throat, unable to remain silent any longer. "It has been well over an hour since ye spoke to your rental agency. Shall I give ye a lift to your car to see if they have shown up yet?"

Smith glanced at his watch, then shrugged. "I wouldn't want to stretch your *hospitality* too far." His toothy smile only heightened the sarcasm in his tone. "I told the rental place to swing by here to pick me up when they came to tow the car."

Caelan squared off, ready to do battle with this lying bastard. He'd been as patient as could be allowed. "Perhaps ye would like to step outside for a wee breath of fresh air. The house sits so far back off the road, they might miss ye if ye dinna watch for them."

He yanked the door open and jutted his chin higher. Once again, his right hand itched for the haft of his sword.

Smith's expression hardened into a predatorial glare. With an almost imperceptible nod, as though he'd arrived at a private decision, he turned to Rachel. "I think Caelan's right. I believe I will have a bit of a walk and watch for the tow truck. It should be along almost any time now. Thank you again for the use of your phone and the wonderful dinner. Not everyone would've been so kind." He held out his hand to her, a smile on his lying lips that made Caelan ready to spit.

Pulling her hands from the dishwater, she quickly dried them and shot Caelan a narrow-eyed glare. For his behavior, he supposed but didn't really give a damn what she thought about the way he treated Smith. She took Smith's hand and offered him a polite smile.

Smith lifted her hand and pressed his slightly opened mouth to the back of it. When she gasped and tried to snatch it away, he held on tight and did it again.

"Get Out!" Caelan caught hold of the man's shoulder and spun him toward the kitchen door.

Smith regained his footing with the quickness of a man who was no stranger to battle. His back to the door, he nodded at Rachel. "What? Along with renting from her, are you her watchdog as well?"

"Caelan. No!" Rachel went to step between them, but it was too late.

Caelan hit Smith with such force that both men exploded out the doorway, taking the shattered remains of the dilapidated screen door with them down the steps into the yard. Both rolled as soon as they hit the ground. Smith drew back to gut punch Caelan as soon as they reached their feet.

Tempted to laugh at the man's useless effort, Caelan retaliated with a well-placed shot to Smith's jaw. The cracking sound and splatter of blood that flew out of the devil's mouth filled him with a completeness he relished.

"Stop it!" Rachel shouted from the doorway, her hands clenched to her chest. "Stop it, I say!"

Caelan ignored her. He wasn't about to stop until Smith's eyes rolled back in his head, and he stopped breathing.

"If you two are going to act like hormone crazed tomcats, then I'm going to treat you like hormone crazed tomcats!" she shouted as she charged over to the garden hose.

A blast of icy cold well water hit Caelan full in the face, stinging like hundreds of needles shot from hundreds of tiny bows. "Damn it, Rachel!"

"If you two start toward each other again, I'm opening fire again," she threatened while aiming the nozzle at them, slowly sweeping it back and forth as if she couldn't decide who to drown first. "I've had enough of this idiocy. Mr. Smith, you go to the end of the driveway. Caelan, you go to your apartment. I don't want to hear one more word out of either of you. Now move it." Her purple eyes flashed with rage, making her even more beautiful and desirable.

"But Rachel..." Caelan took a step toward her, and she shot him full in the face. "Damn it, woman!"

"I warned you. Now go!"

Smith snickered, so she swung on him and blasted him in the face as well. "I've got enough water pressure to shoot your ass down the driveway. Now start walking. I've had enough!"

Coughing, as he wiped the water out of his eyes, Smith raised his hands in defeat and started trotting down the driveway. He paused after just a few yards and turned as though tempted to speak.

Rachel yanked more hose off the rack and started toward him. "Don't think I can't hit you from here."

Hands still raised in surrender, he turned and headed down the driveway at a more leisurely pace.

Caelan cursed under his breath as the gravel crunching under his boots warned Rachel of his approach.

She swung and blinded him with another blast of water, then bolted into the house and locked the door behind her.

As soon as he could see, he dragged himself up onto the porch and tried the knob even though he knew it would be locked. He banged on the door. "Rachel, lass. Please. Let me in so we can talk. I... I can explain."

Nothing answered him but silence.

He turned and leaned back against the door and slid downward until he was sitting on the porch. "Rachel! Please let me in. We need to talk, lass. More than ye could ever know."

She kicked the door hard, rattling it against him. "You're making me crazy! Go home and leave me alone. I don't have time for this kind of drama. I don't need you to screw up my life any more than it already is. Just leave me alone!"

She kicked the door again, then her stomping slowly faded as she raged her way deeper into the house.

Caelan dropped his head into his hands and propped his elbows on his knees. After a deep sigh that did nothing to ease the ache in his heart, he wearily shook his head. "I canna leave ye, lass. I love ye."

CHAPTER 8

"Hawk, this is the bundle, but be careful. There's only one set of bands left on this end," said the voice over the radio, confirming what Rachel had already suspected about the bundle of steel she was preparing to pick up with her crane. She adjusted the spreader beam and slowly set the magnets on it. With patience honed over hours of overtime, she waited for the familiar tug that let her know the magnets had fully engaged with the steel so when she lifted the load, the bundle wouldn't crash to the floor.

"Hey, Hawk! You got your cell phone up there?" squawked her supervisor's voice over the radio. His frazzled nerves heightened the pitch of his cracking tone.

"Yeah, it's up here. But I have it shut off. Why?" She rolled her eyes, knowing the answer before she'd even asked the question. Caelan had been calling her since early this morning, and she'd finally shut it off to silence him.

She carefully tapped the joystick with her palm and deftly maneuvered the bundle of steel down into the railcar, releasing it without so much as a soft thump as it landed on the awaiting dunnage. She was one of the best crane operators at the mill and had earned the nickname *Hawk* for more than just a shortened version of her last name.

"Some guy keeps calling security," her supervisor continued. "He wants you to call him back on your next break. Says it's really important that he get in touch with you. Said it was some kind of emergency." From the background sounds, Joel was in security now, and chances were, he had answered the phone and talked to whoever had called.

"Emergency, my ass," she mumbled to herself before keying the mic to respond to Joel. "Get a number, please. I promise I'll call him back. My break is in about fifteen minutes. I'll put an end to the calls, I promise."

"Thanks, Hawk!"

Rachel recognized the female voice across the radio as belonging to Mercy, the good-natured security guard who was everyone's favorite at the mill.

"Hey, Charlie!" Rachel shouted across the radio. "Can you cover me while I go get rid of a man?" She leaned forward in her seat and watched the man walking on the stacks of steel to the west of her crane. The older man in his bright yellow hard hat looked up at her and gave a thumbs up, then put his radio to his mouth. "Sure, Hawk! Long as you don't make me an accessory. Take her to the landing, and I'll run her while you take a break."

"Thanks, Charlie!"

She hurried to park the crane at the landing and made her way down the several flights of steps. She patted Charlie on the back as she headed out the man door of the mill to the security building.

Joel was still there as she pushed her way through the door. He was nervously fidgeting through several piles of paperwork between glances out the window at the number of trucks waiting to be loaded.

"Here's the number, Hawk," Mercy said. "He sounds sexy!" She gave her a wink as she pressed a yellow sticky note into Rachel's hand.

The number made Rachel frown. It wasn't any of the numbers Caelan had used when calling her cell phone. "Hey Mercy. Can I make the call in First Aid, so I can have some privacy?"

Rachel fished her cell phone out of her coveralls and patiently waited while Mercy calmed Joel down by deciphering his paperwork for him, gave directions to three drivers, and printed load sheets for two other drivers all at the same time.

Mercy waved her toward the door to First Aid. "Just promise me I can have him whenever you're done with him!" She shoved Joel out the door just as he was about to sputter an angry retort about fifteen minute breaks and quickly flipped the bolt on the door so he couldn't get back into the room. "Hurry!" she said as she leaned back against the door.

Rachel rushed into the triage room, punched in the number, and listened to the ringing on the other end, wondering who was going to answer. As soon as she heard the voice, she rolled her eyes and glanced at her phone to make sure it wasn't roaming.

"Don't hang up, Rachel, and no, you're not roaming. This is a number you can call from your area. I already checked." Jayden Smith's voice was crystal clear on the line as though he stood in the room beside her.

"What do you want?" she said, clipping her words and couldn't believe she had wasted her fifteen minute break on one of the idiot males she'd had to souse down in her yard last night.

"I wanted to apologize for my behavior and ask you to give me another chance." His voice lowered to a sultry purr, and she almost pictured a huge jungle cat, with its eyes half closed, hanging on a tree limb.

"Another chance at what?" She glanced at her watch. Five more minutes, and she still needed to pee before she climbed those stairs back up into the crane.

"Another chance for you to find out that I'm not the Neanderthal I appeared to be last night, and I really wish you'd speak to me in more than just four-word sentences." His voice had taken on a bit of a strain, like a spoiled brat used to always getting what he wanted. Jayden Smith was the last thing she needed in her life.

"Sorry. Have to go. Don't call here again. I'm not in the market for complications of any kind right now, and that includes relationships—be they friend or be they foe. I'll give your number to my friend Mercy. You'll really like her. Bye." She ended the call, powered down her phone, and pushed her way back into security.

As she headed out to the restroom, she tossed the balled up sticky note with the number to Mercy, shouting back to her over her shoulder. "He looks like he'd be good in bed, but other than that I bet he's a real jackass."

With a wicked grin, Mercy smoothed out the note and began punching the number into the phone. "Hmm...I'm up for a ride on a mule anytime."

"Emrys!" Caelan bellowed, fueling the shout with every bit of rage and frustration hammering through him. His yell echoed through the woods but went unanswered except for the wind shushing through the trees and the wee birds chirping and chattering. Sam stood patiently by his side, his tiny head cocked as though straining to hear Emrys's response.

Working his way deeper into the trees, he finally came upon what he thought of as Emrys's pond even though it was really Rachel's. Disappointment ratcheted his irritation tighter as he scanned the banks of the wee bit of water and found it deserted except for a squirrel skittering down for a drink. The old druid's usual spot on the limestone shelf overlooking the pond was littered with pine needles, pinecones, and small branches blown free during the last storm. Apparently, the seer had not sat upon his stony throne for a while.

"If that sorcerer traveled back in time without me, I shall wring his ancient neck." A sickening dread churned in the pit of Caelan's stomach as he continued searching through the grove.

"Maizy!" he shouted, deciding on a different tactic to find the man. The golden lab never left Emrys's side. She had even taken to curling up at the foot of his bed every evening, having moved herself into their apartment over the garage. While Rachel was Caelan's soulmate for all time, it would seem Maizy was Emrys's match.

"Why must ye always bellow?" the druid asked from his perch atop a large boulder wedged between a pair of oak trees so huge they had to be hundreds of years old. True to her nature, Maizy sat beside him, faithfully leaning into his side.

"Why do ye refuse to answer when I summon ye?" Caelan leaned against the rock, his heart aching as he stared off into the woods. "I fear she'll never forgive me." He scrubbed his face with both hands and bowed his head. "Pray tell me I've not lost her for good."

"Did I not advise ye to go carefully in this time?" the ancient one gently asked. "Ye canna address things here as ye would address them in the past." Emrys blew out a heavy sigh. "The imbalance in the energies here is taking its toll upon me. Ye must try harder, Caelan."

"It was him who ye saw upon the surface of the pond. The evil one intending to do her harm. The feckin' devil tried to seduce her right in front of me! Was I expected to stand there and do nothing while he devoured her, then spit her out?" Raking his hands through his already wild blonde hair, he bared his teeth, aching with the need to hunt that bastard down and end him.

"Did it ever occur to ye that the man was testing the two of ye, and ye played right into his hands?" Emrys shook his head while staring down at Maizy and rubbing her ears. "I saw it in the waters. He's now drawn to her because she revealed her inner fire when she hosed ye both down. His only interest was her land until he witnessed her anger. And, aye, he's evil, but the man is no fool. He knows any woman capable of such fury can also reach unbelievable levels of passion." He poked Caelan's shoulder, then shook a bent finger in his face. "That also explains why the Goddess has protected the lass. There are few like her left in this time."

The seer frowned, knotting his scraggly white brows as he scratched his beard. "The way I see it, the only thing ye have left in your favor is that the lass does not wish to have a relationship with anyone at all. She still trusts no one. Therefore, she will more than likely spurn his advances."

He worried his staff between his hands, running his bent fingers along the knots and whorls of the wood that seemed to come alive and dance beneath his touch. "However,..." He fixed a grim look on Caelan. "A man like that's appetite will only increase when he is rejected. He will become crazed for that which he canna have."

"It has been almost two months since we arrived," Caelan said, feeling worse than before he'd found Emrys. "Two moons wasted, and I'm no closer to joining with her or convincing her to return with us than I was when we first began. What would happen if I stole her back to our time? Stealing wives is a time-honored tradition in the Highlands, ye ken?" He searched for a glimmer of hope from the old druid.

Emrys rolled his eyes. "We already discussed that. Have ye forgotten? She must come back with us of her own free will. The Fates have made it known to me they are not so fond of that kidnapping habit, and neither is the Goddess." He shifted on the rock and squinted up at the storm clouds gathering.

"Then ye are going to have to tell me how I can win her because everything I attempt is wrong." Caelan held his head and groaned. "Leading my clan is nay as complicated as winning the heart of this one woman!"

Emrys scratched his head with the knot on the end of his cane, frowning as he narrowed his eyes and appeared to be plotting. "I'm thinking that Smith devil will reveal himself for what he truly is. I refuse to believe we've been allowed to come this far to watch the lass hand herself over to that ruthless cur." He pursed his lips and nodded, making his mustache twitch. "Take a step back from the lass. Become her watcher without her knowing it. Only step in if ye see she's in danger. 'Twould be even better if ye can hold off until she cries out and admits she canna help herself. She is a strong woman, your Rachel is, and ye drive a wedge deeper between the two of ye every time ye deny that strength." He caught hold of Caelan's shoulder and tightened his grip. "Can ye do that, my laird?"

Caelan blew out a weary sigh as he pushed off the boulder and attempted to roll the stiffness from his shoulders. "It appears I have no choice, old man."

"If you put that woman through one more time, you're fired!" Releasing the intercom button, Jayden Smith spun in his chair and stared out the glass walls of his office at the city sprawled before him like fresh fruit waiting to be plucked from the vine and crushed.

How dare Rachel Hawkins give out his private number to some sex-crazed woman who said she was some kind of security guard? That guard sounded deranged and possibly dangerous. He made a mental note to hire extra personal guards to travel with him the next time he went to Kentucky.

And how dare Rachel, that little backwoods hick, turn him down when he could show her a better time than she had ever known by the looks of that shack she lived in.

With her looks, he could turn her into an absolute queen, a mesmerizing beauty that would demand the attention of every person in the room as soon as she walked through the door. But no, she was too busy floundering in financial ruin and trying to hang onto land left to her by parents who never wanted her.

Background checks and digging up old skeletons about insignificant individuals were so simple they were almost laughable. Especially, when the private investigator had been persistent enough to find Rachel's ex trying to eke out a living off the worst streets in Vegas and willing to spill everything he knew about her for enough money to get good and high one last time.

Jayden's interest in her had started simply enough. He had merely wanted her land. But now that he'd met the woman, the challenge of winning her had become an obsession. His personal quest and he *always* got what he wanted.

The office door opened quietly, and his assistant silently moved across the plush carpet around to his side of the desk. "These are ready for your signature, sir."

"Thank you." Grabbing a five hundred dollar pen from the stand on his massive desk, Jayden lined up the forms and signed them with his legally given name, *Christopher Jayden Smith Larkin.*

CHAPTER 9

An oddly emotional mix of relief, disappointment, and worry shot through Rachel as she pulled up the driveway and noticed Caelan and Emrys's rusted out old truck wasn't in its usual spot beside the garage. Another confrontation this evening was something she wasn't prepared to handle. Not right now. Her first day back at work had seemed harder than usual, and the soreness in her back reminded her it hadn't been that long since she'd been so injured that she couldn't even move. The sight of both dogs rounding the corner of the barn, barking and wagging their tails made her smile. There was no doubt *they* loved her and could be trusted.

After stuffing the pile of bills she'd pulled from the mailbox into her upturned hardhat, she tucked it under her arm and eased her aching body out of the truck. "Hey, babies! I'm glad to be home too! I love you too!" She squatted down and laughed into their adoring kisses, patting and hugging them until they almost knocked her over with their wiggling.

A grunting huff worked free of her as she stiffly rose and made her way into the house, dumped her stuff on the kitchen table, and plopped down in a chair to unlace her boots. The hard toed boots with the metatarsal protectors probably weighed close to three pounds each. They were always the first thing she shed at the end of her day.

Most of the mill workers changed in the shower house and left their work clothes in their lockers at work. But she preferred to make a beeline for her vehicle and head home, no matter how grubby she might be by the end of her shift. If she ended up covered in an excessive amount of the black mill dust, she'd hose her boots off before coming into the house. But being a crane operator, she was one of the lucky ones who stayed somewhat clean.

She leaned against the table and rested her head in her hand, trying to calm her churning thoughts and emotions about the last couple of months. A long white envelope taped to the outside glass of the kitchen door caught her eye. "How did I miss that when I came in?" She must be more tired than she realized. In her sock feet, she went to the door, peeled the envelope off the glass, and cast a leery look inside it.

"What in the world?" She pulled out three crisp one hundred-dollar bills. Staring at them, she made her way back to the kitchen table, sank into her chair, and gingerly smoothed open the letter that had been folded around the money.

My Dearest Rachel,

Please accept *my heartfelt apologies for my behavior last evening. I have no explanation for my actions. Enclosed you will find money to replace the screen door I destroyed.*

I finally understand *what you wish from me, and I swear to you that from this day forward, I will never be a problem to you again.*

. . .

Your humble servant,
   Caelan Foster MacKay

She swallowed hard, rereading the letter twice more while a disturbing sense of loss and uneasiness knotted in her chest and became heavier with every passing second. With her lower lip caught between her teeth, she swallowed hard and blinked against the sting of tears threatening to burst free. She never cried, but oh how she wanted to sob her heart out right now.

"Get a hold of yourself," she choked out. "This is what you wanted—remember?"

But what did he mean he would never be a problem to her again? Had they headed back to Scotland without even saying goodbye? Or had he finally decided she wasn't worth the effort? What about all those things he'd said about not leaving here without her? And that he was going to *make* her love him? How they were meant to be together? Had it all been lies? Some silly game for him to toy with the stupid American?

"Why are you even feeling this way?" she growled, as she smacked the envelope down on the table. The last thing she wanted was to get involved with a man. All she needed was a reliable tenant for the apartment. Rent money to pay the bills. Rent money *on time*. But if she was honest, it wasn't the loss of the money that upset her. Her heart hurt, burned like an open wound. Her heart burned for him.

"Damn it! Why is everything so freaking complicated?"

She slammed her fist on the table, shoved the letter away, and watched it flutter to the floor. Stubborn Highlander. She didn't want him completely out of her life. She just wanted him to slow down a little. Her life was such a jumbled mess right now. She needed to get a few things ironed out before she walked into any more complications.

She'd always been attracted to him, and the way he'd taken care of her when she was hurt had touched her heart more than she was ready to admit. But he always acted as though she were such a helpless creature, and after what she'd been through the past couple of years, she'd be damned if she would ever be perceived as helpless by anyone ever again.

Pushing up from the table, she went back to the door to see if, by chance Emrys and Caelan had shown up. Her heart sank at the sight of her truck sitting all alone in the driveway. The windows in the apartment above the garage were still dark—empty like dead eyes, eyes bereft of hope.

She turned from the doorway and bent to pick up her boots. The faint crunch of tires on the graveled driveway caused her to catch her breath. "Thank goodness," she whispered, pressing a hand to her heart. The faded blue truck with the rusted out paint job, the one owned by the two Scotsmen, was slowly pulling up the driveway and making its way to the parking spot beside the garage.

With a stumbling hop, she stuffed her feet back into her boots, then hurried out onto the porch without lacing them up. Hair falling down and hands stuffed in her pockets, she bounced in place as Caelan and Emrys emerged from their vehicle.

"Caelan!" she called out, holding her breath to see if he would look her way.

His bowed head immediately lifted. He looked at her and nodded politely before turning away. Emrys waved at her, then mumbled something to Caelan before patting Maizy on the head and heading toward the garage.

"Caelan, if you're not too busy can we please talk?" She nervously chewed on her bottom lip, remembering how he had made that same request last night, not two feet from where she stood, and she'd told him to go away. "I'm sorry I didn't listen to you last night. I found your note. And...and it's not what I want. Can...can you please come over here so I don't have to keep shouting across the yard?"

He stared at her, appeared to take in a deep breath, and slowly blew it out.

She held her breath, clenching her fists in her pockets, anxious to see what he would do.

After an entirely too long amount of time, he turned and ambled toward her as though still unsure if he should come over or not.

She fidgeted with the pockets on her coveralls, tugging at the unraveled edges. Her heart soared when he headed her way, but now what? What was she going to say when he got to her? How could she explain everything when she didn't really understand it herself?

He finally reached the porch, stopped in front of the steps, and stood staring at the ground. His squared jaw flexed as though he were gritting his teeth.

"Caelan," she whispered, while slipping closer to the edge of the porch. From where he stood, they were almost at eye level if the infuriating man would just look up at her. "Caelan?"

Ever so cautiously, he raised his tortured gaze and stared at her with such pain and pleading that she gasped. All time and space seemed to stand still. A brilliant violet light burst into existence and surrounded them in a shimmering, pulsating orb. The light whirled and strengthened, swelling and dancing like a heartbeat as it drew them closer together.

Rachel found herself uplifted and energized as the violet energy swirled around and through them until there was no distinguishing where one of them ended and the other began. The circle tightened, drawing them closer still.

She had to remind herself to breathe. Somehow, she understood everything about Caelan now. Her thoughts and his, her emotions and his, everything melded into one fiery, vibrating frequency that surged through her heart and soul, then traveled through him as well. She watched the violet stream pour from her chest to his, swirl and travel back as though sharing everything between them. Then, the energy faded away, disappearing like dawn's delicate mist hit by the morning sun.

"I think I am in love with you," she admitted softy. She reached for him and pulled him a step closer to brush her lips across his.

"What say ye, lass?" He grabbed both her hands and held her at bay, putting a bit of distance between them. Tipping his head to the side, he reminded her of Sam listening for Maizy barking in the woods.

She couldn't be apart from him any longer. She leapt into his arms, wrapped her legs around his waist, and locked her arms around his neck. "I said I love you."

With a rumbling groan, he tangled his fingers in her hair, tipped her back, and held her there while he stared down into her eyes. "My precious, lass. I had given up all hope of ever hearing ye say that." He crushed her to him, backed her against the porch railing, and ravaged her mouth with his. His passion, fury, and fears poured into her, and she returned the same to him. This wasn't just a kiss, it was their souls touching, reassuring each other that finally, things were as they were meant to be.

As she broke the bond, she whispered, "I thought you'd returned to Scotland. I thought you'd left me."

His rumbling voice, deep, yet both soft and husky, rasped with raw emotions. "I could never leave without ye, my love. But I've done nothing but drive ye away every time I've tried to draw ye closer. I meant what I said about nearly giving up hope. Ye have no idea how badly I need ye. Ye are mine, Rachel. Made for me as I am made for ye."

She pressed her forehead against his and whispered, "Why don't we go inside because I need you too...badly." She hugged him tighter and tucked her face into the warm crook where his neck met his shoulder. Her cheeks burned like fire from the sheer boldness of her behavior. She'd never begged a man to take her before, and, for a moment, she thought he hadn't heard her. Then he scooped her up into his arms.

He strode up the steps, crossed the porch, then turned and bumped the door open with his back. Once inside, he kicked the door shut and turned to bolt the lock. "We shall not have any interruptions this evening," he said in a tone that sent a delicious shiver through her.

"Don't get my boots on the bed!" she squeaked as he strode down the hallway, then sidled them through the bedroom door.

An amused snort huffed from him as he sat in the oversized chair beside the bed and settled her in his lap. "Has anyone ever told ye that ye are a headstrong woman who gives entirely too many orders?"

With one muscular arm hugging her close as if determined to never let her go, he slipped one of her boots off and tossed it to the floor.

"You have," she answered. "Repeatedly. But this time, I have a good reason. My boots are nasty, and I don't want to be rolling around in mill dust while we are...uhm...while we..." Her entire body flamed hotter as she struggled to finish that sentence.

"While we what?" He gave her a knowing grin while hugging her closer and slipping off the other boot.

"Just shut up and kiss me!" She pulled his head down and opened her mouth to his. For someone so strong and burly, his lips slid across hers like sumptuous velvet.

After kissing her until she thought she'd surely melt into a puddle of yearning, he left her mouth and nibbled along her jawline, then tasted his way down to her throat, leaving a trail of fire in his wake.

Her breath caught as he stretched the neckline of her tee shirt out of his way and continued his determined tasting of her. "We have to get out of these clothes," she rasped as she grabbed the front of her coveralls and popped the snaps open. She pumped her legs, kicking to right herself and get out of his lap so she could shed them.

"Slow down, lass!" he laughed. "We have the rest of our lives to enjoy each other." He helped her stand before she dumped herself off onto the floor. His laughter faded to a groan, and the burning intensity of his gaze sharpened as she shucked off her clothes.

"You are staring," she whispered.

"Aye, love. That, I am. I canna help it." He rose and barely traced a finger along her cheek, down across her collarbone, and then farther down her arm. He smiled while running that same finger along the ray of sunlight slanting across her. "The setting sun has painted ye in copper and gold, making ye shimmer finer than the most precious silk." He slid his fingers into her hair and combed his hands through her curls, draping them across her shoulders. "Ye are a goddess, my love. A beautiful goddess that I canna get enough of."

Her heart pounded, making her breathless and even more eager for them to possess each other completely. "I want to see you," she said as she fumbled with the buttons on his shirt. His familiar scent of fresh pinewoods and a very aroused male wafted across her senses, making her mouth water. She circled him, stretching to peel the shirt off his broad shoulders and down his bulging biceps.

Silent and wearing a smile that almost made her dizzy with yearning, Caelan watched her, his heavy-lidded gaze following her every move.

She ran her hands along the sculpted muscles of his back, frowning at a long, jagged scar running along his right shoulder blade. Aching for the pain he must have suffered, she pressed a kiss to it, then hugged closer, soaking in his warmth and reveling in the deliciousness of his skin sliding against hers.

"Lore a'mighty, woman. Ye are about to kill me. Come here and let me love ye." He pulled her around into his arms and clutched her to his chest. He slid his hands down her back, cupped her backside in his hands, and squeezed. "Finish undressing me, my love. Some of my best features are in the front, ye ken?"

She kept her gaze locked with his as she undid his belt, unfastened his jeans, then shoved them down past his tensed hips and muscular thighs until they lay tangled around his ankles.

Kneeling, she pulled each of his feet free and shoved the jeans aside. With a feather-light touch, she tickled her fingers up the inside of each of his legs. She couldn't help but smile when he hissed with a sharp intake of air as she traced his impressive length with the tip of her tongue, then licked a circle around the head.

She cupped him in one hand, while stroking with the other, and swallowing him as deep as she could. The harder she sucked and swirled her tongue around him, the tighter his fisted hands tangled in her hair.

"Come to me," he growled as he grabbed her up and tossed her across the bed.

His eyes were filled with longing and the love she'd felt from him in the strange violet glow. Their gazes locked as he covered her body with his. Her breasts belonged against his hard muscular chest, and she hugged her legs around him, arching to hurry him along to where she needed him most.

"The taste of ye," he groaned, while nuzzling her neck and rocking against her, "your scent—lore a'mighty, everything about ye turns me into a ravenous beast raging to possess ye."

He lifted his head and glared at her. "Ye've undone me this time, my precious, seductive lass," he said with a wry grin. "But I will have my revenge before this night is through."

She raked her nails down his back and arched into him again, bucking to get him inside her. "Less talk, my fine Highlander. More action."

A determined glow lit in his eyes like an unextinguishable flame. He pushed into her with a long, slow shove, groaning as he buried himself completely. "By the Goddess, we are made for each other."

He drew back out and plunged in again until they rocked together in the ancient dance. Their bodies melted into each other, as did their souls. Rachel crested and spiraled into mindless bliss first, but with her cries, Caelan quickly followed, roaring his release.

As he rolled to one side, he hugged her tighter. She buried her face in the curve of his neck, agreeing wholeheartedly. His touch, the length of his body entwined with hers, was something she was loath to be without.

He pressed a kiss to her forehead as he reached down, snagged hold of the sheet, and pulled it up over them. "I love ye, my precious one. More than ye will ever know." He tightened his arms around her and rained kisses into her hair.

"I love you, too," she admitted softly, thrilled that she no longer feared saying it. "I never thought it possible I'd ever love anyone, but you made me whole. Healed me." She kissed his chest and breathed him in, floating on a cloud of utter contentment.

Caelan rocked her even closer. "We both are whole now," he whispered. "'Tis a painful thing when half your soul is gone from ye." He shifted against her with what sounded like a satisfied sigh. "But when ye find that half and come together as one—there's nary a greater feeling than that in all creation."

CHAPTER 10

The rude blaring of Rachel's alarm clock startled Caelan to full wakefulness as if someone had shouted a battle cry. She flailed away from him, slapped at the thing until it went quiet, then rolled back over and snuggled back into his arms. "I wish I didn't have to go to work today," she mumbled, hugging herself tighter against him.

He tightened his arm around her and kissed the top of her head. "Stay here with me today. Surely, that mill of yours can survive one day without ye."

With a jaw cracking yawn, she lifted her head and gave him a sad smile. "The mill will do fine without me, but my paycheck won't be fine without today's eight hours of pay."

"Ye fret too much about money. Everything will be fine now that we're together." She didn't realize how fine it would be. He was tempted to tell her, but something stopped him. His gut warned that their bond was still too new, and he might lose her if he didn't go slow. Her trust needed to be unshakeable before he explained they were heading back to the past, to fourteenth century Scotland.

"One of these days, I might not need to worry about money," she grumbled with another yawn. "But today is not that day." She treated him to a glancing kiss, slid out of bed, then headed into the bathroom. Squeaking pipes and the sound of water pelting the wall told Caelan she was headed for the shower. She peeped out of the bathroom while brushing the snarls from her hair. "Don't you have to work today? I don't want to cause you to lose your job."

He couldn't resist a smile as he scooped his jeans up from the floor and slipped them on. "Ye need not worry about that, lass. I assure ye my job is quite secure."

Before she could turn back into the bathroom and head for the shower, he gave her a suggestive grin. "What time do ye have to be at work?"

"We don't have time," she said, regret lacing her tone. "But tonight…" She gave him a suggestive look of her own.

He pulled her close and confirmed the date with a powerful kiss that hinted at even more—if only they had the time. Once he made her properly breathless, he drew back and smiled. "Until tonight then, lass."

She gave a heavy sigh and backed toward the shower. "Shame we can't jump to tonight and skip the working part of the day."

"Aye, lass." He clenched his teeth to keep from revealing anything more. "A damned shame we canna jump across time."

"I dinna ken how to tell a woman from this time that I need her to come home with me to 1379." Caelan shifted in place, watching a sleek turtle, more black than green from the muck at the bottom of the pond, crawl up onto the large limb sticking up out of the water, and stretch its wee head toward the sunlight dappling down through the trees.

While Caelan enjoyed a sense of contentment this morning, nay, it was more than contentment—it was a feeling of completeness—yet still, worry and dread about the next task looming on the horizon threatened to steal his joy. He eyed the rippling rings spreading from the turtle's perch as another turtle joined the first. An ache for his home filled him. He missed the sea's crashing waves around the castle of Clan MacKay.

"What can I say to her that'll not sound as if I've gone mad?" he asked Emrys.

The druid frowned as he idled his way around the bank of the pond, stroking his beard with every footstep. "It may not be as difficult as ye think. There is something mystical about this place. I saw that violet orb surround the two of ye yesterday evening. Perhaps the lass won't think it so strange if she's open to the energies."

"We haven't talked about the light that brought us together and helped us see each other's hearts." Caelan resettled his stance and adjusted that dratted seam in the crotch of his trews that was doing its damnedest to split the hard rising the memory of last night gave him. "We nay talked verra much yesterday evening."

Emrys shook his head and rolled his eyes as he settled himself down on his limestone ledge. "Ye best set your mind on more talking with the lass. We've but a short time left here in Kentucky."

He offered his staff and inclined his head toward the deepest end of the pool. "Take this and stir the waters. With any luck, the energies of this place will guide ye."

Caelan clenched his fists while eyeing the staff. To take hold of that thing would be like grasping hold of a poisonous adder. "I canna call to the powers of this place."

Emrys pushed himself to his feet, stepped down off the ledge, then shook the staff at Caelan. "Ye ask me to advise ye, and then ye refuse to listen! So, ye've become a coward, then? Has traveling to the future stripped your manhood from ye?"

"Ye forget your place, druid!" Caelan growled. "When have ye ever known me to cringe from a battle?" He snatched hold of the staff and barely controlled the urge to snap it in two.

Emrys tipped his head to a submissive angle and slowly backed away. "Forgive me, my laird. I was merely frustrated that ye lost your belief in the ways. After all, ye ordered a chapel built next to the keep and brought a priest in for those in the clan who might find comfort from it."

"I can believe in both, old man. A wise leader keeps his mind open to all possibilities." He strode to the darkest waters of the pond, lifted his face to the heavens, and sent up a silent prayer to every benevolent power he had ever known. After breathing deeply to slow the pounding of his heart and clear the chaos from his mind, he touched the tip of the staff to the pond, the waters dark in the shadows of the trees.

At first, nothing happened. Caelan focused harder, holding Rachel clearly in his mind. Shimmering colors, golds, silvers, reds, and violets appeared where the rod touched the water, flowing out and spreading as though pouring out of the staff. Then the image of an overwrought Rachel came into focus. Eyes wide with fear, hands held up in terror, she backed away from something that was still too smudged and foggy to make out. Then the snarling face of Jayden Smith cleared in sharp detail. He was the one making Rachel retreat.

Rage sent Caelan's blood to a slow boil. "I should have killed that bastard when I had the chance." Teeth clenched, he tightened his hold on the cane, envisioning his hands around the man's throat.

The image disappeared but was replaced by one of Rachel sitting on an ancient stone bench, her face buried in her hands. As Caelan studied the vision closer, he recognized the garden as the one enclosed by the protective walls of his castle. Rachel was weeping, her shoulders shaking as though her sobs would never cease.

He looked up at Emrys, his heart turning to lead in his chest and sinking like a weight to the pit of his stomach. "What do these images mean? It looks as though she returns with us but ends up miserable. Will she not be happy with us in the past? Will she not be able to join us and settle in like one born in that time?"

Emrys frowned, his wild white brows knotting over his troubled eyes. He took the staff back from Caelan and slowly shook his head. "I canna tell ye what the images mean. Only that what ye have seen will come to pass." His gaze dropped to the ground. "Her weeping in your garden could be explained easily enough since we dinna ken what has come to pass right before that moment. Perhaps we should not have looked for guidance. Sometimes, following your heart is best."

Caelan narrowed his eyes, glaring at the old man. "So, what ye are telling me is that we've merely complicated matters by toying with your wee crystal ball here?"

Emrys bowed his head. "Aye. My deepest apologies, my laird."

"Hey, Hawk! What am I supposed to do with all these roses?" Mercy's voice filled the crane cab, drowning out the local radio station currently playing one of Rachel's favorite songs.

"If they're from Smith, then find out if any of the guys in the mill want to take them home to their wives." Rachel released the mic on the radio and added, "Or call Mr. Smith's office and leave a message for the roses to be shoved where the sun doesn't shine—preferably with the thorns fully intact." She adjusted her safety glasses higher on the bridge of her nose and stretched to peer down at the bundle below her magnets.

"And all these balloons?" Mercy's voice was taking on a decided strain in her struggle to keep from giggling over the radio.

"Pop them," Rachel said as she picked up the bundle of steel, maneuvered it over the roll line, and positioned the long bundle of channels for cutting at the offline saw.

"And then there's the candy?" Mercy had given up on trying not to snicker. She merely keyed off the mic to keep her fit of giggles from clogging the airwaves.

"You haven't eaten it yet?" Rachel trolleyed the crane back to the stacker and parked to wait for another bundle of finished product to add to a stack.

"Well, I might have tried a piece or two," Mercy admitted over the radio.

"Knowing this crew, you shouldn't have any trouble getting rid of the candy." Rachel kicked back in the chair, propped her foot on the control box, and blew out an irritated huff. This was the third day in a row that Jayden Smith had disrupted her shift by pelting the security office with gifts meant for her. The only way she had kept her supervisor off her back was by pointedly refusing to acknowledge the gifts, and anyone who wanted the stuff was welcome to take it home with them.

Why was this guy so persistent? She hadn't even seen him since that night at the house when he and Caelan had gotten into their wrestling match. Something was not quite right about this sudden hot and heavy pursuit from him. *Stalker dude* was getting on her nerves, but she wasn't sure how to get rid of him and didn't really have anything to tell the sheriff that the man would take seriously. After all, the guy had only showered her with gifts and calls to go out with him. The sheriff would laugh her out of his office if she filed a complaint about that.

She hadn't told Caelan about it and had sworn Mercy and her entire crew to secrecy. The knot in her chest loosened and her heart lightened, warming and filling with joy as he came to mind. No. She wouldn't tell Caelan. Their wonderful moments together would not be ruined by something as ridiculous and annoying as Jayden Smith. She couldn't remember when she'd ever been this happy and wasn't about to jinx it.

"Hey, Hawk! You're backing up the line. Are you going to get this bundle or what?" one of the stacker crew shouted over the radio. "Come on, Hawk!"

"Mess with me and I'll swap shifts with Josh," she threatened. "You want to listen to his mouth for eight hours?" She lifted the newly banded bundle, eased it over to the transfer car, and carefully released it to its new location.

"No way!" a guy in the stacker crew shouted amid laughter in the background. "You sit up there and daydream about your Highlander as long as you want! We can make steel some other time."

Good-natured heckling was part of the job, and Rachel didn't mind. Working with her crew at the steel mill was like being suddenly blessed with a herd of little brothers who liked nothing better than to aggravate her at every opportunity. But she also knew if she ever got into a bind, any of the guys on her crew would quickly come to her aid.

After a glance at her watch, she trolleyed the crane to the landing and began filling out the end of shift check sheet so the next operator would know if she'd had any problems with the crane during her time at the stick. With her things gathered and tucked under her arm, she climbed out of the crane, looking forward to getting home to Caelan.

After that first unbelievable night, when she'd finally given in to her emotions, she'd discovered him capable of a depth of caring and love she thought existed only in fairy tales.

Physically, he'd taken her body to ecstasies she'd never imagined possible. She shook her head, smiling as she flashed hot at the thought of it. Who knew a body had so many sensitive spots capable of exploding into bliss? Emotionally, he was healing her soul, helping her to become whole again.

"Try this one. It's unbelievable even if it is from Mr. Smith." Mercy interrupted Rachel's inner chatter by stuffing an enormous piece of chocolate into her mouth.

Rachel wasn't about to admit that the chocolaty caramel delight tasted fantastic. "I don't want anything from him," she reminded the grinning security guard while trying to chew the treat down to a size she could swallow. "Anything he sends is to be distributed as you see fit. As a matter of fact, since you enjoy aggravating people so much, why don't you call him and tell him how much you love all his gifts, but that you prefer candy only?"

Mercy tipped her head toward the gate while trying to pry a caramel bite out from between her teeth. "You can tell him for me. He's in the parking lot. Been there since noon."

"What? Why didn't you warn me?"

"I just did."

Rachel leaned across the counter and squinted out the large window overlooking the lot. Mercy was right. Jayden Smith was there, leaning against the side of an immaculate BMW.

As if sensing her gaze upon him, he whipped off his sunglasses, which probably cost more than her annual salary, and gave her a predatory smile.

Tucking her hard hat under her arm, Rachel stormed out of the security office. Time to end this ridiculous game.

"Wait till you get off company property to belt him, or they'll make me call the cops!" Mercy shouted, then quickly slammed the door and pulled the shade to block her view of the lot.

"What are you doing here?" Rachel spat at the man before she was halfway out the employee's only gate. It was taking all her self-control to keep from slinging her hard hat at him and knocking that smug look off his face.

"I've been trying to get in touch with you for days, beauty. Sent gifts. Left messages. Nothing seemed to get through. So, I decided to show up in person and tender my apology personally so you'd come to your senses and give me another chance." He tipped a nod at the other workers slowly filing out through the gate and making their way to their cars.

"You all right, Hawk?" one of the grubbier workers called out.

"Fine, Stump. Go home and give that new grandbaby a hug for me." Rachel faked a smile at the kindly man who was short and squat but burly—just like his nickname. *Stump.*

"I accept your apology," she told Smith as she turned back to him. "We all had a bad night, and what's done is done. Get in your beamer there, point it toward Chicago, and don't stop until you see Lake Michigan." She forced another smile she didn't feel. "See? All cleared up. On your way, Mr. Smith."

"Have dinner with me tonight, and I'll leave you alone." He flashed that smile of his that made her wonder if he'd sprout fangs at the scent of blood.

"Sorry." She shook her head. "Thank you, but I already have plans. If you start now, you could probably reach Chicago before midnight. I hear that Stop and Rob at the off ramp is running a special on coffee if you buy one of their mugs. Plenty of caffeine and a tank load of gas to be on your way. Who could ask for anything more?" She turned and headed for her truck with her teeth clenched. Something deep inside told her it would not be that easy.

"Come to dinner with me, and I'll show you a way out of this financial mess your ex left you in. Then you and your throwback Highlander can raise all the backwoods babies you want." Smith cocked his head to one side, his smile melting into a cruel sneer. "I thought you'd have better sense than to turn me down, but I guess I was wrong about you. You're just another stupid little hick that doesn't have the sense to come running when I snap my fingers."

A chill shot through her. She slowed her steps. How did he know about her finances? About her ex?

"We could have enjoyed each other, you and I," he continued when she didn't turn and face him. "But relationships usually are a pain in the ass, even when it's just sex for a few weeks." He laughed. "At least I'll still end up with your land. That's all I *really* wanted, anyway."

Rachel swallowed hard, trying not to choke on the fury knotting in her throat. "What did you just say?"

"You heard me or is there so much of that mill grit in your ears that you're deaf until you get home and dig it out?" He took his handkerchief out of his pocket and made a production of wiping his hands.

"I think you better stay the hell away from me," she said through bared teeth. "And stay the hell off my land. I'll be stopping by the sheriff on the way home and seeing about a restraining order." Rachel couldn't remember the last time she had felt this enraged. Not at her parents. Not at David. Not at anyone who had ever crossed her. But this man who thought he was so much better than everyone else had her shaking where she stood.

"You might want to rethink that, my lovely little mill rat. Your sheriff does what I tell him to do. You see, I introduced myself to you as Jayden Smith, but perhaps you're more familiar with my business name. It's on all those gorgeous subdivisions and developments in this area. Does *Christopher Larkin* ring any bells in that grubby little head of yours?"

He popped his sunglasses back on and slid into the creamy white leather seat of the BMW. Before closing the door, he smiled, started the engine, and lowered the window. "By the way, dirt bug, I've had my investigators do more legwork on you so, I'm sure things will move along quickly. We'll be completing matters in a few weeks—maybe even a few days." He pulled up beside her and flashed another malicious sneer. "Or as you would say in your own delightful backwood's vernacular, *time to pack your shit and git, girl!*" With a chilling laugh, he raised the tinted window and tapped the horn twice as he pulled the sleek car out onto the road.

CAELAN SPOTTED Rachel before he'd even pulled into the employee parking lot. She sat in her truck, both hands on the steering wheel, staring straight ahead. Mistress Mercy, the security guard, had told him Rachel had rolled up the windows, locked the doors, and ignored everyone who'd stopped by to peck on the window and ask if she was okay.

According to the lady security guard, some workers had overheard Rachel's exchange with Larkin and quickly gone back to report it. Mistress Mercy begged him to understand that there was nothing she could do. Come to find out, the bastard Larkin owned a controlling interest in the steel mill. Nobody could afford to cross him. She said she would have warned Rachel if they'd known who Jayden Smith really was.

When it grew late and Rachel hadn't come home, Caelan had called the mill and found out what had happened. He wished he'd known before Larkin got away. He parked his truck beside Rachel's. "I wish I would have killed that bastard when I had the chance," he grumbled under his breath as he got out and slammed the door.

His heart lurched at her tear-stained face. "Rachel, lass," he coaxed. "Open the door and let me in to hold ye."

As if waking from a trance, she faced the window and met his gaze. Her enormous violet eyes were so dark they were nearly black.

Sorrow filled them. She slowly blinked as though finally realizing who he was, then twisted in the seat, unlocked the door, and slid over to the passenger side as Caelan climbed into the truck. Without a word, she dove into his arms and buried her face in his chest with her arms tucked in so he could completely cocoon her in his protective embrace.

"I don't know what to do," she said in a hitching whisper.

"Tell me what happened, love. Tell me so I can help."

From the depths of his shirt, in slow hiccupping bursts, she gradually choked out the entire story. Without lifting her head, her voice fell a hush lower as she explained her history and how her circumstances had come to be such a mess. With a lunge that surprised him, she pushed free of his embrace, hugged her knees to her chest, and buried her face in her arms.

"You can leave now," she said, her voice bleak and hollow. "I understand completely." She shuddered with a pitiful sniff. "You know why people die, don't you? It's not because they're sick or hurt or old. It's because they lose hope. Whenever there's nothing left to hope for, nothing to look forward to, there's no more reason to live. Hope keeps you alive."

Caelan took a firm hold of her and forced her to meet his gaze. "I'll not have ye giving up because that ill-bred cur threatened ye. Ye've battled valiantly this long. Now that I'm here to battle at your side, we shall win this war together."

"I'm a loser, Caelan," she said, as though the confession pained her. "I just told you everything about myself. It's all true. The failures. Lies. Stupid choices. If you have any sense, you'll get the hell out of here as fast as you can." A sob escaped her as struggled to wriggle from his grasp.

"All I see before me is a strong woman who I love more than I can ever explain. Ye will be my wife and the mother of my children. Ye are the very breath that keeps me alive. We will figure a way to beat this bastard, I promise ye. But I'll not have ye talking as though all hope is lost." It was time, he decided. At least, time for part of what he had decided to do. He shoved his hand deep inside his shirt pocket, fishing for what he hoped would strengthen their union. He paused before pulling it out and revealing it. "Give me your hand."

Rachel's brow puckered with confusion, but she held out her hand.

He placed the intricately woven band of gold, silver, and bronze onto the ring finger of her left hand, sliding it smoothly over her knuckle, and seating it. It fit perfectly. Their bond was meant to be.

"Promise ye will be mine for all eternity," he said softly. "Swear to me by the Goddess and by the moon above. Then place the ring that's still in my pocket on my finger, and I shall swear my oath to ye as well."

She stared at the ring on her finger, then shifted her gaze to the larger version he had fished out of his pocket and held out to her.

When she didn't move or speak, he felt compelled to babble even though babbling was something he never did. "These are ancient, my love. Forged an age ago for the lairds of Clan MacKay and their soulmates. The swirls and knots of silver, gold, and bronze come together to not only symbolize the Goddess but also love, fidelity, and infinity, as well."

She sniffed as she lifted her gaze. "I swear by the Goddess and the moon and by my very heart and soul that I will be yours throughout eternity." Her fingers trembling, she fumbled to pick up the ring and slid it onto the ring finger of his left hand.

Her eyes went wide as he placed the palms of their left hands together. He intertwined his fingers with hers as he said, "*Gràdh a-nis agus gu bràth.*"

"What does that mean?" she whispered, staring at the rings that seemed to meld their hands together and send a warm, tingling heat through them.

"*Love, now and forever.* I swear I will always love ye and always find ye through the centuries. No matter how many incarnations our souls go through. We are bound forever now. Through all time and space, we will find each other much easier than we did this time. At least, I hope so." He kissed the end of her nose. Her look of amazement made him smile.

"You're an astounding man, Caelan Foster MacKay." She tilted her head to one side, a tear slipping down her cheek to the corner of her sad little smile.

"Aye, and ye are mine forevermore, Rachel Hawkins MacKay." He twitched a shrug. "Although, my clan will insist on making it official in the Church, once we return to Scotland." He caught one of her teardrops on his fingertip and kissed it. "From now on, I shall kiss all your tears away. I swear it."

Her eyes became even wider and shone with the threat of more tears. "Scotland? But I can't. Not until...what about all this mess? Sam and Maizy? My job? Passport? What about..."

Caelan silenced her with a kiss and didn't raise his head until he was certain she was completely breathless. "Dinna fash yourself, my love. I have a plan. But for now, let's go home and have our pagan honeymoon tonight. Then we shall have a second one when we're back home in Scotland."

He reached over and buckled her in securely, then fastened his seatbelt and started the truck. As he pulled past the gate, he shouted to the midnight guard on shift, "I'll be back to get the other truck tomorrow!"

CHAPTER 11

"Tell her everything first. This notion ye've come up with might not even be necessary." Emrys shook a knobby finger in Caelan's face. "Ye dinna have that much time left. This fool plan of yours not only wastes precious time but valuable resources."

"This *fool plan of mine* as ye call it, old man, will give my wife peace of mind, clear her name before she leaves, and also allow her the sweet taste of a revenge well played." Caelan jotted a few more numbers in another column of Rachel's ledger. Thank the gods and goddesses his father had insisted he be tutored at a young age even though the knowledge of ciphers and reading had to be practically beaten into him. "Lore a'mighty, I dinna see how the woman survived as long as she has."

"If ye tell her she's traveling across time, then she won't have to worry about any of this mess anymore!" Emrys waved a hand across the neatly laid out piles of invoices, canceled checks, and receipts.

"I know Rachel," Caelan said while squinting at the scrawl across a receipt so he could match it to an entry in the ledger. "She'll not be at peace if she knows that bastard Larkin is pissing on her trees to mark them as his own."

Emrys blew out a heavy sigh and dragged a chair out from the table to sit. With a defeated groan, he propped his head in his hands. "So ye need me to bring back enough gold to clear her debt and buy her lands. Everything must be transferred to your name. Is that what ye wish?"

"Aye," Caelan said, while running his fingertip down another column of numbers. "I spoke with a solicitor—I mean, a *lawyer*—in the next town who can take care of all the paperwork for right now, as well as the paperwork for after we've crossed over and Larkin discovers we've gone."

"There must be no errors," Emrys warned. "Ye ken well enough that a man as rich and conniving as Larkin didn't get there by being honest." The old man ran his hands through his shaggy white hair until it stood on end.

"That, oh grand and mighty druid to the MacKay, is where ye need to shine. Cast a binding spell on all the contracts, bequests, and wills so they can never be broken. If memory serves, that was your second most favorite magick next to time travel—was it not?" Caelan sat back in the chair and folded his arms across his chest.

Emrys took on a sly look, pursing his lips as he pushed up from the table. "I shall do as ye request, my fine laird. Obtain the gold by tomorrow night's full moon—but only *after* ye tell Rachel how and, more importantly, *when* we will arrive in Scotland. I shall do no magick until she knows the entire truth of things."

"Ye old bastard." Caelan slammed his fists on the table, shaking the neat stacks of papers back into disorderly piles. "That is blackmail."

"No." Emrys shook his finger again. "That is what ye should have done before ye bedded the lass outside of the dream plane. By all the Fates and Furies, have ye no honor left in your bones?" Anger dripped from Emrys's every word. "What happens now if ye tell her the truth and she refuses to accept it and cross over, yet she is carrying your child? Then what shall ye do when ye have to leave not only your soulmate here, but your son or daughter as well? What were ye thinking, man?"

Caelan let his mouth sag open, completely at a loss for words. Then he shook himself, refusing to even consider such a terrible thing. "The time has not been right. Ye ken that as well as I. I thought if she and I spent a little more time together, then somehow, it would all come together."

"Time is a luxury of which ye are quickly running out. Need I remind ye that ye came to the year 2007 with only a set number of days to accomplish this task?" Emrys shoved away from the kitchen table and started toward the door to the back porch. "I shall return at sunset tomorrow to see if ye've done as I've said, ye ken?" He paused in the doorway and looked back at Caelan. "Tell her the dogs may come. Kindred spirits may pass freely without harm."

He shook his head and mumbled as he stepped out the door, "Mayhap, that will somehow help your case."

THE MORNING SUN glistened across their rings, the metal seeming to warm his flesh as he smiled down at their hands lying together on his bare chest. More thankful than he had ever been in his life, Caelan watched the mystical energies send a rainbow of colors dancing across the ceiling. The symbols shaped into the metalwork embraced the shafts of sunlight, then set them free again, strengthening the promise of the eternal circle, the infinite hope, and the endless gift of true love.

It soothed his soul to stroke Rachel's silky hair as she slept nestled in the curve of his shoulder. Her leg curled around his with a possessiveness that hardened him to readiness as she shifted in her sleep.

Lore a'mighty, he could stay like this forever. With an almost silent groan, he thought over how he needed to convince his beloved lass that traveling back in time to the Scotland of 1379 was no great feat at all. He had to make her see how wonderful and full their lives would be—raising a castle full of rowdy bairns and growing old among his proud and caring people. She needed to understand how leaving all the conveniences of this time also meant leaving all the complications. Tensed beyond measure, he shifted and ran his free hand through his hair, a bleak realization hitting him that energy from their rings no longer danced across the ceiling. An omen, perhaps? Goddess help him, he prayed not.

"You're fidgeting," Rachel said around a yawn, then nuzzled his neck with warm kisses before shifting higher to nip his ear.

"Ye keep nipping at me, and I shall do more than fidget," he promised as he rolled her over onto her back. He smiled down at her. "I fear I must beg ye show me a bit of mercy this morning, though. We need to discuss the details of our trip."

She arched upward and ground her hips into him, grinning impishly as she tickled his sides, then slowly raked her nails down his back the way he loved. "You said we didn't have to leave until the end of October. We've got lots of time to work out the details before then."

Caelan grabbed her wrists and rolled to a sitting position, pulling her to a neutral spot beside him on the bed. Goddess, help him. He couldn't concentrate when she did the things she did. "Rachel, I am serious. This is a talk we should've had days ago. I have not been entirely honest with ye."

"Oh, hell. You're married, aren't you?" She spat the words out so fast, at first, he wasn't sure what she said.

He frowned at her. "What say ye?"

"I said, 'You are married'," she repeated, baring her clenched teeth.

"Aye. I am." He wasn't sure what the problem was. Of course, he was married. To her. He nodded. "We two are married in the old way, but we'll still need to say the vows at the altar and record them in the Church when we get home. As laird of my clan, I am expected to have my wedding vows sanctioned by the Church."

She closed her eyes, scrubbed her face with both hands, then dropped them into her lap. "Okay. Well, that's good. But what have you been dishonest about? Are you really from Scotland?"

"Aye."

"Are you really Caelan Foster MacKay?"

"Aye."

"Is Emrys really your uncle?"

"No."

"Aha!" She poked him in the chest, irritation flashing in her eyes. "Will you just tell me already and stop making me drag it out of you? I haven't even had my shower or any coffee yet!"

Damn it to hell. His timing was indeed poor. He should have thoroughly pleasured her in bed, allowed her a shower, plied her with that disgusting swill she called coffee, and *then* explained the concept of time travel to her. He rubbed the grit of sleep from his eyes and sent up a prayer to the Goddess for guidance. "When we travel to Scotland on Samhain, at midnight, during the seventh full moon since I arrived in Kentucky, we will not need a passport, airline tickets, or luggage. All we need is ourselves, Emrys, and the dogs. We will go to the pond deep in the woods, and when Emrys speaks the words, we will go back in time to the year 1379, to Scotland, to my home, and to my clan where I am their laird." He held his breath and waited for her reaction.

"Did you inhale too much of the ether yesterday when you worked on the tractor? Because that sounds like one hell of a dream you had." She arched both her eyebrows nearly to her hairline as she slid out of bed, grabbed her robe, and slid it around her shoulders. With a leery glance back at him, she slowly ambled toward the bathroom.

He pulled in a deep breath and braced himself for the worst. This was not going well. "It is no dream, lass. In fact, this all started months and months ago because of the same dream of ye that haunted me every night. For nearly a year, ye came to me, teased me with your beauty, and tormented me by never allowing me to catch ye. I drove the clan mad, making them search for this violet-eyed goddess of my dreams. I even had my most trusted and wisest druid search through all his mystical sources for this wonderful lass I could nay forget."

She went a little pale as she fisted her hands at her sides. "And this druid's name was?" She chewed on the corner of her lip, her eyes telling Caelan that she already knew the answer.

"Aye, it was Emrys. He found ye in the Mirrors of Time. Showed ye to me and worked a spell with the Fates. The spell granted us seven moons to come forward, win your heart, and then give ye the choice to return to my home and my time with me." He pushed himself out of the bed, grabbed his jeans, and pulled them on. This wasn't going well, but, at least, she hadn't run out the door screaming.

"You said give me the choice. So, we don't have to go back to Scotland 1379? We could stay here, right?" The color returned to her cheeks, and she smiled as she blew out a relieved sigh. "I know the name of a good psychiatrist. His office takes payments, and I'd be happy to go with you."

Caelan tensed, his heart aching. She believed him mad, thought none of it was true. "This is not pretend, Rachel. It is real. And *ye* have the choice whether or not to go, my love, but only ye can choose. Ye may return to my home, the love of my soul, as my heartmate and make me the happiest man who ever lived, or ye may stay here in your Kentucky of 2007. With your dogs, your conveniences, and without Emrys and myself. The old man and I will be sent back to our time, whether or not ye choose to accompany us." As he watched her thoughts and worries play across her face, he felt as though he aged all the years between 1379 and 2007. All he could hope was that he'd captured enough of her heart to ensure she couldn't live without him, either.

"Caelan," she started, then stopped, pulled in a deep breath and blew it out. She gentled her tone as though speaking to a child. "I hope you realize how much I love you. But I don't see how what you are saying is possible. You cannot be from the year 1379." She offered him a sympathetic smile. "How about bacon and pancakes this morning? You rest while I fix it."

A determination to make her believe filled him, raging within him like a battle needing to be won. He closed the distance between them and took hold of both her hands. "The day before Emrys and I showed up on your doorstep, ye and I were together in your dreams. It was the first time we loved each other and enjoyed each other's touch as we have these past few days. Do ye remember, lass?"

Her eyes went wide. She yanked her hands out of his and clutched the lapels of her robe, pulling it tighter around herself. "How do you know that?" she whispered as she backed up against the dresser.

He kept his voice soft and low, sensing she was about to bolt. "Because Emrys sent me to love ye in your dream plane so that ye would know me when we appeared in this time."

"That is not possible," she choked out as she stumbled toward the bedroom door.

"What about the violet light that surrounded us? The energies that flowed through us when we permitted ourselves to admit our true feelings? Have ye forgotten that night? How the light united us?" He wanted to touch her but realized she would never allow it. Not now. His heart ached for her to believe. If she didn't—

With shaking hands waving him away and her head bowed, she whimpered like a frightened pup.

Caelan couldn't hold off any longer. He closed the space between them, lifted her face to his, and brushed his lips across hers. "Believe me, Rachel," he whispered. "I beg ye."

She backed up a step and shied away from him, turning to the wall.

"I'll go for a bit of a walk," he suggested, unable to come up with anything else to do to give her time to come to her senses. "Think about it, aye? Please know I love ye with all my being, dear one. I swear ye have nothing to fear. Never would I ever let any harm come to ye."

She hugged herself tightly and stared at the floor, not saying a word as he walked out.

"Goddess, I beg ye," he said under his breath as he strode down the hall, through the kitchen, then out the door. "Dinna let me lose her. I canna bear it."

∼

The setting sun drew even with the ridge just as Emrys emerged from the woods. True to his word, the druid was right on time. He ambled along, touching the ground with his staff, not to support himself but seemingly for some other purpose known only to him. As he crossed the yard, he narrowed his eyes and knotted his brows as his gaze lit first on Caelan where he sat on the edge of the porch, then rose and took in the dark windows of the house.

"Where is she?" he asked, his tone revealing that he sensed all was not well.

"Ye tell me." Caelan stared at the ground. He'd sat here for hours, waiting for her return while his hopes and dreams dwindled to nothingness before his eyes.

"What did she say when ye told her?" Emrys asked. "How did she react?" With a groan in honor of his stiff old bones, he lowered himself to the porch beside Caelan. "How bad was it, my laird?" he asked with a solemn quietness.

Caelan huffed a mirthless laugh; his gaze focused on the ground but his mind's eyes watching the terrible scene over and over. "At first, the lass thought I'd gotten caught up in a dream or maybe gone daft for whatever reason. But when I reminded her of our time together in the dream plane before ye and I arrived, it frightened her. I could see it in her eyes."

"Frightened her?" Emrys stroked his beard and twisted his staff, digging its tip deeper into the soft earth beside the porch. "Was she frightened about the time travel or afraid she'd fallen in love with a madman?"

Caelan cocked his head and glared at the old druid. "Have I ever told ye how much of a comfort ye are during times like these? Always saying the *wrong* thing?" Damned old wizard. He closed his eyes and held his head. How could everything go so wrong so quickly? And when it seemed things were finally going right?

"Damn it, man!" Emrys grumbled. "Ye ken what I mean. 'Tis important to know how much she knows and believes in the old ways. Answer me now. Was she frightened about traveling to the past or because she feared ye crazed?" He stamped his cane and caused blue sparks to rise from the soil and crackle across the ground.

Caelan grabbed the ancient one's arm and stilled him with a dip of his head at the end of the glowing staff. "Mind yourself, man! This land must lie along the ancient lines. Dinna let your temper set something in motion that neither of us can control."

Emrys pulled his arm out of Caelan's grasp and smoothed his crumpled sleeve. "Mayhap that's what's frightened your lass. If this land's been in her family for years, then it's not the old ways making her afraid. Her granny would have taught her about that and made it natural to accept. But traveling to the unknown past, giving up all the niceties and safety she's accustomed to, that's what has her fearful."

"She did not say. Stood staring at me, growing paler the longer I talked. That's why I gave her space and time to think a bit. Told her I'd go for a walk. I'd hoped that when I returned, she would be calmer and more inclined to accept what I said." Caelan rose from his seat on the porch and walked with his uneasiness, pacing around the yard.

Emrys shook his head and scratched the tip of his cane in the dirt. With a pained look at the empty driveway, he gripped his staff with both hands and steadied himself to his feet. "I'll still travel back this moon and get the things ye require for your plan. We'll move forward as though she's chosen to return with us. I canna believe the lass has left for good or run away from ye without an explanation. That is not her way. Your Rachel is fearless."

"We shall see, old man," Caelan said with a defeated sigh. "We've naught but a short while left, and then we'll see." He gave the old druid a half-hearted clap on the shoulder, then climbed on the porch, and entered the dark, lonely house to continue his vigil alone.

CHAPTER 12

Rachel rubbed her gritty eyes, then squinted harder at the multiple images of Scotland pulled up on her laptop. Hours had passed, endless hours that she had lost track of while sitting in the booth at the back of the diner. Gallons of coffee had kept her upright as she downloaded everything she could find about the history of the land and the plausibility of time travel.

Almost everything she found on both subjects unnerved her even more than before she started. Scotland's history was brutal and bloody. She'd read of Robert the Bruce and his battles, of the Jacobite uprising, of the Highland Clearances, and the cruelties inflicted upon the people through the battles and struggle for power and land.

The information she'd found on time travel left a knot in her throat that she couldn't quite seem to dislodge. Quantum theory, Einstein's research scientific data, actually supported what Caelan was stating that they had not only done but were about to do again.

She propped her head in her hands and stared down at the keyboard. Why wasn't anything in her life simple?

"Honey, are you sure you don't want something to eat? All this caffeine and acid from my diner coffee is going to eat a hole clean through your gut." Pamela, owner of the diner, head waitress, and also one of Rachel's best friends since elementary school, plopped her more than ample behind down onto the bench across from where Rachel sat.

Rachel leaned back and stretched her arms over her head. "Thanks, but no, Pamela. I don't need anything. But your coffee is doing wonders at keeping me going, and I really appreciate you letting me camp out back here. What time is it anyway? I didn't even notice it had gotten dark."

After a glance at her watch, Pamela gave a dimpled smile and reached across the table to pat Rachel's arm. "Nearly midnight, girl. I flipped the closed sign over a long time ago, but you stay here as long as you like. Since I live upstairs, I'm going on up to bed. I've got an extra room with a bed or there's an old couch back yonder where I crash sometimes when my knees play out, and I can't carry this load up the steps." Pamela patted her fleshy rump. "If you decide to go home, just lock up for me, okay? You know where I keep the extra key. If you decide to stay, then sleep wherever you like." The woman edged sideways to slide her plump girth out from between the table and bench. She paused one last time before passing through the door marked *Private*. "I don't know what's going on with you, Rachel, but I wish you the best. You've always been a good friend, and I can't count the number of times you've bailed me out and never asked to be repaid. God bless you and watch over you, girl."

Rachel blinked against the sting of unshed tears as she watched Pamela limp from the room. Even though they were the same age, Pamela had always seemed years older. She'd dropped out of high school to raise her brood of brothers and sisters after her alcoholic father beat her mother to death then shot himself. But Pamela kept the family together with the help of a few big-hearted social workers.

Poor living conditions, no healthcare, and poor DNA had also saddled Pamela with a myriad of medical problems. Never complaining, Pamela always worked hard, was grateful for what she had, and helped others whenever she could. The woman never asked for anything in return.

"And I thought I had problems," Rachel mumbled into her coffee while listening to Pamela's pained groans and huffing and puffing as she labored her way up the back stairs of the diner.

Rachel closed her laptop, shoved it aside, then rested her forehead on top of her folded hands on the table. How in the world could all of what Caelan said be true? How could a laird from the year 1379 have recurring dreams about her, hunt her down with a druid, travel to the future to seduce her, and then tell her she had to choose to come back with him or he had to go back alone? What the hell kind of screwed up fairy tale was that?

Why on earth would she want to go to the past—permanently? No television, no computers, no deodorant, and, oh hell no, no coffee. Toothpaste, makeup, tampons—all gone. No showers, razors, tater tots, and, heaven help her, no ice cream!

Even worse, what if she decided she wanted to have children? The dangers were mind-boggling. And what if they got sick? At the rate women and babies died throughout history, it was a wonder humans survived at all.

She lifted her head, shook herself free of the mounting panic, and drained the last dredges of coffee from her cup. Sliding out of the booth, she scooped up her laptop and purse and headed toward the door. At the counter, she paused and fished out a crumpled twenty-dollar bill. She smoothed it out and weighed it down with a salt-shaker, hoping it would cover all the coffee she'd consumed in the almost twenty-four hours she'd sat in that booth. Heading out the door, she checked to make sure no one was around, then took the extra key from the hiding place and securely bolted the lock.

As she clambered into the truck and took hold of the steering wheel, the blue, white light from the security lamp hit her wedding band and made it sparkle. She'd been quick to run down the list of the many things she would miss if she went back in time, but she'd avoided acknowledging the biggest gain of all if she found the courage to make that leap.

Never in a million years would she have dreamed a man like Caelan existed anywhere but in a fairy tale. He was as thoughtful as he was stubborn. As tender-hearted as he was barbaric and as gentle as he was brutish. He was an amalgam of opposites and contradictions that added up to the most loving, caring individual she had ever met. How could she live without him?

She closed her eyes and inhaled deeply, remembering the contentment, comfort, and feeling of being loved she experienced every morning when she woke up in his arms. Did she really want to go back to waking up to nothing more comforting than Sam and Maizy's cold wet noses nudging her in the side?

Whenever she thought about Caelan, her soul stirred beneath her breastbone as though straining to reconnect to her other half. A dull, constant ache had filled her ever since she'd left the house without telling him, *Yes. I will go back with you.* Neither her heart nor her soul was happy without him.

She stared out the windshield at the full moon, her love for Caelan battling with the security she felt in this era. For some unknown reason, a distant memory of her grandmother pushed its way to the forefront of her thoughts.

She saw the ancient woman sitting in an old rocking chair on a smaller front porch than the one that was there now. The tiny, gray-haired lady was furious and holding tight to a small leather-bound journal with her knobby, arthritic hands. Her toothless mouth was clamped shut. Her cloudy eyes stared forward as the young adults inside the house argued over which one was going to haul the old woman to the old folks' home, and which one was going to tell her she wasn't coming back.

"Come here, sweet girl," Granny said to seven year old Rachel with a crook of her finger.

Peeping around the corner of the house, her dress streaked with dirt and torn, and her face stained with tears, little Rachel had fought valiantly against her mean parents, trying to make them leave Granny alone. But they wouldn't listen. Just shoved her away and told her to go outside.

Unable to resist her favorite person in all the world, Rachel ducked her head and ran into Granny's waiting arms. "I hate them! They're sending you away, and I'll never see you again. I hate them, and I'm gonna put one of them spells on them like you do!"

"Shhh," Granny said, her frail hug tightening around Rachel. "Hush now, sweet girl. You know better." Granny smoothed Rachel's tangled curls away from her face and smiled down into her eyes. "You always get back times three what you send out. Remember that, Rachel. For the good of all, harm none."

"B-but..." Rachel hiccupped and sobbed in her precious grandmother's embrace, committing the smell of lavender, sage, and lilacs to memory. "It's my fault they're sending you away. They say you're just not right, and you shouldn't be 'round me no more. I hate them!"

"Look at me, gal. Our time together is over for now." With a trembling hand, Granny wiped the tears from Rachel's face. "But when you need me the most, I'll return and help you. You just wait and see." She bent and kissed Rachel on the forehead. "Now you run and take Granny's book with you. Hide it where it will never be found, so you'll have it when I come back to help you. Run now. Hurry, sweet girl. They're coming and mustn't see you with that book or where you hide it. Run!"

The last thing Rachel remembered was running from that porch with Granny's leather journal hugged to her chest. Busy with her mission to hide it, her parents hauled Granny away without even allowing her to say goodbye, and whisper that she'd hidden the book *real good*. Rachel swallowed hard. She never saw Granny again.

She gasped in a shuddering breath as she snapped out of the trance, her hand to her throat as she wheezed with a heart wrenching sob. It had been years since she'd thought about the awful day they had taken Granny off. Why would that terrible memory come to her now?

Sniffing back tears and shoving the raw memory back into the shadows where it belonged, she started the truck while her mind whirled in all directions. But even in her sadness, she couldn't resist a faint smile. Granny had been such a talented, wise woman. Country folk had come from all over to beg her for healing and her love potions.

Maybe that was why she hadn't been all that shocked about the mystical aspects of Caelan's story. She'd spent the first seven years of her life being raised and instructed by a woman known far and wide for her healing powers and her abilities to help with the elemental issues. Granny had been a proud and powerful witch.

It was only when Rachel had exhibited even stronger talents in the mystical arts that her parents decided it was time to lock the old woman up in a nursing home. Imprisoned inside a sterile world of glass, plastic, and ceramic tile it had taken Granny's soul only three months to vacate her body and seek refuge on a more welcoming plane of existence.

A heavy sigh pushed free of Rachel as she turned the truck toward home. "Where in the world did I put that book?" she asked her reflection in the rearview mirror, frowning as she tried to remember. A tiny plan, delicate and new, began itching at the base of her brain, and if she could find Granny's book, she just might figure out if she could do it.

FULLY ENGULFED IN A JAW-CRACKING YAWN, Rachel slid out of the truck. Thankful to be home, and a lot calmer and determined than she had been when she left. She tried to close the truck door quietly to keep from rousing the dogs into a barking frenzy. As she stepped back from the truck and turned toward the house, she screeched as Caelan scooped her up into his arms.

"I feared ye had left me for good." He buried his face in her hair and held her clutched to his chest, her feet dangling in midair.

"I can't breathe," Rachel said, while trying to shift the laptop wedged under her chin.

He loosened his hold but kept her pinned to his chest and her feet well up from the ground. "If I let ye down," he asked in a voice rasping with emotion, "will ye swear not to leave me? Never again?"

She tilted her head and caught sight of his weary face revealed by the porch light and the light of the full moon. Guilt nudged her conscience before she reminded herself that the situation wasn't entirely all her fault. "I haven't quite figured everything out yet, but no. I promise I won't take off again."

Ever so slowly, he allowed her to slide lower until her feet touched the ground, and she stood in front of him. He rested his hands on her shoulders, gripping tighter as he drew her closer. "Of your own free will, you are choosing to travel to the past? To be my wife? Say the words, Rachel. I canna believe ye until ye say the words."

She tamped down a fresh wave of guilt over the lie she was about to tell and pushed *Plan B* to the back of her mind. With his worried face framed between her hands, she nodded. "Of my own free will, I choose to travel back in time to be with you, my beloved husband."

Caelan threw back his head and let out a Scottish war cry that echoed across the Kentucky hillside. Sam and Maizy came running, barking, and ready for battle. Emrys stuck his head out the apartment window, his white hair even wilder than normal.

"What the bloody hell is going on?" the old druid shouted. "Is one of the rival clans invading?"

Caelan grabbed Rachel around the waist and spun her around until all the coffee she'd drank threatened to come back out.

She beat on his shoulders. "Stop! Before I puke!"

He halted but still held her high in the air. "She agreed," he shouted. "It is done. She is coming home."

"That was entirely too easy," Emrys mumbled before pulling his head back inside. "The lass is up to something. I'd bet my eyeteeth on it."

Rachel heard what he said but was relieved when Caelan ignored it. She shot a narrow-eyed look at the window that the druid had disappeared into and made a mental note to watch him. She would not allow him to ruin her *Plan B*.

STILL BREATHING hard from climbing the rugged incline, Rachel leaned back against the tree, straining to listen for any sound of anyone following her through the woods. Weariness and worry plagued her. Weariness from not sleeping well, and worry because the pregnancy test had come up positive.

"But the pee sticks aren't foolproof," she reminded herself even though intuition told her the test was spot on. Being pregnant would explain a lot—and she and Caelan hadn't exactly been steadfast about always taking precautions. She shivered away the thought and forced herself to make her way deeper into the trees.

Even though she was exhausted, she had to perform the ritual that had surfaced from her memories before the sun rose, and *before* she forgot the ritual again. It was the only rite she fully remembered without the aid of Granny's journal. Hopefully, it would work and not only lead her straight to the book itself but also confirm if the pregnancy test was right and provide even more information. Granny had always accurately predicted a woman's offspring whenever asked if it was a boy or a girl.

She paused at the hidden spring behind an outcropping of limestone and splashed the icy water on her face and throat. When this was over, she would return home to Caelan, curl up against his warm, welcoming body, and sleep forever.

When she reached the clearing, she remembered from her childhood, Rachel smiled wistfully. "I still miss you, Granny," she whispered into the breeze. Knowing she had little time, she removed all her clothing and reverently unfolded the carefully preserved cloak she had retrieved from the trunk tucked away in the attic.

The deepest of purple velvets; it perfectly matched her eyes and settled around her shoulders as though made for her. She freed her hair and let it tumble down her back as the moonlight spun silvery lights and threads through her curls. She took it as a good sign that what part of her pale skin that wasn't covered by the cloak seemed to glow as though she were lit from within. It could be the pregnancy, the gift of magick Granny had passed down to her, or both, but she hoped that for certain it was the magick. As she stood in the clearing, the woods went silent and the breeze disappeared as though, at long last, their mistress had returned.

"Face north," Rachel told herself, hearing Granny's voice in her head. She lifted her hands and recited the ancient words, thanking the spirits of the north, the earth element, for blessing her with their powers and time. She turned clockwise and halted at the point of the east, repeating the movement and paying homage to the spirits of the east, the air element. To each direction, she acknowledged and welcomed them to her sacred circle: south for fire, west for water. As she finished, the glowing blue energies she remembered from long ago swirled around her.

In the center of the circle, arms raised and eyes closed, she allowed the cloak to slide off her shoulders and puddle around her feet. She opened her eyes and held out her hands, baring herself to the energies and offering her glowing white aura to swirl and mix with the blue.

When a familiar warmth, a faint violet aura brushed across her shoulders, it made her smile. She knew this power would do her no harm. This spirit guide, her precious Granny, still loved and protected her as she had done while she lived. The violet light swirled around her body, encircling her head like the gentle hand of a loving parent touching their favorite child. Then the aura tickled her under the chin and touched her cheek as Granny had always done during life.

After greeting her in such a loving way, it surrounded her body and shifted to a blinding brightness for several seconds, then faded. Rachel held her breath as the energy circled her waist, rose, and touched her forehead. It repeated this motion three times. *Boy*, whispered through her mind each time.

Rachel swallowed hard. Three boys. Heaven help her. She carried triplets. Struggling to focus, she reached for the shimmering violet light. "Where is the book, Granny? I don't remember," she whispered.

You know where it is, sweet girl. It is in the place you fear. Then the aura warmed around her one last time, then shot up into the stars.

"The place I fear," she repeated, missing the violet light as the other energies slowly faded. She'd have to think about that, but first, she had to undo the circle. She donned her cloak and once more faced north. But this time, she turned counterclockwise and bid all the powers farewell and thanked them for blessing and protecting her circle. When she sensed everything had returned to its natural state, she wearily returned the cloak to its protective packaging and pulled on her jeans and sweatshirt. She shoved her feet into her shoes, then yawned and stumbled back down the hillside toward the house.

"Witch!" Emrys accused as he stepped out from behind a great oak. He glared at her as if ready to challenge her to some sort of magickal duel.

She almost laughed at the thought of it. Her weariness had driven her to the stage of downright silliness. Too tired for the confrontation, she squared her shoulders and glared right back at him. "What is it you Highlanders always say? Aye and so what!"

"Dinna mock me, girl! Ye've not the full training to have any idea at what ye're playing at!" He shook his finger, barely missing the end of her nose.

If the man wasn't so old, she'd shove him back on his ass and leave him in the woods. But she couldn't. Granny would never forgive her. "As you no doubt just witnessed, you sneaky old man, I know a bit more about the craft than you'd probably care to admit." She resettled her stance and protectively tucked her cloak under her arm. "Look—I'm tired and in no mood to argue with you right now. Unless you're going to burn me at the stake this very minute, I'd suggest we save this conversation for another time."

Emrys puffed up to his full height and raised both his arms, causing storm clouds to gather and block the light from the moon. Lightning streaked through the clouds, and thunder rumbled as the wind blew harder.

Rachel rolled her eyes and pinched the bridge of her nose, rubbing the corners of her tired eyes. "I am so not impressed and not about to engage in an *I can do anything you can do contest* either. I consider that a waste of time and disrespectful to the surrounding energies."

Emrys cracked a slow smile and lowered his arms. "I see your grandmother taught ye well. By the way, the triplets? Be they sons or daughters?"

Rachel blew out a heavy sigh while still rubbing her eyes. "Caelan should be proud. He has three sons started, but let's not tell him that just yet, okay? I have no idea how I'm going to handle this, and I'm afraid of what he will say."

Emrys grinned, hugged one of his scrawny arms around her shoulders, and offered to carry her cloak. "Three sons? Ha! That Highlander will finally learn to be careful of what he wishes for. Dinna worry, lass. There will be plenty of folk at the keep to help ye care for them. Everything will be just fine."

"I hope so." She stared at her feet as they trudged along, hoping the druid couldn't read minds. If he could, he would soon discover her plan to break their curse, so he and Caelan would remain in the present time with her.

CHAPTER 13

"And I need your signature and initials one more time right here please, Mr. MacKay." Gerald Randolph, the lawyer Emrys had thoroughly researched by studying the man's history on the surface of the pond, pointed at yet another line on what felt like the fiftieth sheet of at least the seventy-fifth copy of the sheaf of papers Caelan and Rachel had signed this morning.

"Will that do it, then?" Caelan asked, as his oversized hand almost swallowed the strange wee pen with which he scrawled his name across the bottom of the page.

"Everything is now completely as you requested it, sir," Mr. Randolph assured. He rose from his chair and extended his hand while bobbing his head happily. "Any time you need us to handle your financial and legal needs again, you just call us. I'll see to anything you need, sir. Yes, sir, anytime you need us, you just give us a call."

Caelan barely narrowed his eyes at Rachel as she pretended to gag behind the lawyer's back. He smiled and shook Mr. Randolph's hand, then accepted the folder containing copies of all the papers. "Thank you, Mr. Randolph. I can assure ye, I will keep ye in mind any time I'm in this area again."

He pressed his hand to the small of Rachel's back and steered her out of the room before Mr. Randolph noticed how often she rolled her eyes whenever he spoke. Caelan breathed easier as they stepped outside. Finally, it was over. His precious Rachel was completely out of debt, and no longer had to worry about Larkin taking over her lands. What was even better was that it was also set up so that when they traveled to the past, all their holdings would be used to set up the aptly named Hawkins-MacKay Wetlands where no construction or hunting would be allowed. Larkin would be furious when the two hundred plus acres of river bottom land slipped right through his greedy fingers.

"Shall we go by the mill so ye can turn in your resignation in person or will ye mail it to them?" Caelan glanced at her as she sat beside him in the truck, nervously chewing on her bottom lip.

"What happens if we decide to come back? Would we be able to get the land returned to us?" she asked without looking at him.

It was then he noticed her pallor and the slight sheen of sweat beading across her upper lip. She kept pulling in deep breaths and blowing them back out as though about to be ill.

Caelan pulled the truck over, put it in park, and stopped the engine. He laid his hand on hers and tried to keep the worry out of his voice. "There is no coming back, lass. Once we travel to the past, we shall be there the rest of our days."

She jerked her hands away, dove out the truck door, and scrambled down into the ditch. Holding her hair back from her face, she bent and heaved, losing every bit of the impressively huge breakfast she had eaten at the diner.

He ran to her side, wrapped an arm around her, and helped hold back her hair as she continued to gag. When she finally stopped vomiting, he carried her back up the embankment, then sat them down in the grass beside the truck.

"Rachel," he said softly. "Please dinna tell me ye have changed your mind about coming back with me. Have your fears made ye ill? Is that what's wrong?" He struggled to read the overwrought feelings flashing in her eyes. While he longed to know what was wrong, he feared hearing the answer.

Tears slipped down her cheeks as she struggled to her feet and stumbled her way around to her side of the truck.

"Rachel?"

"Leave me alone and get in the truck."

He scrambled to his feet and went to her, but when he tried to help, she slapped his hands away. Her behavior shocked him. Earlier today, she'd been fine and seemed happy and excited about all their plans. "Rachel, love! Tell me what's wrong. Ye're scaring the living shite out of me."

"Damn it! I'm pregnant!" she shouted. "Now, will you just leave me alone? Once again, I have screwed up. Literally this time." She climbed into the truck, planted herself in the seat, and folded her arms across her chest. Huge silent tears rolled down her cheeks as she stared straight ahead.

Pregnant. Caelan wanted to roar with joy but clenched his teeth instead. In her current mood, he didn't think she would appreciate such a reaction. But a wee bairn of their own. His heart threatened to explode with happiness. Fighting for a calmness he didn't feel, he started the engine, turned the truck around, and drove the ten-minute drive straight home. Once parked in the driveway, he got out on his side, walked around to Rachel's, opened the door, and stood there, waiting.

Still staring straight ahead, she hiked her chin higher. "What?" she asked without looking at him.

"I am waiting." He kept one hand on the open door, and the other on the side of the truck, effectively hemming her in.

"For what?" she growled, crossing her legs and wriggling in the seat as though she was about to wet herself.

Now, he understood her new habit of needing to relieve herself so often. And her appetite. It all made sense. But he didn't say so. If he did, she would kill him. Instead, he said, "I am waiting to hold the woman I love and thank her for giving me a child."

She burst into tears anew, yowling like a wounded animal. "You're going to think *thank her*. I'm giving you three boys all at once. We're having triplets." She covered her face with her hands and sobbed.

"Three? Three *sons*? Are ye certain?" Caelan slapped his forehead and stumbled back against the truck. "Blessed Goddess, holy Fates!"

She keened with another high-pitched, heartbreaking sob that made both dogs howl.

"What in the name of all that is sacred is all this infernal caterwauling?" Emrys called out as he emerged from the house. The screen door banged shut behind him. He picked up speed, shuffled over to Caelan, and poked him in the chest while bobbing his snowy white head. "I ken what this is about now. What did ye say to her? Ye should be proud, ye fool! Three sons! The woman is going to bear ye three sons, and ye've reduced her to sobbing. Ye should treat her like the queen that she is, and yet, ye stand there as though ye've lost every bit of wit and wisdom ye ever hoped to have."

He shoved around Caelan and gently urged Rachel from the truck. "There, there now lass. All will be well. Come inside and lie down for a wee rest. I promise ye, all will be well." As he led her toward the house, Emrys glared back at Caelan and mouthed the words for him to stay put.

"Stay put, my arse," Caelan groaned while scrubbing his face with both hands. How could he stay put when he had as much condemned the woman he loved with all his heart and soul to certain death? He wanted to howl along with the dogs, keening his sorrow and pain across the centuries.

After several long moments later, Emrys ambled out through the screen door, letting it slam again. "Would ye care to tell me what the devil has gotten into ye? We find the woman of your soul. We travel across time so ye can win her. Ye woo her, win her over, wed in the old way, and she opens her womb to ye. And now here ye stand there looking like ye've had your entire world taken away." The old druid grabbed him by the shoulders and tried to shake him but failed.

Caught up in his anguish and unable to believe the cruelty of it all, Caelan stared down at the old druid as though suddenly realizing he was there. He leveled a pained glance on the house, then tipped his head toward the cab of the truck. "Copies of today's paperwork are in a folder on the seat. It will all have to be redone."

Emrys gave him a bewildered look. "Why?"

"Because we are going back to Scotland without Rachel. We must work out the financial details, so she and the bairns have the land and all the money they need. I'll not have them wanting for anything, ye ken?" Caelan struggled not to break down and weep for the first time in his life.

"But ye said ye could nay live without the lass. That ye needed her to complete ye." Emrys allowed his voice to trail off, giving up on further argument.

"It is because I love her that I do this," Caelan said, his voice breaking. "I refuse to bring her back to our time to watch her die trying to bring my sons into this world. How many women of our time die when they try to bring forth a single bairn? If she carried a single precious wee son—I still would have feared for her, but I would have hoped in the promise of our joy. But three? In our time? Ye ken as well as I what her chances are."

He turned away from the seer, sagged across the hood of the truck, and held his head in his hands. He had to keep Rachel and the bairns safe. No matter the cost.

"Ye're not even going to tell her or give her the choice to have the babies here or try to have them in Scotland with ye?"

Caelan didn't bother lifting his head. "No. She must think she's going with us until the last possible minute. I dinna wish for her to suffer any more unhappiness than necessary. She'll suffer enough once we're gone. I am counting on ye, Emrys. Ye have to help me make her think she's coming with us. Can ye do that?" He turned his head and leveled a hard glare on the druid, silently demanding his oath.

"Aye, my laird. It will be done." Emrys turned to go, then paused before he entered the woods. "And when we've returned, I will be sure the Mirrors of Time watch over her and the wee ones so ye can see them as they grow."

Caelan nodded his thanks, not trusting himself to speak. He

walked to the house, stepped up on the porch, and quietly let himself inside. He made his way to the bedroom door and fought back tears. Rachel was asleep, curled up into a ball with the pillow clutched to her chest. He eased into the bed behind her, wrapped her in his arms, and buried his face in her hair.

~

Rachel stirred in Caelan's arms, shifting him to immediate wakefulness. She moved slowly, easing her way to the edge of the bed as though trying to escape without his knowing.

"Where are ye going, my love?" he asked in a husky whisper as he pulled her back against him and buried his face in the softness of her hair. He breathed her in, imprinting her sweet scent of warmed vanilla to memory, so when he left, he could bring it back to mind and remember the comfort of holding her.

"I was going for a walk," she said. Nervousness and despair echoed in her tone. "I need some air and time to think...time to figure out what to do." She gently pulled away from him again without a glance back. It was almost as though she couldn't bear to meet his gaze.

Caelan swallowed hard, struggling to control the raging tempest within him and do what needed to be done for the safety of her and the bairns. "What do ye mean, Rachel?" He caught her arm. "Look at me, love. Tell me."

She kept her head bowed, refusing to meet his gaze. "I'm sorry I wasn't more careful. Please understand that I didn't mean for this to happen, and I'm sorry I made you so unhappy with the news I hit you with yesterday. But I already love these babies, and if you don't want them, I'll figure out a way to raise them on my own."

He rose in the bed, took her by the shoulders, and turned her to face him. "Why would ye think I'd nay want our babies?" He worked his mouth, swallowing hard as he tried to choose the proper words. "I know I reacted badly, and I am sorry. It was only because I love ye so, and the danger of bringing three bairns into this world terrifies me."

He pulled her close and kissed the top of her head, then added in a rasping whisper, "And I fear nothing, my love. Not like I fear losing ye and the wee ones."

She wrapped her arms around him and hugged him tightly. "I'm afraid too," she whispered, "but it's too late to worry about that now, I guess. Caelan—I am so sorry."

"Stop telling me ye're sorry, my precious lass." He tilted her face up to his and gave her the tenderest of kisses. "Ye've done no wrong, and everything will be all right. I promise ye." A sense of dread and dark mourning tightened like a band around his chest as he remembered his instructions to Emrys. But there was no turning back or weakening and changing his mind. To the devil with that because if he was selfish, Rachel and the bairns might very well die—in fact, there was more than a slight chance that they would. Somehow, he had to put her at ease, at least, until time for them to part. He pressed his forehead to hers. "Everything will be right as rain, my own. I swear it."

"I WANT THE TRUTH. What is going on with Caelan? I know he keeps nothing from you." Rachel stood behind Emrys, determined to get an answer out of the stubborn old man. Something was going on, but she couldn't quite put her finger on it. Caelan hadn't been the same ever since she told him about the babies. At first, she'd thought it was because he struggled with the idea of his pending fatherhood. But no, the longer his odd behavior went on, the more she sensed something else stirred inside her hard-headed Highlander's heart.

Emrys stared up at the sky for a long moment before slowly turning to face her. "Ye ken he loves ye, lass, and already loves his sons. Ye've no idea of the bond between a Highlander and his family. I promise ye he is not disappointed that ye've opened your womb to him. He's but worried about your health and the safety of the bairns."

Rachel narrowed her eyes and studied the old druid, tilting her head to one side and reaching out to him with her senses. The ability to read minds would be so helpful right now, but unfortunately, she didn't possess that gift. Emrys held something back—but what?

"I'm worried too," she admitted. "I've read how many women and babies died during childbirth back in your time. But what am I supposed to do?" Maybe she could trick the sly old goat into telling her whatever gnawed away at him. She had to find Granny's spell book. Surely, there was a way to keep Caelan and Emrys in this century. Break that strange MacKay curse and bind them to this time to prevent them from being pulled back into the past.

Emrys lifted his chin, twitched his whiskers, and narrowed his eyes at her. "What are ye up to, lass? The hairs on the back of me neck are standing on end, and that only occurs when the cosmic energies are about to be disturbed."

"I'm not up to anything. I'm just worried about Caelan."

"Trust him," the old druid advised. "Caelan will always keep ye safe, and ye must always keep in mind how much the lad loves ye."

A heavy sigh escaped her as she realized she would not get a straight answer out of the seer. Her instincts nudged her deep in her bones. Whatever was going on, whatever the truth was, he wasn't about to tell her. "I love him, Emrys, and I just hope he'll always keep that in mind as well."

Emrys frowned and narrowed his eyes even more, then slowly shook his head and ambled out of the room.

"Tell me about your castle. Is it as drafty and cold as the pictures look?" Rachel idly tickled a finger through the hair on his chest as rain pattered against the windows.

One hand propped behind his head, the other cupping the irresistible nakedness of her bum, Caelan nuzzled his cheek against the top of her head, committing the moment to memory, memorizing every sensation to treasure all the rest of his days. "Aye, they can be wicked cold and drafty at times, but we keep the fires roaring in the hearths, and the tapestries over the windows help keep the north winds out when they decide to blow. Castle MacKay is one of the best in all the Highlands for keeping the bitter cold at bay."

He swallowed hard and closed his eyes, praying for the strength to keep the farce going for just a few more days. So far, he and Emrys both had acted as though they were helping Rachel to prepare to come with them to Scotland in 1379.

"I know there won't be a Thanksgiving, but I guess there will be a...what do you call it...Yuletide? You're going to have to guide me with the customs of your time. By the way, how are you and Emrys going to explain my appearance? Neither of you has ever told me what I'm supposed to say about that. Won't your people find it odd when I just show up? I'll sound strange with my American accent."

Suddenly, she rolled off the bed and bolted for the bathroom. She slammed the door behind her, but Caelan heard her retching. He cringed for her suffering and prayed at least that part of it would end before he and Emrys left her. Goddess forgive him for putting the lass through such hell. He covered his eyes and clenched his teeth to keep from groaning with his guilt and sorrow.

"I had hoped by now that I'd stop this foolishness," she said as she emerged from the bathroom. "According to everything I've read and my personal calculations, I'm well into the second trimester. I guess I should have seen my doctor before quitting the mill and losing my insurance. The health department is okay but not nearly as good as a private doctor." She weakly dragged herself back onto the bed and curled up beside him. "Oh!"

"What?" Caelan hovered over her, brushing her hair back from her face.

She placed his hand on her side just in time for a distinct thump to tap his palm. "One of your sons. A foot or a hand. I have no idea which."

The barely perceptible mound of her stomach seemed to shift like a wave rolling within it. "The lads are swimming!"

She laughed and propped up on an elbow as the bump in her middle undulated again. "I was getting a little worried, but I guess it's taken them a while to learn to work together in such a cramped space."

Tears escaped him, but he whisked them away before Rachel saw them. His heart ached as though it had been ripped from his chest and twisted in two. These braw lads, his precious sons, would never know him. He could only watch them grow through the Mirrors of Time. With a deep inhale to rein in the storm battering within him, he sternly reminded himself that at least they would be safe, them and their mother both. That was all that mattered.

He leaned over and pressed a kiss to Rachel's forehead. "I'm going to fix ye a bit of tea and toast to settle ye. Lie here and rest, if the lads will settle down and let ye catch your breath for a bit." Rising from the bed, he paused at the doorway and glanced back, the ache in his chest almost unbearable as he watched her shift to find a more comfortable position to catch a bit more sleep.

Fists clenched against dropping to his knees and mourning what he could never have, he forced himself to turn away and head down the hall to the kitchen. He leaned against the counter, closed his eyes, and bowed his head. How in the world could he walk away from her now, when he had felt his sons move within her womb? How could he leave the woman of his heart behind and return home without her?

He lifted his head and stared up at the ceiling, reminding himself it was best for Rachel and the bairns. How many of the men of his clan were already on their second and third wives because of the dangers of bringing forth bairns in his time?

Wasn't that the very reason Fergus, his battle-worn war chief, had kept his woman Florie at arm's length until her time of bearing the wee ones had passed? The man couldn't stomach the thought of losing her.

Caelan snorted as he filled the dented teakettle with water and placed it on the stove. Why did there have to be three bairns? He couldn't remember a single woman in all the surrounding clans who had survived birthing more than one babe at a time. Twins or more always brought death. Always. He'd attended more funerals of mothers with their bairns than he cared to count.

As the kettle started to gurgle and hiss out a column of steam, he wiped a weary hand across his face. He was doing the right thing. He felt that in his bones. But Goddess help him, how was he ever going to survive it?

CHAPTER 14

In *the place she always feared.* It had to be up here in the attic because she had always hated spiders. Still did. With her shoulders wedged between two of the main trusses, Rachel tried one more time to reposition the crowbar and loosen the oblong floorboard haphazardly nailed to the beam. Once again, the crowbar slipped and nearly dinged her right between the eyes as it popped free. "Shit!"

"If ye're having so much trouble removing that board as a woman grown and wielding a piece of iron, how in the world would ye have hidden your grandmother's wee book there as a mere lass of seven summers? Especially if ye hid it in haste?" Emrys's tone held a distinct note of sarcasm that irritated the living daylights out of her. "And I still canna understand how ye could nay remember where ye put it."

"Traumatic childhood memories are best kept buried and forgotten," she snapped, even though she agreed with him. She didn't understand how she could forget something so important either. "And if you can't help with anything other than snide remarks, go away." She had searched the house high and low ever since the night in the woods when Granny's spirit had visited her.

She knew in her heart if she could find that book, she could keep Caelan and Emrys in this time. They would all stay here in the year 2007 and live out their lives in relative safety with *modern* conveniences and medicines. Raise their babies without the worry about them dying from illnesses already researched and resolved. Granted, this time held dangers all its own, but not so many as the past.

This way, she could also protect Caelan and her sons from Scotland's bloody history. She paused and rubbed her stomach like a wishing stone, tears burning her eyes at the thought of her sons and the future they would have if they were born in fourteenth century Scotland and grew up in the past she had so carefully researched.

"Ye canna be thinking anything good with that look on your bonny face." Emrys's gruffness tore her from her worries as he gently pulled the crowbar from her hand.

"I just want to find Granny's book to take back to Scotland with me," she hurried to explain. "I'm frustrated because I can't find it. She blinked away the tears and moved to another corner of the attic. "You said I couldn't take anything through the portal but myself and the dogs. Surely the Fates would allow me to bring my grandmother's book."

"Perhaps." Emrys narrowed his eyes at her and scratched his beard. "Ye seem more than a little obsessed about it, ye ken? Even got your aura glowing a bright purple. Highly charged with energy, ye are."

Rachel wanted to tell him to *hush* but bit her tongue before the words slipped out. He was much harder to fool than Caelan, and it made her nervous.

"What about that wee box over there? See it wedged under that eave?" The old druid pointed. The corner of a barely visible wooden container was shoved so far back beside the chimney that it looked to be part of a supporting beam.

"That's it!" The memory flooded back to her. She made her way over to it, dropped to her knees, and worked at the tightly wedged box until she was able to wiggle it free. It refused to open once she held it in her lap. Years of dirt, debris, and good old Kentucky humidity had caused the lid to seal itself better than any glue.

"You are going to open," she told the box. She grabbed the crowbar, wedged the end of it into the box's wooden seams, then whacked the container against the floor as hard as possible. As it splintered into pieces, a worn leather book slid to the floor. Rachel lifted it with reverence, dusting pieces of wood and dirt off the cover. Happiness filled her as it warmed to her touch. "Hello, Granny."

She carefully opened it and turned the pages. Memories of her grandmother flooded her mind and heart as scents of spices and florals wafted up from the small leather tome.

"A precious book," Emrys said while peering over her shoulder. "Makes me yearn for me own library back at the keep."

"I thought druid rituals were never written," Rachel said without looking up from the yellowed pages. "Taught from master to apprentice by memory and rote only?"

"Aye, it is," he told her, still sounding wistful. "But with no apprentice and as old as I'm getting to be, I began recording things years ago." He worked his hands as though itching to touch the precious grimoire. "Now that ye've found the wee book, what do ye mean to do with it?"

She smoothed the worn leather cover shut again and hugged it close. With her thumb mindlessly rubbing back and forth across it, she tucked her nose closer to the spine and inhaled Granny's scent as she closed her eyes. "I'm going to keep it with me to share with my sons. That way, I can at least introduce them to the one good ancestor from my side of the family. I'm sure their father has lots of tales of the brave warriors on the MacKay side."

It wasn't a lie. She would use the book to introduce her sons to their great grandmother. Now just wasn't the time for Emrys to find out her plan to keep himself and Caelan with her here in the future.

"Aye Caelan will have many tales for the lads." He cleared his throat and turned away, as though overcome with emotion.

Rachel eyed him. His behavior had turned decidedly odd. "Are you all right, Emrys?" What was the man hiding?

"Fine, lass. I'll be going now to see if Caelan's come back from town yet." He moved carefully across the exposed beams toward the ladder, his gait slow and uncertain.

"Okay. Be careful on that ladder." Rachel pulled in a deep breath as she reopened the book. While thumbing through the soft, worn pages, she found herself smiling.

"Here," she said in a breathless whisper. She tapped the page and ran her finger slowly down a column of faded, flowery scrawl. She squinted at the paragraphs in the attic's poor light, barely able to make out the words.

"Tonight should be close enough to the full moon, but I have to get them up to the pond." She caught her bottom lip between her teeth and read the passage again to be sure.

"This is definitely the way. I know I can get Caelan there." She nervously chewed on her lip. "But Emrys has to be there too."

Downstairs, the screen door slammed, startling her from her plotting. She closed the book and tucked it into the crook of her arm. As she picked her way across the attic floor and headed for the ladder, she kept mumbling under her breath, "Come on, Granny. Tell me how I can get them to the woods. What would get Emrys moving at midnight at an *almost* full moon?"

RACHEL CAREFULLY BACKED down the ancient attic ladder, only holding on with one hand as she held tight to her grandmother's book with the other. A surprised squeal escaped her as Caelan scooped her into his arms before she made it halfway down.

"Woman!" His face dark as thunderclouds, he turned her in his arms and gently stood her in front of him. "What the devil goes on in your head? Ye've no business climbing up and down such a rickety contraption in your condition! Ye might fall and injure yourself or the babes or both! Can I not leave ye alone for five minutes?"

"Calm down," she laughed, while patting him on his chest. "I've climbed up and down that thing a thousand times." She turned away to head to the kitchen, a sudden pang of hunger reminding her she'd forgotten to eat lunch.

Caelan grabbed her arm and spun her around to face him. "I dinna care how many times ye have done anything around here. This is the first time ye've done these things with bairns in your belly. 'Tis a dangerous time, Rachel. Ye must be more mindful. I'll not have ye hurt because ye refuse to listen to reason. Act with caution, ye ken? I canna always be here to catch ye if ye fall!" His eyes were wild with terror, as though some unseen enemy he couldn't fight was stalking her, and he hated being helpless to protect her.

She had never seen him so upset, and it tore at her heart that she was the one responsible for making him that way. Pulling him into a tight hug, she melted against him, snuggling as close as she could.

"I'm sorry," she whispered. "I promise I'll be more careful since it's not just me anymore." The tension seemed to leave him, and she listened closely as his heartbeat calmed even though he held her tighter.

He stroked her hair and inhaled as though breathing in her scent. She found it strange but didn't say a word. Not when she'd just upset him so.

"Just promise me ye will take care," he begged, his voice husky with emotion. "I canna bear the thought of anything happening to ye or the bairns. Promise me, aye?" He tangled his fingers in her hair and held on tight as though fearing she would disappear.

She leaned back and touched his face. "I promise with all my heart and soul to be more careful and *try* to stop being so hard-headed."

He angled an eyebrow higher while cocking his head to one side. "I suppose a half promise is better than no promise at all."

She gave him a teasing thump on his chest, then returned to her quest for food. "I am not all *that* hard-headed—at least, not as hard-headed as some people I know. Which reminds me, how was your trip to town? You said you had to get the lawyer to redo some of the paperwork. What was wrong with it? I thought everything was taken care of." She hoped she'd understood all the legal jargon correctly when she'd read that as long as she and Caelan were alive and well—and in this time—the property and money would remain in their names and not become a protected wetland foundation.

Caelan groaned and fidgeted beside her, raking a hand through his hair as his irritated scowl returned. "My trip was for naught. The documents I needed to change had already been sent to some such place to be recorded or filed or something, and they have yet to return." He shook his head, frustration flashing in his emerald eyes. "Some such nonsense about waiting periods and filing times. I dinna see how anything gets done in this century."

She pulled a bag of chocolate sandwich cookies and the jar of peanut butter down from the cabinet and moved to the kitchen table. "That's how lawyers stay in business. All the filing and re-filing and waiting periods and such. They're the only ones who can keep up with all that mess. Do you want some?" She offered him a cookie she had smeared with peanut butter.

"No, thank ye." He wrinkled his nose, making a face as if she was eating dirt.

"It's good," she defended.

"Must be the bairns that think so," he said as he poured her a tall glass of milk to go with them.

"Thank you." She accepted the drink with a smile. "You know…it's supposed to be a beautiful night with the moon nearly full. You and Emrys need to see the view of the farm in the moonlight—from the pond before we cross over into the past." She rose from the table and started clearing away her mess, carefully avoiding Caelan's gaze as she laid the groundwork for her plan. "Since I've stuffed myself with cookies and peanut butter, there's no way I'll be hungry for supper at the regular time. How about if I fix the three of us a good old-fashioned picnic? Fried chicken and all the fixings? We can take it up to the pond and enjoy a moonrise supper. You, me, Emrys, and the dogs. How about it? Granny and I used to do it a lot when I stayed with her in the summer. It's so beautiful up there. What do you say?"

She snapped her mouth shut when she realized that the more she babbled, the more she sounded like she was up to something. She'd never been a convincing liar as a child and apparently, her skill at lying hadn't approved as an adult. Turning from the kitchen sink, she risked meeting Caelan's watchful gaze.

"What are ye playing at, lass?" He leaned against the doorjamb with his arms folded across his chest.

"What?" She lifted both hands in the air and forced as innocent a look as possible. "It's just that I know we're going to be leaving soon, and I used to go up there with Granny every summer. This might be the last chance for me to relive that memory."

She silently sent up a prayer to her grandmother to forgive her for playing the homesick pregnant female card and hoped Caelan would fall for it. It was the only thing she could think of to get everybody up there. She'd accidentally used the term *moonrise,* and if Caelan repeated it to Emrys, well, then she knew the game would be over before it even began.

He dropped his gaze to the floor and scrubbed a hand over his face as if suddenly stricken with an overwhelming weariness. "Aye, lass. A picnic tonight would be a fine thing indeed. Forgive me for not understanding how much it meant to ye. I'm afraid it's been a verra long day. I'll go to the apartment and tell Emrys of your invitation."

She couldn't help but grin. "Great! Do me a favor and keep Emrys occupied until time to go to the pond. He gets underfoot worse than a toddler sometimes. Just bring him and Maizy to the pond at midnight. Sam and I will have everything ready and waiting. Would you be able to do that?" She held her breath while waiting for his answer.

"Aye, lass," he agreed with a tired smile. "I can do that with no trouble at all." He kissed her on the tip of her nose, laid a gentle touch on her stomach, then quietly let himself out the screen door with a hitching sniffle.

"Are you getting a cold?" she called after him.

He cleared his throat and answered without looking back at her. "Nay, lass. No cold at all." But his voice broke and sounded strange.

"It almost sounded like he was about to cry," Rachel mused aloud but forced herself to shrug it away. Everything would be all right after tonight. He would probably be angry for a while, but hopefully, would forgive her when she explained all her reasons for trapping him here in this time—the most important thing was that they would be here together where everything was so much safer.

"It will be all right," she promised herself as she started putting together the most important picnic of her life.

CHAPTER 15

"Sam!" Rachel snapped her fingers at the sneaky little dog just as he nosed his way under the towel covering the picnic basket. "Stay out of there. You know you can't have chicken bones, and you also know how important this is. We discussed it all the way up here, remember? Now, behave yourself while I finish things up."

Granny's book lay open on top of a boulder. Rachel leaned closer and squinted at the flowing script in the moonlight, double-checking every step. She had to follow everything to the letter. Nothing could be left to chance. Just as the little black and tan dog poked his head into the basket again, she scooped him up and moved the basket to a higher perch on a rock.

"I need you to behave. Please?" she implored him as she set him back on the ground.

Back at the book, she picked up where she'd left off. "Salt for protection. Done." She counted the steps off on her fingers while frowning down at the passage. "Area cleansed with sage—done. Candles lit. Circle open and blessed by the directions, and the crystals are ready. All I need are the guests of honor, and it will be time to seal them here."

She dabbed at one of her fingers that was still bleeding. She'd had to prick them with the tip of her athame to spread drops of blood around the perimeter of the pond. That had been the worst requirement of the spell, but a blood ritual was strong and well worth it to keep Caelan here.

Sam's ears perked, and he stood at full attention, his tiny body as proud and stiff as though he were a Doberman.

"I hear them," she whispered to her faithful watchman, smoothing down his hackles as she crouched beside him. "Don't worry. Soon, everything will be okay."

Maizy came bounding out from between the ancient, gnarled oaks that bordered the path. She barked once, as though announcing Emrys and Caelan.

"There's my girl!" Rachel rubbed the exuberant dog's velvety ears, laughing as Maizy took turns between licking her hands and excitedly nudging Sam with her enormous square head. The yellow lab was always very careful to hurt no one's feelings or leave anyone out of her greetings.

"What is this?" Emry's gruff tone caused the hairs on the back of Rachel's neck to stand on end with an almost burning tingle.

She slowly rose from her kneeling position by the dogs, hid her hands behind her back like a guilty child, and tried in vain to calm her nervousness with deep breathing. A glance at the moon and a scan of her directional position according to the stars and the keystone of the pond told her she needed to move. With a forced smile locked on the men, she meandered to the northern edge of the clearing toward the largest stone outcropping.

"Emrys. Caelan. This is where Granny and I used to have the most wonderful midnight summer picnics when I was a little girl. Isn't it beautiful?" Their wary expressions made her heart pound faster. They weren't buying off on her stroll down memory lane.

Moonlight flooded the still water of the pond, setting it afire with pure white light. Even though the powerful moon wasn't waxed to complete fullness, it shone bright enough that the flames of her ritual candles paled in comparison. Energy crackled in the air, making everyone's movements create the slightest hint of neon blue lightning. It was as though the forest held its breath in anticipation of what was about to happen. The flints of time were prepared to strike and spark into a raging inferno.

"Dinna play with me, lass," Emrys barked, then stamped his staff on the ground.

As soon as the old druid's ancient rod hit the energy-charged ground sprinkled with Rachel's blood, a rumbling came from deep within the earth. The wind picked up, swirling through the surrounding trees.

Caelan's eyes flared wide, and he grabbed hold of Emry's arm as the ground trembled hard enough to vibrate pebbles into motion. "Shield your temper, old man, lest ye kill us all!"

Hair whipping around her with the fiercer blowing of the wind, Rachel gave Emrys a curt nod. "You're on my land now. Not only my land, but the land of my ancestors—protected by my blood. My proof glows in the moonlight."

She stretched out her hand and waved it in a sweeping arc around the pond and the clearing. Everywhere a drop of her blood had fallen to the ground glowed with a blinding, silvery light. Caelan, Emrys, both the dogs, and she stood inside the gleaming circle of blood.

The old druid shook his head, his knuckles whitening with his tighter grip on his staff. He caught hold of Caelan and leaned against him for support against the increasing tempest.

"Ye should have trusted me enough to ask me, lass," he told her, "or at least channeled your grandmother and asked her. This will not work, and now ye may have killed yourself."

Caelan grabbed Emrys and shook him, shouting above the howling wind. "What are ye saying? What has she done?"

"She's cast a spell to keep us here. Used a blood ritual. Is that not right, lass?" Emrys pulled himself away from Caelan and fought to move closer to where she stood at the stone mound with the dogs.

Warily watching the druid make his way toward her, Rachel fought to remain standing as the glowing circle of her blood spun faster around them.

"Is that true?" Caelan moved to her side, shielding her as much as possible from the flying debris caught up in the wind.

"Yes, it's true!" she shouted, her composure snapping. She'd had enough of the subterfuge and effort to save them from themselves. "I am tired of allowing everything else to control my life. That's the way it's always been. I've finally found someone I love, and I will be damned if I let you be torn away and sent back to a disease-ridden, war-mongering past where you're going to suffer and die, and my sons will suffer and die. If I keep everyone here, I can protect all of you. I can save you from needless torment!"

She screamed at the top of her lungs to be heard above the wailing wind. Her silvery circle of blood had reached a dizzying speed around them, and losing her equilibrium was making it difficult to stand.

"What ye dinna understand," Emrys shouted, "is that ye've opened the portal rather than closed it. Ye've also angered the Fates because, in this prophecy, ye passed back through time at Samhain. This is not Samhain, and ye do not wish to pass through the portal at all. Do ye ken my meaning?"

"I will not die, and you know it, old man," she yelled back at him. Tears burned her cheeks in a steady stream at the failure at which he hinted. She could not be going back in time. That would not happen. The old druid couldn't possibly be right. The spell said it would seal the portal, not open it. Granny's book was never wrong. Rachel dropped to the ground and covered her face with her hands.

"Is she right? What is she saying?" Caelan grabbed Emrys and shook him again as the old man stared off into space.

"She is right," Emrys shouted. "She carries the life forces of three innocents inside her. The Goddess Brid would never allow the bairns to be punished for the actions of the mother."

All hope was gone, Rachel admitted to herself. She had failed. She didn't even bother lifting her head as she spoke. "My punishment is banishment to an uncivilized time where I will be forced to watch every person I love, suffer and die from things I could have saved them from if only I could have kept them here." No sooner had the words left her than the howling winds ceased and the silvery border of blood disappeared.

"It is done," Emrys whispered.

Gone were the tree frogs merrily chirruping around the pond in Kentucky. Gone were the crickets' songs and the distant hum of boats as the tourists enjoyed the warm moonlit night on Kentucky Lake. The only sound was the nearby gurgling of a burn as it splashed over the rocks. The sky was a velvety darkness, unmarred by security lights or lights from homes. The only illumination was the moon, and the stars spattered above them. The air still had a bit of a bite to it, and the ground was damp and chilly. Summer nights were often quite cool in Scotland.

"Only a bit farther, lass. Can ye make it or shall I carry ye?" Caelan cast a worried look at Rachel's downcast face, wishing she would say something. Talk about what happened. The only time she had spoken since they passed through the portal was when either he or Emrys asked her a direct question. Other than that, she stared at the ground and plodded along.

"I am fine." Her mouth returned to its thin, hard line, and the way the muscles rippled in her cheek revealed she clenched her teeth.

"Rachel—"

"I said I am fine," she snapped, her eyes flashing in the moonlight. "Why wouldn't I be? I've just received a life sentence with no hope for parole. What do you want from me, Caelan? I'm cursed to spend the rest of my life witnessing the people I cherish more than life itself suffer with things I could've prevented, and there isn't a damn thing I can do about it. Forgive me if I'm not belching butterflies, prancing like a unicorn, or shitting rainbows!"

Before he could counter that outburst, she started in again. "It doesn't matter that I might not even survive the birth of my children. What matters is that I'll have to see them suffer with something that could've been avoided." She pulled in a deep breath and walked faster. "And what about Scotland's bloody history? How long can I even hope for you to survive before you leave me widowed? And if our babies live to adulthood, it'll only be so they can be hacked to death in some war too." A heart-wrenching sob escaped her as she kicked a rock out of her path.

She shot a fiery glower at Emrys. "What did I ever do to make the Fates want to punish me like this? Or am I just a toy to amuse them when they're bored? Tell me that, Emrys? Tell me!"

The old druid opened his mouth to respond, and she cut him off.

"Never mind! I don't need any of your sanctimonious, holier-than-thou speeches. Spare me!"

Sam tugged on her pant leg and whined.

Thank the Goddess for the dog, Caelan thought, fearing to nettle his lovely wee bear any further.

She bent, picked up her loyal companion, and cradled him to her chest. The pup whined again while licking her face as though assuring her everything would be okay.

"I'll carry you a bit, Sam," she said, her fury gone, and defeat making her shoulders sag. "I know you must be getting tired."

"Scotland is beautiful, Rachel. Especially this late in the summer." Caelan braced himself for another rant. Perhaps if the lass got it all out of her system, she would feel better for it.

"I'm sure it is," she agreed in a dull, dead tone that worried him even more than her fury. She nuzzled her face against Sam's furry neck, as though the dog were her only reason for living.

Caelan ambled along beside her, wishing she would let him in, let him help her. Even though they had only been in the past a little while, she had already used her fears to build a wall between them. He saw it as plainly as if she erected it of stone, and he understood her fears. Hadn't he planned to leave her and the wee ones behind for their safety and wellbeing? But now that she was here, they needed to draw closer to one another, not far apart. Together, they could strengthen each other. Isolated, they would surely lose all hope.

She needed to realize that there were no guarantees in life, no matter what era in which you lived. He understood that now and was grateful that she was with him, here at his side, in his homeland. Together, they could withstand whatever life gave them.

Hope filled him. As soon as the winds had died down from the portal, he had realized they were once again on Alba's blessed soil. When he had touched Rachel's hand, he'd sensed not only the beating of her heart but the beating of his three sons' wee strong hearts as well, and they all beat in time with his own. That's when he knew her spell hadn't gone wrong at all but, in fact, had gone perfectly right. It was up to him now to convince her of that small matter as well.

He reached for Sam. "Here. Let me carry the wee pup. Ye are weariness itself, and we've yet a ways to go before we reach the keep."

The dog flattened his ears, bared his teeth, and growled.

"I need to hold him right now, Caelan, and he knows it." She stared at the ground and kept walking, lightly stroking the head of the tiny protector in her arms.

Emrys caught up with Caelan and tugged him aside while whispering, "Ye're going to have to start all over again with the lass. Go with care, aye?"

"I fear it will be more difficult this time," Caelan whispered back. "She's terrified and has decided all of us are going to die and leave her here alone." He watched her mindless plodding, her not looking at the beautiful, rugged hills, or even noticing the ancient burial cairns off to the side of the path. It hurt his heart for her to be so defeated. She had longed to travel to Scotland and see all these things, and yet, she walked blindly past them all.

"Can ye guarantee her ye will never leave her alone?" Emrys asked after a hesitant glance at Rachel. "I caught her researching Scotland's history on that computer of hers, and the things she read aloud to me curdled my gut and chilled my old bones."

"Why would anyone want to live forever, old one?" Caelan cast Emrys a sideways glance, his jaw locked defensively.

"Spoken like a true warrior, but ye must think about what the wife of that warrior feels or the mother of that warrior's sons. Rachel was not raised to be a warrior's wife or to raise a warrior's sons. She takes no pride in sending her children to battle. She wants them safe and alive to a ripe old age."

"Both of you need to just shut up," Rachel said without looking at either of them. "I've lost all hope—not my hearing."

Caelan shoved the old man aside and shook a finger at him in a demand for silence. He stared at the woman he loved, trying to understand what was going through her mind. With a slow shake of his head, he swore an oath to himself. He and Rachel would be happy once again. He had not come this far just to lose his heartmate.

As DAWN BROKE over the horizon, they topped the last hill that had shielded Castle MacKay from view. Rachel rubbed Sam's ears while staring across the meadow at the large foreboding keep. How in heaven's name would she ever adapt to this time?

Built on top of a cliff facing the sea, it was obvious the fortress had been planned out carefully to protect its clan against any intruders. The front entrance was only accessible by a long bridge built over a deep ravine. It reminded her of the pictures she had seen of Dunnottar.

With her eyes shaded with her hand, she barely made out the tiny figures walking along the top of the outermost wall. Torches flickered in the duskiness of the early hour as the inhabitants of Castle MacKay greeted the coming day.

She could feel Caelan's pride and excitement as he stood beside her.

He pointed across the way. "Look there at the main gate stands Fergus ready to mount his horse. He watches to ensure that all is well guarded and only those who can be trusted enter the keep."

With a nod, she clutched Sam even closer than before as they all made their way down the hill. She could not do this. A derisive snort escaped her. What choice did she have?

They had only covered a few yards down the hillside when she heard a shout go up from the wall. Apparently, they had been spotted. With any luck, they would shoot her first, she glumly thought before the movement of her sons reminded her she needed to live for their sakes.

Men on horses streamed out the gate and pounded across the bridge. Caelan pulled her behind him. "Stay behind me for a bit, aye? Till they ken ye are my wife."

She didn't answer, just buried her face in Sam's neck, tears stinging in her eyes when he trembled and whined. "Me too, Sam," she whispered. "Me too."

"Caelan! Is it yourself, man?" shouted an enormous man, his flaming red hair shot with gray. He sat astride a monstrous black horse and was in the lead.

"Aye, Fergus, and it pleases me to see how well ye've tended the keep." Caelan stepped forward with his hand raised.

Fergus dismounted as the rest of the men reined in their horses. He caught hold of Caelan's arm and thumped him on the back, while a wide smile split his auburn beard. His ruddy eyebrows rose to his hairline as his gaze lit on Rachel.

She suddenly felt more than a little self-conscious, standing there in her jeans, sandals, and the mound of her belly stretching her tee shirt tightly across her front.

After a polite nod her way, Fergus turned back to Caelan. "And this would be the lady of your dreams?"

Caelan drew her to his side, his arm protectively around her. "Fergus, I would like to introduce ye to my wife, Rachel, and her wee friend Sam."

Fergus bowed, then smiled warmly at her. "'Tis a fine pleasure indeed to meet the woman able to tame this man. Welcome to Castle MacKay, Lady Rachel."

"Thank you," she said softly. "It's a pleasure to meet you." She shifted uncomfortably as she noticed the other men appeared to be quite taken aback by her clothing. She nodded at them and forced a smile.

They bowed their heads and smiled back, but their smiles didn't reach their eyes.

Lovely. Rachel swallowed hard. Not only would she be forced to acclimate to the time, but she'd have to watch her back. They didn't trust her, probably even feared her. Thought of her as a witch—which she was, but that was beside the point. Either way, without Caelan's protection, she would be toast. Literally. On a stake in the middle of a bonfire.

"We nay brought ye a horse, for we didna ken if that was yourself coming down the hillside. There has been more trouble of late, but we can discuss it later. After ye get your fine new lady wife settled in the keep." Fergus bowed to Rachel again, then turned to the other men still on their mounts. "Alec. Ian. Dismount and give your horses to the laird and his lady."

Two men jumped to the ground and led their horses to stand in front of Caelan and Rachel.

"And I am to walk?" Emrys growled with a stamp of his staff. "I shall set a curse on your arse, Fergus. Ye always vexed me!"

"Walk? Why I figured ye would cast a spell, old man, so that ye could ride upon the winds." Fergus grinned as he led his horse to stand in front of Emrys.

"Ye are a rude, insolent cur. Did your mother give up on teaching ye any manners when ye were a lad?" Emrys shook his staff at him once again, then mounted with amazing ease, considering his age.

Rachel eyed the horse and backed up a step. Sam growled, expressing her feelings about the situation perfectly. "I'm afraid I don't know how to ride. Sorry."

Caelan lifted her into the saddle, then launched himself up behind her. "Ian, ye can either ride or give Fergus your mount. My wife and I shall ride together."

The tall, quiet youth grinned as he glanced in Fergus's direction. "Aye, I'll walk. I'd never hear the end of it from old Fergus if I don't. He greets worse than a wee bairn if he has to go anywhere afoot."

After cuffing Ian with a glancing blow, Fergus settled into the lad's saddle. "When ye've fought as many battles as I have, boy, then ye can talk to me about traveling afoot. I've earned the right to ride wherever I go, and I dinna intend to let anyone forget it."

"Ah, 'tis a fine thing to be home," Caelan breathed into Rachel's ear as he gently pulled her back against his chest.

Little Sam rumbled and growled while hugging himself tighter into her arms. She pressed a kiss to him and whispered, "I know. I don't like it either, but we have no choice."

A hint of relief washed across her when she spotted Maizy trotting along happily beside Emrys's horse as though she'd followed him all her life. *At least one of us is adapting*, she thought as she tried to settle more comfortably in the saddle.

"Rest easy, lass. We'll be inside the keep soon enough. After ye have the bairns, ye can learn to ride. I know just the mare for ye. She's as gentle as a wee kitten and will be perfect for ye to get to know." Caelan kissed the back of her neck as they started across the bridge spanning the deep ravine.

Rachel snapped her eyes shut after a glance down and sunk back even tighter against his chest. *Don't puke*, she repeated over and over to herself. If crossing this was the only way out of the keep, she'd never be able to go anywhere unless they blindfolded her.

When the horse's hooves thudded on solid ground once more, she opened her eyes to curious faces on both sides of the path. She was tempted to close her eyes again but chided herself at the cowardly thought. Word had traveled fast that the time-traveling laird had finally returned with his wife. She might as well face this and get it over with. He had promised they would be friendly. She prayed he was right.

They halted in the outer courtyard—or bailey. She couldn't remember for sure what they called it. More clansmen, women, and children poured from every doorway and out from around every corner. Panic mounted, making Rachel's heart pound.

Caelan dismounted and held up his hands for her.

She ignored him, trying to breathe and on the verge of passing out. They all stared at her as though she were some sort of magickal creature he had captured during his travels.

"I don't belong here," she told him while tucking away from his reach. Take me back to the woods. I'll try to go back when the moon is full."

Caelan stepped closer, love and worry filling his eyes. "Ye ken as well as I that ye canna do that," he reminded softly. "It'll not work, my love." He reached for her again. "Ye belong with me, and I belong here. Give it a chance, dear one. I beg ye."

She blinked hard and fast, trying to hold back her tears. "They already hate me," she whispered. "I sense it."

He took hold of her waist, slid her down into his arms, and gently steadied her to the ground. After a tender kiss to her temple, he whispered back, "They dinna hate ye, lass. Ye are new, and they are simply curious about ye."

A woman stepped forward, approaching Rachel with what looked to be a genuine smile—at least it sparkled in her eyes. "Welcome, m'lady. We have watched for ye ever since the laird told us he was off to bring ye home." The kindly matron eased forward, as though she believed Rachel to be a wounded animal. She shot Caelan a stern glare, then turned her smile back on Rachel. "I be Florie. Your maid who will tend to all your needs. Ye need not fear me, m'lady, I swear it."

Rachel noticed Sam had stopped growling and was actually wagging his tiny tail. She trusted the little dog's instincts more than she trusted anything else right now. She offered Florie a smile. "I'm Rachel."

Florie bumped Caelan out of the way with her broad hip as she wrapped her arm around Rachel's shoulders. "Shall we get ye to your chambers, Lady Rachel? I ken ye must be far gone weary. While ye have yourself a wee nap. I'll find some proper clothes for ye to make ye more comfortable. Walking for miles while growing with child, ye must be more than a wee bit exhausted."

As Florie led her away, Rachel glanced back at Caelan.

Caelan nodded his approval, smiling when Sam jumped out of her arms and ran to his side. "Florie will take good care of ye, lass. Rest and I'll join ye soon."

CHAPTER 16

"Where is she?" he worried under his breath. From his seat at the head table overlooking the hall, Caelan watched the archway where Rachel should have entered long ago. Familiar faces filled the large gathering room, but his beloved lass had yet to appear and take her place at his side. He missed her as though they'd been separated for an age, aching to have her warm presence beside him to reassure himself she had really joined him, and he'd not just dreamt it. He worried for her, needed to see with his own eyes that she was well, and had not decided to hate him for ripping her away from everything she knew. "Where the devil is she?" he said louder, while scowling at the doorway.

"Still in your rooms, my laird," a quiet voice behind his chair whispered. "She refuses to come down. Said she canna bear it."

Caelan shifted and angled an expectant brow at Florie. Her explanation worried him even more. The only comfort he drew from it was that Florie was one of the few castle women whose heart he deemed patient and kind enough to help Rachel become accustomed to her new life. Adapting to Rachel's time had been quite the chore. He feared his lady love would struggle to embrace his world especially while under the stress of becoming a mother to three bairns.

"And why can she not bear to come down?" he asked quietly to ensure no one overheard. If anyone dared make his Rachel uncomfortable, he'd snap their necks for them. He angled an ear closer to Florie while scowling at anyone foolish enough to meander too close to overhear the private conversation.

Florie scrunched up her face, looking slightly bewildered and perhaps a wee bit embarrassed about failing him. She hid her words behind her hand as she whispered, "She said she refused to meet your people looking like an oversized, purple pen...pen..." Her scowl tightened, and she jerked her head from side to side. "That word she used—I dinna ken it. What in heaven's name was it?" She tapped her chin and stared at the ceiling as though the answer might be written across the huge dark rafters spanning the width of the hall. "Pen-yadda? Pin-yatti?" She shook her head again. "Something like that, my laird. Lady Rachel appears to be troubled by her appearance even though she is loveliness itself, what with her rounding with your wee bairn."

Caelan groaned with a heavy sigh. Goddess help him help his lady love. Near as he could tell, Rachel considered herself a large piñata. She had shown him one in a shop window and explained how they were used. Why would she think such a thing? As Florie said, his beloved was beauty itself.

"My laird?" Florie whispered again, still behind his chair.

"Aye?" Caelan scrubbed his weary eyes, trying to come up with a way to make things better.

"What exactly is a pen-yadda?" Loyal, good-hearted, and kind, Florie was also curious to the point of almost being a danger to herself.

"I shall have Lady Rachel explain it to ye sometime," he told her as he pushed himself up from his chair. "Perhaps I should have been more thoughtful with my lady and escorted her down to the hall. I shall fetch her now, aye?"

"Aye, that will be a fine thing, my laird." Florie gave him a sympathetic nod that failed to make him feel any better.

CAELAN OPENED the door to his private chambers and forgot to breathe. There she stood, staring out the window, even more beautiful than when she had teased him in his dreams.

She wore a gown of the richest purple, a deep amethyst, only rivaled by the vibrant violet of her eyes. Its high waist caught up beneath her full breasts by a golden braided rope allowed the supple material to flow gracefully down over her rounded middle, proudly displaying that she carried his precious wee bairns. Her breasts, full and tempting, mounded about the low-cut neckline, making his mouth water as they swelled and shifted with her every breath. The velvet sleeves were closely fitted to her long, slender arms and came to a point atop her hands. A gossamer mantle, shimmering and golden, was attached to her shoulders and flowed in a regal train behind her. Florie had caught up her hair in a mass of gleaming ebony curls and placed a hammered collar of polished gold around her neck.

"Ye are loveliness itself, Rachel. I canna take my eyes from ye," he said softly as he stepped into the room and closed the door behind him.

"I can't do this, Caelan. Not yet. I'm sorry, but I'm just not ready." She paced back and forth in front of the window, rubbing the mound of her stomach as though it were a wishing stone.

He crossed the room, took her in his arms, and cradled her close. "The clan has prepared a proper wedding feast, my love. They wish to meet ye and toiled hard to pull such a thing together so quickly. Would ye deny them the joy of knowing ye? Of discovering what a wondrous woman the Fates chose for their laird?" He tried to soothe her with a tender kiss on her forehead. "I promise everything will be all right. Just give them the chance to know and love ye."

Her beguiling, warm vanilla scent stirred him to nuzzle the silky curve of her neck. He cradled her even closer and whispered, "Come to the hall with me. Show them how blessed I am to have ye as my wife. Ye are loveliness itself."

She pushed away, her large, beautiful eyes gleaming with unshed tears. "I am not loveliness. I am the size of a beached whale, and now that we're back here, you're going to find someone else, and I'll be stuck here, and I have no one to turn to, and…" She hiccupped as she was wont to do each time she worked herself into one of these spells that had become commonplace the farther along she traveled in her journey to motherhood. She grabbed a cup of water from the bedside table and downed it while holding her nose.

Caelan took the cup from her, set it on the table, and eased her back into his arms. He kissed her hard and long, pouring every ounce of his love and need for her into the bond. She clung to him, desperation in the kiss that she returned. His heart ached to make her understand he was nothing without her, and no one could ever take her place in his heart or his bed.

He pulled back and looked into her eyes. "I did not travel across time and space merely to bed ye, get ye with child, and then toss ye aside." He cupped her cheek and brushed his thumb across her bottom lip. "I came for ye because ye are part of my soul, my love, and I intend to keep ye for all eternity. Now wipe your eyes, aye? We shall enjoy our wedding banquet, then return here to give our marriage bed a proper christening." He gave her a smile that he prayed she would take to heart.

She stepped back again, easing out of his embrace while smoothing the folds of her gown. Her mouth flattened into a tight line, and her gaze fell as she brushed a stray tendril of hair behind her ear. With a strained cough and one last hiccup, she returned to the window and stared outside.

He could tell that her eyes saw nothing but the life she wished she still had. The sight of her mourning her time clenched icy fingers around his heart and squeezed.

"Florie is nice," she said in that dead tone that made him ache with regret. She squinted as though trying to see something in the distance. "But the rest of them, they stare and whisper. They look at me with fear in their eyes—like I'm a tainted relic that's going to curse them."

Caelan pulled in a deep breath and forced himself to remain calm. She needed understanding now. She needed patience. Emrys had warned it would be difficult for her to adapt—especially with her condition that made her even more sensitive to the upheaval of leaving her time.

"They merely need to know ye, lass," he reassured gently. "Meet ye and speak with ye. Once they see the wonderful woman ye are, they will be the family ye never had."

She didn't respond, just continued staring out at the sea. The waves crashed outside, mimicking the turmoil within the room. "If they're so eager to welcome me with open arms, why did Emrys tell me to keep my past and Granny's journal a secret?" She hugged her middle as though trying to shield her children. "They think I'm a witch, Caelan. I see it in their eyes, and I know what happens to witches in this era." She finally glanced back at him for the briefest moment, the sadness and fear in her face stealing his breath. "If they accept Emrys's magick, why can't they accept mine?" She barely shook her head. "I'm not safe here. I can feel it."

He joined her at the window, remembering the same warning from Emrys. "My clan...our clan," he corrected, "is superstitious. Some find it difficult to accept Emrys and his ways. That is why the old seer has been kept under the laird's protection. If not, some would have seen him banished from the clan years ago." As soon as the words left his lips, he knew he shouldn't have uttered them. Damned fool, he was. "I will keep ye—"

Her glare cut him off. "You knew their superstitions and yet you still brought me here? Knowing I could be in that same danger. What if something happens to you, and I fall to them? What about our sons?" Her jaw tightened and her eyes brimmed with tears as she tightened her arms around her stomach.

He took her back into his arms and lifted her chin to force her to look him in the eyes. "Ye are allowing fear to steal your power, lass.

Fight it. Ye are so much stronger than ye believe. Ye will never find peace as long as ye look for the ill in every situation. We are together because of our love, and we will be safe because I will make it so. Ye must trust in me, Rachel. Ye had started to before we came back through the portal. Can ye not do so again?"

She shifted with a despondent sigh and sadly shook her head. "I've read too much about this time. I may never get past the fear."

"Trust me," he whispered, then kissed the tip of her nose. "Come now. Let me introduce my wondrous wife to my clan."

Rubbing her forehead as though it ached, she linked her arm through his. "Fine," she said with a heavy sigh that twisted his heart. "I'm as ready as I'll ever be, I guess."

CAELAN DID his best to ignore the acrid scent of the smoke rising from the brazier in the corner as he paced around Emrys's chambers. "She'll not even let me touch her. No holding her and no consoling her. We've been here weeks now, and she still turns her face to the wall every night and cries herself to sleep." He raked a hand through his hair, then scrubbed his face. "Her misery is killing me, and it canna be good for the bairns. Tell me what to do."

"I warned ye it would take a while for the lass to adapt. She never planned to be here and did not come willingly. Ye must be patient." Emrys didn't bother to look up from his book as he idly stroked his beard. "Ye must also remember that she's growing heavy with your children. As she nears her time, her emotions will be even worse. Make her feel as safe as ye can. She knows too much about Scotland's history that has not yet come to pass. Try to keep her thoughts away from those things."

Caelan pounded his fist on the table, then reached over and slammed Emrys's book shut. "I need your help, damn it. I dinna need idle advice about being patient and understanding. I *am* doing those things, but it's nay helping her. Not a feckin' bit! I need her smiling again and looking at this as her home. I need her happy."

Emrys glared at him, his bushy white brows twitching. "What do ye ask of me, my laird? Cast a spell that will turn her into a meek, accepting wife?" He stiffly rose from his seat and jabbed a bent finger in Caelan's face. "Did ye think it was going to be a mere feat of going to the future, whisking her back, then all would fall into a nice, tidy routine? Are ye that big of a fool to think that any woman worthy of the MacKay line would be easy to uproot from her era and replant over six hundred years in the past?"

Mumbling and cursing under his breath, Emrys threw more herbs on the burning coals in the brazier. As the smoke became more bitter and thickened anew, he turned and faced Caelan. "Ill tidings are brewing, and ye best work harder at winning back your wife's heart, mind, and soul. Go carefully, Caelan, for ye can still lose it all even though she joined ye in this time."

Caelan slammed his hands onto Emrys's chest, caught hold of his robes, and yanked him closer with a hard shake. "What have ye seen? Tell me so I can keep her and the bairns safe. I will let nothing risk them!"

"I have said all that the Fates will allow," Emrys said, jutting his chin to a defiant angle. "If I reveal too much and change the tapestry of time, they will take away my visions completely. But know this— that which we should fear the most does not always come from outside forces. Sometimes our greatest enemies, our greatest challenges, come from within."

He yanked his robes free of Caelan's fists and returned to his seat by the fire.

Caelan gritted his teeth as he strode to the door. "If anything happens to her, and ye have seen it, and not warned me, the Fates will not be able to take your visions away because I will take your life."

"I saw the woman, and I tell ye that she is an evil brought into our midst." Roderic, the bastard half-brother to Laird Caelan MacKay, glanced around the village's only inn as he whispered around his tankard of ale.

Chieftain Cormac of Glen Marren leaned forward and narrowed his eyes in disbelief. "Me and mine attended the wedding banquet. The lass looked harmless enough to me." He belched and patted his stomach. "Already round with child, so the laird must be pleased she's fertile."

"What about how she got here?" Roderic insisted. "How could a *normal* woman accept that a druid was going to take her back in time to be with her husband? Would your fine daughter have accepted such an unnatural thing so easily?" Roderic allowed himself a cruel smile as he purposely reminded Cormac of his daughter's rejection by the laird. He knew the man was still sorely disappointed that his daughter had not been taken to wife by Caelan. The match would've been advantageous for both clans since Cormac's lands joined the MacKay lands at their northernmost border.

Cormac frowned as he stared down into his mug. "Nay. Not my Calynda. She would never accept such a heathen tale. She would've run screaming to the Church for protection." He pursed his lips, his scowl tightening. "But Emrys has advised all the clans in a fair manner for as far back as any of us can remember. A druid, he is, yes. A follower of the old ways. But never has he brought ill upon a soul."

"As far as we know," Roderic said, stoking the man's doubt. He waved to the barmaid to bring two more ales. Sowing seeds of ill content was thirsty work. "What of that maid who disappeared from the cliff by the sea? Her body never was found. If she merely lost her footing, as some have said, her body would have snagged in the jagged rocks below, ye ken?" He leaned closer and lowered his voice, feeding on the fear growing in Cormac's eyes. "But the moon was full that night, remember? It was just before planting time and had Emrys not just told the clans they needed a sacrifice to ensure a good harvest? What better sacrifice than that of a pure maiden?"

"Aye, the poor wee lass was never found, and the crops did do well that year." Cormac's knuckles whitened as he clenched the handle of his drink. "But what can we do? Laird MacKay is powerful, and if his wife be a witch, what will keep her from laying curses upon us? Upon our descendents, even?"

"Trust me, old friend, we will bide our time until the proper moment. Then we will scourge the land of this evil and put things right as they were meant to be. Tell me you are with me. Tell me I can count on your clan in this cleansing of the land." Roderic held out his hand and waited for Cormac's pledge of loyalty.

Cormac nodded once and shook his hand. "Aye, Roderic. Ye have my oath and that of my clan's."

RACHEL STRUGGLED to rise gracefully from the bench in the garden. A relieved huff escaped her as she rubbed her aching back and stretched. She'd always prided herself on exercising and keeping active. She might not have always been what society considered the perfect weight, but she was healthy. The babies rolled within her as if wrestling with each other for space. With a push on the rib they'd made sore with their constant stretching, she cut loose a quiet groan. "I never realized I was training to give birth to a herd of oxen."

She eyed her handiwork with distaste. All this discomfort on that hard bench for a bit of embroidery. Fancy stitchery was not her wheelhouse. Of course, neither was good old common sense stitchery either. Thank goodness, since she was the wife of the laird, she wasn't expected to do the sewing required to keep clothes on her back.

"Good thing too," she said to no one in particular. "If I had to sew my own clothes, I'd be walking around in cloth sacks." She patted her leg so Sam would jump up so she could rub his ears. At this stage in her pregnancy, her ability to bend and reach anything below her knees was laughable. The little dog placed his paws on her knee, then jerked around, bared his teeth, and growled like a miniature buzz saw.

Rachel eyed the huge clansmen headed her way, trying to place him and remember his name. The back of her neck tingled and her babies went still, a surefire sign that he wasn't one of the MacKay's wishing to befriend her or play nice. Since traveling back in time, her instincts had sharpened. Probably as a means of survival and protecting her sons. Whenever her body warned her that all was not well, she listened.

She pointed at the bench. Sam leapt up on it so she could scoop him up and hug him to her chest. "Protect me, my brave friend," she whispered. Precious Sam might be tiny, but he could do some damage and make a lot of noise.

"Good day to ye, Lady Rachel," the man called out as he continued toward her. Close to seven feet tall and dressed in dark trews and his everyday plaid, he closed the distance between them like a panther stalking its prey. His hair was black, shot with silver, and his eyes were an unnerving, icy grey. But it was his predatory gait that caused her to step back and place the stone bench between them.

"Good day to you, sir," she politely responded while cursing herself for not remembering his name.

"Roderic," he offered with a curt nod. A sly smirk played across his mouth and his cold grey eyes narrowed.

Rachel smiled and played as if she had just remembered him. "Well, of course, Roderic. Please forgive me. I have a lot on my mind of late." She patted her stomach. "The babies already keep me busy, and when I'm weary, my memory fails me."

"I understand, m'lady, but ye should always remember me. After all, I am Caelan's half-brother. Next in line should anything ever befall our fine laird—heaven forbid, of course." With the speed of a striking snake, he smoothed an errant curl back from her face and tucked it behind her ear. His smile turned colder and gleamed with malice. "But rest assured, m'lady, if anything so terrible were to happen to our laird before he had a son of age, I would not only take over his leadership of the clan but also his duties as your husband."

He drew closer but halted and thought better of it when Sam snapped at him as though ready to eat him alive. As he stepped away, Roderic laughed while glaring at the dog. "Ye will not always have your wee protector. We shall meet again at another time, my lady."

As the disgusting man turned to leave the garden, Rachel concentrated very hard on the back of his head. When he walked out from beneath the arbor, a trio of ravens swooped in from beyond the castle skirting wall and pelted him with droppings.

He ran and cursed in what she assumed must be Gaelic. His less than elegant exit from the garden made her smile but worry still tightened like a knot in her chest. She sank onto the bench and hugged Sam closer.

"Take care, lass," Emrys warned as he and Maizy stepped out from behind the rose bushes. "That one there is pure evil and would as soon see ye burned for being a witch as he would to bed ye for being a beautiful woman. It would make no difference to him either way."

"He means Caelan harm." A vicious chill ran across her, making her hug her middle. "And he'll kill our sons if given the chance."

"Dinna fash yourself, lass. Caelan knows about Roderic and has been watching that cur for years." Emrys lightly touched her shoulder and aimed a smile at her middle. "'Tis a grand thing we came back when we did. Your lads are growing and making themselves more known every day." He cleared his throat and tilted his head. "Do ye ken when the three will decide to make their appearance?"

"By my calculations, probably not until after the first of the year, but it's hard to tell with triplets. They might come early." She eyed the old druid, resenting him for trying to change the subject. She was not a child that needed placating. With his help, she rose from the bench and gathered up her pitiful excuse for embroidery. "Are you going to tell Caelan about Roderic, or am I? He needs to be warned."

"He already knows, lass, now stop worrying. Ye need to concentrate on taking care of yourself and those three bairns." Emrys motioned her forward in a silent entreaty for her to join him on a stroll.

"I'm fine," she said, deciding she would warn Caelan herself. Emrys was useless. "The boys are more than fine. They just need more room with each passing day." She rubbed her back as she waddled along. "I've come to grips with the fact that I'm never going to fit in here." She blew out a heavy sigh and shrugged. "But I've never fit in anywhere, so I guess it doesn't really matter." Ambling along, she scowled at Emrys, tugging on his arm to make sure he listened. "My only goal is to keep my sons safe, and Caelan safe for as long as I can—considering this place's history. I don't expect to be happy. Never. It's my fault I ended up here, so I can't blame anyone but myself."

"Are ye truly that miserable, lass? Is life here as bad as all that?" Emrys eyed her with a worried look.

She stopped walking and faced him. "I don't deserve a man like Caelan, and I was a fool to believe I could keep him in my life. Although, if I could've kept him in my time, I might've had a fighting chance at it. So, let's just say I've resigned myself to his loss—whether it be by the sword, disease, or something as simple as him finally opening his eyes to how I failed to protect him." Releasing Emrys's arm, she turned to head back to the keep, Sam following closely on her heels.

RACHEL LAY ON HER SIDE, facing the wall rather than him, a position she had taken up as soon as they settled into the keep. Caelan hated it, ached to know how to make things better for her, and lift her spirits. He only prayed that once the bairns arrived—safe and healthy, all the powers of the universe willing—that Rachel would find her way back to him.

"I know ye canna be sleeping," he whispered into her hair, nestled against her back and wrapping an arm around her. At least she allowed him that. As he stroked her swollen stomach, his sons rolled and kicked as though ready to be free of their cramped quarters. "Our wee scamps grow livelier by the day. Have ye been able to rest at all, my love?"

"I have to get us back," she whispered, making his heart clench.

Ever since Roderic had taunted her in the garden, she had been more uneasy. Caelan toyed with the idea of banishing the bastard, but several in the clan listened to his lying tongue and would cast their lot with his. It was far better to keep the coward close and under a watchful eye than have him gathering forces across the Highlands. More than one clan had been weakened by infighting. Caelan refused to allow Clan MacKay to go down that path of destruction. He knew how to manage the man.

He eased up onto his elbow and peered over at her as he smoothed her hair back from her face. "Ye canna go back, love. Ye ken that is impossible. The Fates will not allow it, and like it or not, they are stronger than your magick. This is your home now. Our home. We shall thrive here with our bairns and grow old together."

"You don't know that," she growled, shoving him away. "Don't make promises you can't possibly keep. It's always the same from you, the same old placating tone, the *pat her on the head and make her happy* lies. You have no way of guaranteeing any of it, and I'm sick of listening to it!"

She threw back the bedclothes and struggled to flounder her way out of the bed as quickly and with as much grace as her unbalanced roundness would allow. Her eyes flashed with angry violet fire as she turned and pointed at him, jabbing the air as though stabbing it with a dagger. "Lame promises might work with the women of this time and those who hang on your every word, but I know the truth. I read about what happens."

She shoved her wild mane of curls out of her eyes and growled again as she searched for a ribbon to tie around the unruly mess. "Damn, what I wouldn't give for even one freaking rubber band right now!" She stormed over to the curtained-off corner hiding the chamber pot cabinet. "And a *real* bathroom. Wonderful running water—hot and cold. But, no, I have to squat over the chamber pot because I have to piss every freaking five minutes since your sons use my bladder for a trampoline. Or if I really feel like getting fancy, I get to use a garderobe that we in Kentucky would call an indoor outhouse!"

Caelan rolled back and stared up at the canopied ceiling of the great oak bed. Emrys and Florie had warned him about a breeding woman's temper swings, and that Rachel would grow tetchier as her discomfort grew. If the bairns weren't due to come until after Yule, the entire clan could be in danger of losing their lives in a matter of weeks.

She emerged from behind the curtain, her lovely eyes still flashing purple venom. As she approached the bed, she chopped the air with her hands, keeping time with each of her words. "Roderic plans to kill you, lay claim to your clan, claim me, and do who knows what to our sons. He so much as said so in the garden, and all you do is smile and tell me we're going to grow old together and raise our bairns? How stupid do you think I am?"

Hands on her hips, she narrowed her eyes into a deadly glare, waiting for him to dig himself deeper into the hole in which he appeared to, currently, be trapped.

He chose his words carefully as he nonchalantly piled the bedclothes across his lap so his beloved wife couldn't see how much her fiery tirade excited him. It had been so long since they'd loved and lore the woman's passion was unmatched. The sooner he calmed her, the sooner he could try to channel her fire into a more enjoyable outlet.

"Rachel," he began, then stopped and cleared his throat. *Start again and dinna talk to her like she's a child.* "As I'm sure Emrys already told ye, Roderic and I have been sworn enemies since he sprang from my father's mistress's womb." Caelan fought to control both his voice and his yearning for her as she circled the room like a caged lioness. "Da took a mistress after my mother died while bringing me into this world. He swore he'd never wed another because my mother was his one true match. But Da was a lusty man, and Roderic's mother filled a need. When she brought forth her bairn and found it nay changed my father's mind about marrying her, she abandoned Roderic on the steps of the keep, telling everyone that the only reason she'd brought the bastard into the world was to secure a place at the head table for herself."

Caelan rose from the bed, then halted as Rachel's eyes narrowed even more and her lips thinned as though she'd draw a weapon if he drew any closer.

"So ye see," he said as he sat on the edge of the bed. "Roderic resents how he was abandoned because he turned out to be a useless pawn."

"Doesn't look to me like he's that much worse for the wear. He's still here." Rachel propped her arms on the shelf of her belly and tapped her foot on the stone floor.

Caelan sensed that what little patience she possessed was nearing its end. "Aye, the clan took him in, but the man will always be known as a bastard. As ye have said yourself, ye ken how cruel Scotland can be for one so labeled." He held his breath, praying her murderous mood would pass as it usually did.

She massaged her temples while pacing the room. "I understand his bitterness and jealousy, but that doesn't negate the fact that he's a danger to you and our sons. I'm not worried about myself. If he bothers me, I'll just cover him in bird shit again." She dropped to a pillowed bench, buried her face in her hands, and gave way to her tears. "No one takes me seriously in this century. None of you listen. Not ever."

Damnation. Not the tears. Caelan rushed to her side. He'd rather her rant and rave, throw anything she could hoist into the air, and threaten to cast every spell she might ever hope to know, but, by the Goddess, don't let her cry. He dropped to his knees alongside her. "Shh now, Rachel, love. Hush now, my precious one. It will be all right, and I'm not just saying that to make ye stop crying."

She sobbed harder, keening out a high-pitched wail.

As he rose to sit beside her on the bench and tried to pull her into his arms, someone knocked on their bedchamber door.

"What the hell now?" he roared while smoothing Rachel's hair and gently rocking.

Florie entered the room with a tray of sliced fruit and cheese but halted as soon as she took in the situation. She slid the tray onto the table beside the bed and rushed to Rachel's side. "Are ye ill, m'lady?"

She gently lifted Rachel's face to hers and shook her head with concern. "Are ye in pain? Is it the wee ones?"

"No, none of that." Rachel snuffled, then burst into another hiccupping tirade of tears. "I'm sick with misery and frustration because no one will listen to the danger that my husband and my sons are in, and there's nothing I can do about it because of this stupid century where women are expected to do nothing but b-b-breed and accept whatever fate hands them while walking around spouting sunshine and shitting rainbows!" She turned away from Caelan, covered her face with a pillow, and howled anew.

"Lore a'mighty," Caelan whispered, then shook his head. He looked at Florie and prayed the woman could help.

"I see." Florie narrowed her eyes at him, then grabbed hold of his sleeve and urged him to his feet.

"What did ye say to her?" she hissed as she herded him into the large solar just off the bedchamber. The morning sun streamed in through the tall, narrow windows but it failed to knock the chill from the air.

Caelan shrugged, feeling much like a lad falsely accused of stealing bannocks from the larder. "All I did was tell her everything was going to be all right. I assured her we would all be fine and grow old together and raise our bairns."

"So ye talked to her like she was a daft idiot, did ye? Have ye no more sense than that fool Emrys?" Florie shoved him toward the hearth and pointed at the wood piled beside it. "Feed the coals, man. Ye dinna wish her to grow chilled, do ye?".

"Woman, ye forget your place. I am the laird here." But he hurried to do as she said and soon had a good fire crackling. "What are ye thinking?" he demanded with a glance back over his shoulder.

"I'm thinking if the laird had a brain in his head, he'd be doing whatever it took to keep his wife happy since she's more miserable with each passing day. Have ye thought of telling Emrys to let Lady Rachel work in his library or help him translate his books? She might find that a comfort rather than all the other things she's been unable to do." Florie gave him a sad shake of her head. "Poor lamb. Ye should have seen her face when she burned the bread, knotted the weaving, and scalded the tallow while trying to make the candles." She jabbed a finger at him. "She needs help to find her place so she will feel like she belongs."

Caelan rubbed his chin, mulling over the suggestion. Could Florie be right? If Rachel had something to do that she enjoyed, then maybe that would ease her into her new home and help her settle until the babes arrived. Then she'd have three very important things keeping her days filled.

"Emrys will not like it," he said as he continued scrubbing at the stubble along his jaw.

"Are ye not the laird?" Florie tapped her foot impatiently on the floor.

"Some people appear to have trouble remembering that," Caelan replied.

"YE SHOULD HAVE SEEN HER, FERGUS," Florie said, her voice soft as silk in the darkness. "It nearly tore my heart in two, finding her there, weeping all alone in the garden. The poor lamb needs kindness right now, the company of women, and yet none draw near to her." She blew out a heavy sigh. "'Tis unlike the women of this clan to be so cold and cruel."

Fergus kissed the top of her head and tightened his arm around her, pulling her closer. "I have seen Lady Rachel off to herself entirely too often. The clan holds her at arm's length, I fear. Her keeping such close company with Emrys does not help her cause. She's playing right into the hands of all the rumor-mongers intent on stirring suspiciousness and fear at every corner."

"She healed one of the stable lads yesterday," Florie said, propping her head in her hand and frowning down at him. Even in the dimly lit room, he read the concern in his lover's eyes. She poked him in the chest. "The herbs she gave that wee bratling stopped the pain in his bowels, and the ungrateful idiot nay even had the courtesy to thank the lady for her troubles!" She poked Fergus again. "Can ye believe that wee fool was convinced she'd stolen his soul since he no longer felt any pain?"

He smoothed her tousled gray curls away from her face, smiling as he rubbed his thumb across her lower lip. "Florie, ye ken as well as I about the superstitious lot we have among us. Look how the laird, and his father before him, sheltered Emrys all these years—for the old one's protection."

He pulled her head down to his and nuzzled kisses to the tender skin behind her ear. "Leave off worrying about the laird's wife, love. Ye've wakened me fully, and now I'll never sleep until ye sate me once again."

"Ever since my time of breeding ended, ye've been insatiable, my fine lover." She pressed her ample curves even tighter against him and smiled as she lowered her mouth to his. "Whoever said an older man could not keep the cold at bay all night long, never met a man such as yourself."

CHAPTER 17

"When I was headed up to the laird's solar to build his morning fire, I overheard the MacKay praising Lady Rachel for working spells with old Emrys." Maery, the youngest and prettiest maid in the keep, leaned closer to Ian as she whispered this latest tidbit of gossip.

"I canna believe the MacKay allows his lovely wife to do such a thing," Ian said. "The woman is heavy with his sons." He tried to pull Maery deeper into the pantry to steal a few kisses before they both continued their chores.

"Are ye calling me a liar, then?" She slapped away his roaming hands, then shook a finger in his face. "I heard it with me own ears, I tell ye! I also overheard Mistress Florie telling the MacKay about his wife and all her failings. The woman canna do anything. Heaven knows I've righted her messes several times now. Why—she canna even do the simplest needlepoint!"

With his hands around the maid's shapely waist, Ian pulled her tighter against him. "Ye should nay be so sharp tongued about the lady. She is not from this place and was not taught such things. It's nay her fault she canna learn everything all at once when it takes many an entire upbringing to master one of those tasks."

Maery jutted her chin higher and held his kisses at bay. "Fine. But how do ye explain Lady Rachel working spells? Some even say she stole young Angus's soul to cure his belly pain."

Ian blew out an irritated snort and set her back from him. "All I ken for certain is that Lady Rachel seems verra kind, and ye would do well not to let Florie or Fergus hear ye wagging your tongue with such tales against her. It could be dangerous for the lady, and ye verra well know it."

Maery stuck out her bottom lip in an irresistible pout, leaned in closer, and slid her hands slowly up Ian's chest. "It's just that I worry for ye, Ian. I ken how much the laird depends on ye, and I'd hate for ye to fare ill in case the lady is a witch." She ground the softness of her curves against his hardness, something she had never done before. "I heard tell she told the birds to shite on Roderic in the garden. 'Tis unnatural, it is. Ye ken that Roderic thinks well of ye too. Watch yourself, aye?"

Ian groaned and cupped both her breasts. "Dinna fear, Maery," he whispered as he lowered his mouth to hers. "I'll keep a watchful eye. Now treat me to the sweetness of your charms."

"So, these are the infamous mirrors. Why three?" Rachel knew the answer, but Emrys had dodged earlier questions and given patronizing answers. Time to distract him and act as though she didn't have a clue about anything. She assumed the role of a *silly woman*, standing in front of the Mirrors of Time with her head cocked to one side as if she was mimicking one of her dogs.

The dark surfaces of the looking glasses swirled and stared back at her. She sensed them sizing her up and did her best not to smile. Whether it was because she was pregnant, had traveled back in time, or fully embraced her magick, her abilities became stronger by the day. She embraced it and intended to use the gift to its fullest to protect Caelan and her sons. *Silly woman.* She'd make that old druid think *silly woman*. With her eyes opened wider to seem as innocent as possible, she repeated herself, "Why three?"

"About that question, lass—search your mind, aye?" Emrys said in a lofty tone that threatened to make her lose her temper. "Even a novice should ken that answer well enough." He wrinkled his nose and settled deeper into his chair.

Rachel meandered back and forth in front of the mirrors to distract him. It was obvious he was irritated about letting her enter his domain. Probably resented having to babysit the emotionally explosive, hormone ridden, pregnant wife of his laird. Granted, she did have trouble controlling her bitchiness, but who wouldn't in this situation? The love of her life and her sons were in danger—and on top of her being ripped from every convenience she had ever known, she was cursed with swollen ankles, an aching back, and the never ending need to pee. And there were no chocolate sandwich cookies or peanut butter!

Emrys looked up from the manuscript in front of him, his gaze following her as she moved back and forth in front of the mirrors. "We found ye in the future. That is the only hint I'll be telling ye."

Before she caught herself, she rolled her eyes. Game over. Time to warn the man he was about to die. "I realize you don't want me here. I get this is your *kingdom*. But if you continue talking to me like I'm some half-witted child and treating me as though you wish you'd never laid eyes on me, then consider yourself warned that I will declare war—and I will win it." She moved closer, narrowing her eyes. "I won't run crying to Caelan nor will I tell Florie, but I promise you, you will regret the day you were born." She cast a casual glance back at the mirrors. "If you'd like to research a little into my ancestry, you'll find a bit of my DNA is a tad evil. Some witches in my family were burnt at the stake and for good reason—they deserved it. Although my Wiccan beliefs are *harm none*, I'm willing to make an exception if it comes to not only my survival here in medieval Scotland but also that of Caelan and my sons. Understand?"

They both stared at each other for what seemed like several full minutes, neither blinking, both barely breathing. Finally, Emrys slowly closed the ancient book on the table. "I am well aware of your line. Their powers were unmatched."

With the aid of his staff, he pushed himself up from his chair. "'Tis a shame there was no one to train or guide ye after ye lost your grandmother." He wearily rubbed his eyes, then pinched the bridge of his nose. "I am none too certain it be a good idea for ye to hone your powers. It could cause ye to end up on one of those burning stakes yourself."

"And you think I haven't thought of that?" She returned to wandering around the room, eyeing the dusty covered crocks and stoppered containers lining the shelves. While a small part of him might be trying to protect her, she was also well aware that he made it a habit of running a con whenever it stood to benefit him. He always got the choicest meat pies, finest pastries, and the first ales pulled from the kegs because of the useless herbs he had convinced the serving maids would grant them eternal youth.

She cleared her throat and gave him a knowing smile. "I appreciate your concern for my wellbeing, but since we've been here, my paranoia has increased tenfold. In fact, that's the main reason I'm in your *sanctuary* right now. The more I can learn, the more empowered I become. So the best way you can keep yourself safe is to teach me."

When realization flashed in the old man's eyes, she picked up the ancient tome from his table and started leafing through it. "Now, what are we studying today?"

"Why do ye keep moving about so?" Caelan whispered to Rachel as she shifted and rearranged the pillows in her chair yet again. The woman had been in motion for the entire hour she'd sat at his side. "Ye said ye wished to be here."

She shot him a narrow-eyed look of disgust and rocked from side to side with her hands propped on the shelf of her stomach. "You wear three, six-pound cannon balls around your waist, and we'll talk about sitting still." She elbowed him in the ribs as she added, "And each of those cannon balls has two arms and two legs that are in constant motion." She wiggled again, grimacing as she arched her back. "And why didn't you tell that man that he should treat his wife better?"

Caelan forced a smile at those gathered in the great hall as he grabbed her hand and tucked it affectionately into the crook of his arm. "Because his wife should treat her husband with more respect and not spend so much time wandering to the adjoining field to visit her neighbor's husband."

The rumbling of distant thunder filled the room, making him tense with worry, since it was an unseasonably cloudless day. "Rachel," he warned through clenched teeth. As she neared the time of the bairns' arrival, the more unpredictable she had become with nature's forces. She'd admitted to always having an affinity with the natural energies, and apparently, the ebb and flow of her emotions were meshed even more tightly with the world around her here in the past.

She cleared her throat, pursed her lips, and pulled in a slow, deep breath. "Sorry," she whispered. "It's okay now. I've got a handle on it —oh, shit!"

She squeezed his hand as a flash of lightning nearly blinded all in the room and was immediately followed by a clap of thunder so loud that it nearly shook the stone walls of the keep.

"What has angered ye so?" He followed her line of sight to the end of the hall and found the object of her inner storm. Roderic stood just inside the archway, sneering as he returned Caelan's glare.

"I wish to remind the laird that he has yet to return to the northern borders of his lands as was promised nigh on a year ago," Roderic bellowed as he strode forward. Each of his steps added a punch to the words as he spoke. "Many of the villages suffer neglect. The people are abused by those who know the laird only pays attention to his lovely violet-eyed wife."

The winds outside increased to a loud, moaning howl that sent the maids and serving lads scurrying to shutter every opening against the storm.

Those gathered to seek justice from the laird milled around the hall uncomfortably, casting worried glances up at the narrow windows cut high in the walls. The sky had gone black with Rachel's fury, then splintered with blinding white flashes of lightning whenever Roderic tried to speak again.

Emrys rushed from the stairwell behind the dais and moved to Rachel's side. "Ye must reign in your emotions, lass. I ken the man has threatened those ye love. But he's baiting ye. Dinna give in to him."

Caelan stood, pulling Rachel to her feet along with him. Perhaps it was time to battle his bastard brother to protect his wife and sons. "I will not return to the northern border until my sons are arrived safe, and I see them and my wife well settled and protected here in our home. Ye threatened them, ye bastard, and I will not leave her defenseless against the cowards who side with ye." Thunder rumbled softer across the silence of the room. "I shall have Fergus investigate your claims." Caelan glared at his father's illegitimate spawn. "Although I feel certain he will only find that it is yourself abusing our people." He hugged Rachel closer and couldn't help but smile as one of his wee sons thumped against him.

"Your wife can tend to herself, my laird." Roderic tipped his chin upward with a glance at the darkened windows. "If she's nay conjuring up a storm to match her mood, then she's covering her enemies with bird shite."

A collective gasp echoed through the vastness of the hall as all gathered there shifted to fix wide-eyed stares on Caelan.

"How dare ye insult our lady!" Emrys lifted his staff high in the air, his eyes flashing an unholy blue. "Ye always were slow, Roderic. The day the ravens shat upon ye was I not in the garden with Lady Rachel?"

Roderic narrowed his eyes at the druid with his staff glowing as though it were about to shoot lightning at any moment. "Aye," he growled. "Ye were there."

"And am I not here with my staff aimed at the heavens as we speak?'

"Ye were not in the hall when the storm first broke, old man. We all ken that well enough." Roderic shifted in place as he appeared to realize the hum of whispers around him had turned in Emrys's favor.

"Emrys was in the room behind the dais where he always stays during great hall," Caelan bellowed, daring his half-brother to challenge him. "My father always made ye welcome, since his blood runs in your veins. But because of your actions against my beloved wife, because of your threats to her and my unborn sons, ye are no longer welcome on MacKay land. When ye act like a lying bastard, I have no choice but to treat ye like one. Ye are hereby banished—and take the cowards who side with ye with ye."

The muscles of Roderic's jaw twitched, then he bared his teeth with a low, throaty grown. Eyes dark with hatred, he slowly flexed the fingers of his hand closest to his sword. "Hear me, brother," he said, sounding ready to spit, "when next I darken this hall again, it will be to lay claim to it as the next chieftain of Clan MacKay."

He drew his sword and backed toward the entrance of the hall just as Florie walked through the archway. With a quick sidestep, he grabbed her up against his chest and held the blade across her throat.

"Only a coward hides behind a woman," Caelan roared, fury pounding through him. "Release her!" He charged down from the dais. The steel of his blade rang out with justice as it sang its way free of the sheath.

"Maybe cowardly," Roderic sneered as he backed farther out of the hall, dragging Florie with him. "But I am a live coward at that."

"I have had enough!" Rachel thundered over the storm, her voice echoing with a terrifying power that seemed to come from the heavens.

"Rachel! Think what ye're doing, lass." Emrys reached for her arm, but energy crackled all around her, shoving him back a step.

"Release Florie and go in peace," she warned. "Do her harm and die." She seemed to float as she moved across the floor toward Roderic.

"Ye speak bravely with your husband there and his steel drawn," Roderic barked with a cruel laugh. "Thank ye for the offer, m'lady. But I shall keep this lovely shield until I am safe away." He continued backing his way out of the room, adjusting his hold on Florie as he moved.

Rachel eyed him, tilting her head to one side as she propped her arms atop her stomach. "Step away from him, Florie. He can't hurt you."

Florie's eyes went wide with disbelief as she clenched Roderic's sword arm with both hands. "I beg your forgiveness, m'lady. But I dinna find comfort in your advice while the bastard has his blade still at my throat."

Roderic sputtered with laughter as he bumped against the archway leading out into the bailey. "So, ye are as daft as they say. The violet-eyed wife of the laird—bonnie as can be but nothing in her head. No wonder the man's taken with ye."

Rachel lifted one dark eyebrow and smiled.

"Lore a'mighty," Caelan said to Emrys. "What is she about to do?"

"Brace yourself, my laird," Emrys warned. "Soon there may not be a stone of this keep left standing."

"Sons a bitches!" Roderic threw down his sword, shoved Florie away, then bent, cradling his blistered hand between his knees. The haft of his sword glowed as white hot as though it had just been pulled from the forge. "Witch!" he hissed, glaring at her with hatred and fear.

"Know this Roderic," she said in the same powerful voice of earlier. "I protect my own. Do not force my hand further. Be gone from here, as Caelan said. Go in peace and live well." She turned her back to him and started back to the dais.

The entire clan watched her, backing away as if fearing she would turn on them next.

She tensed, her chin tilting up as though intently listening. She turned just in time to melt Roderic's dagger in midair right before it would've slid between her shoulder blades. As the dagger melted, Caelan heaved his sword across the room. It sank deep into Roderic's chest, nearly cleaving the man in two.

Rachel bowed her head, appearing disappointed and troubled

rather than victorious. She lifted a hand to her forehead and slowly shook her head.

"Better to die by the hand of a man, than lose my soul to a witch," Roderic barely sputtered through bloodied lips before his eyes glazed over in death's stare.

Caelan stood taller and glared around the room. His clan had sorely disappointed him this day, the narrowminded lot of them. "The stench of your cowardice makes me ill," he growled. "My stomach turns at the fear I see reflected in the eyes of the best warriors this clan has ever known. I am ashamed of ye. The MacKays have always had druid advisors to their lairds. And those druids have wisely seen to the betterment and wellbeing of this clan and its future. Why now, when ye see your laird has wed a fine wise woman from across the seas, a powerful druidess in her own right, a caring woman willing to protect us, why do ye shrink from her as though she carries the plague?"

"Why did ye not tell us, Caelan?" Fergus MacKay stepped out of the shadows with his arm tight around Florie.

Caelan narrowed his eyes at the man. Of all people. His faithful war chief. Even Fergus had turned on him. "Ye kent well enough that I traveled forward in time to win her and claim her as my own. Emrys made ye all aware when he returned to secure the last items needed before we all returned together." He moved to Rachel's side and pulled her close, trying to ignore the subtle trembling he felt running through her as he addressed his clan.

Fergus threw out his chest and walked to the center of the room, gently pulling Florie along beside him. "Aye, we understood your bride would come with ye from another place in time. But ye never told us she was to be as that one there." His dark eyes narrowed at Emrys, then he returned his focus to Caelan.

"My woman says the lady is a truly lovely soul but canna make herself be at ease here unless she uses her powers," a husky voice shouted from beside the hearth, speaking in haste lest Caelan home in on their identity.

"They hate me," Rachel whispered her hands holding her belly tight as tears streamed down her face.

Her suffering tore Caelan's heart from his chest and made his blood boil. "Never would I have believed my clan could be so heartless and cruel," he forced through clenched teeth. "How could ye be so cold and unwelcoming to one who so badly needed help to feel at home here? I promised her ye would welcome her and make her never regret coming here to bear my sons. Ye have shamed me and shamed our bloodline. I can no longer stomach the sight of ye!"

He strode forward, ripped his massive sword out of Roderic's chest, and started swinging it in a mighty circle, clearing a path through the hall as his kin dove to miss the lethal blade. "Be gone from this keep," he bellowed. "Be gone from this hall and a curse upon ye if ever I lay eyes upon ye again. Ye have shamed me before my wife and my unborn sons. Your dishonor will be told to them as soon as they are lifted from their mother's womb. I shall rear them up to spit upon your memory and dance upon your graves."

"Caelan stop!" Rachel shouted while standing in the middle of the hall with her arms extended and her hands held palms up. "I should be the one to leave. We both know I never wanted to come here. They're right. I don't belong here. I thought loving you and loving our babies would be enough, but it's not, and it never will be. Where I am going, you and Emrys cannot follow. I'll return for the birth of our sons so you can meet them, and then I'll leave with them again. When they are old enough, I'll send them back to you, and our break will be complete. They're more yours than mine, anyway. They're going to be the greatest of warriors. All three of them. I have seen it."

She stood there, her tears streaming. Her chin dropped to her chest, and she slowly spun, counter clockwise with her arms extended and her hands palms up.

"Rachel, don't!" Caelan dropped his sword and rushed to grab hold of her, only to be thrown across the room by a powerful energy surrounding the love of his life. "Emrys! Stop her! I command ye!"

"I canna interfere here, my laird," the old druid said, his voice hollow and filled with reverence. "She travels to a plane I am forbidden to even peer into." He bowed his head, turned away from her, and covered his eyes.

Caelan fell to his knees and crawled to her with a hand raised. "Dinna leave me, my precious one. Ye are my heart, my soul, my life's breath. I beg ye, Rachel, please."

"I love you, Caelan," she said, her voice breaking, "but this is the best for you and your clan."

A blinding white light shafted down from the heavens, exploded into a protective orb, and surrounded her in a myriad of glittering points of light. When all went dark again, and she was gone.

Caelan stared at the space where only seconds ago his beloved one had stood. He crawled to the spot and flattened his hands on the stone still warm from the strange energy. She was gone. Her and the wee ones. Gone just as quickly from his life as the blink of an eye.

He threw back his head and roared with an unbearable pain unlike any he had ever known before.

CHAPTER 18

"He'll not eat," Ian said. "All he wants is enough ale to blind him and numb his pain. I'll not go back in there again. Last time I carried a tray of meat in there, he nearly took me head off with it." Ian plopped down on a stool beside the long worktable in the center of the kitchen while Florie prepared yet another tray for their heartbroken laird.

She rounded on the youth, waving her knife as though ready to slit his throat. "Ye will do as I tell ye, and I'll hear no more out of your mouth, or I'll have Fergus take a strap to your arse! Dark times have fallen upon this keep what with our lady leaving and our laird in mortal pain." She turned back to her task, arranging a fine display of meats that she knew were Caelan's favorites.

Still shaking her head, she clucked like a nesting hen. "Poor man's drawn and haggard since his lady left. Locks himself in old Emrys's library." She arched a brow and waved her knife again. "Emrys told me he spends all his days searching through the mirrors for her."

"Many say he's lost his mind," Ian said while bowing his head. "He mourns for her and the babes." He crossed himself. "I am ashamed of us, and the pain we caused him with our untrusting ways."

"She could have cursed us for the way we treated her," Florie continued while adding a basket of bannocks to the tray. "But instead, she accepted our unfair judgment of her and left for the good of the laird and the clan. I am ashamed of us as well. She should have turned us all into toads and tossed us into the fires of Hell."

Ian filled a pair of pitchers with ale. "All remember now how it wasn't her who killed Roderic. Lady Rachel merely heated his hand enough to make him drop that blade from your throat. Our laird killed that bastard and rightly so after Roderic attempted to kill his lady. Would any of us have done any less had it been our wives being attacked?"

Fergus hung his head in shame. "I should never have spoken as I did that terrible day." He reached over and covered Florie's hand with his. "Did ye see the pain and humiliation in our lady's eyes, her weeping as she watched us all turn against her? I am ashamed as well."

"Well, one of ye take this to your laird and shame yourselves no more." She slid the tray toward them, then sniffed and wiped her eyes. "I'll follow ye with the pitchers of ale. With any luck, he'll at least keep the tray in the room with him if we bring it all to him together."

Winding their way up the cold dark steps of the tower, Florie, Ian, and Fergus shivered as a cold unholy wind seemed to swirl around them. Ever since Lady Rachel had left, MacKay land had been cast into a dank and gloomy darkness. The castle seemed like a dead body whose spirit had left, and now all that remained was an empty shell. No matter how many torches were lit or how many fires were stoked, the bone-cracking chill refused to leave.

When they reached the uppermost room in the north tower, Florie shook her head at Emrys sitting outside the door to his own library. The old man's chin rested on his chest and his hands were folded in his lap. The yellow dog from Lady Rachel's time lay on the floor at his side, her noble head resting on his feet. Neither of them moved as Florie, Fergus, and Ian approached, so exhausted were they in their vigil.

"Emrys are ye hungry?" Florie asked softly so as not to startle the old druid.

"No. I want nothing." He didn't even lift his head, just dropped his hand to Maizy's and fondled the loyal dog's ears. "And I would leave him be if I were you. His madness deepens."

"I told her to leave him alone, but she'd not listen," Ian said.

Fergus cuffed the lad on the back of his head. "Shut it!"

"She promised to return when the time came for the bairns to be born," Florie said. "She promised to send his sons back to him when they were older. Has he forgotten that? He must stay strong for the bairns." Florie cast a worried look at the bolted door, prepared for Caelan to storm through it at any moment.

Emrys made a face and slowly shook his head. "He must have them all. A MacKay canna live without the other half of his soul as long as she is alive. His heart knows she is somewhere out of his reach, and he canna bear it. It's in his ancestry. A weakness or a strength depending upon your point of view."

"Where has she gone to, Emrys?" Florie whispered while leaning closer to the bolted door, hoping for movement on the other side as proof the laird still lived and breathed.

The old druid pushed himself to his feet, his bones popping in protest. He rubbed his back and grimaced in pain as he shifted from side to side. "It is my belief she has gone to the blessed Brid for protection. Where else would the mystical mother of triplets hide? That is the only place I am forbidden to look with the Mirrors of Time, and no druid will ever have any power there." He stretched more and rolled his shoulders. "Lady Rachel chose wisely. I only hope that while she is there, the Goddess will impart some wisdom to our lady, so she truly will find her way back to us when it is time for her sons to be born rather than change her mind and stay away."

Emrys continued rubbing his back as he squinted out the tiny slit of a window cut in the turret of the castle hall. "I pray the Goddess will not allow Rachel to bear her children anywhere but here, and Caelan will need to be present. I only hope that Caelan is still sane enough by then and can convince Rachel to stay. Perhaps the Goddess will help her in that decision as well."

"Emrys," Ian whispered as a bolt slid to the side and the heavy oak door creaked open.

Florie gasped and covered her mouth.

Caelan's eyes were red-rimmed and bloodshot. His dull, grimy hair hung in matted braids. A scraggly beard covered his face but failed to hide his sunken cheeks or the dark hollows under his eyes. "I can hear all ye say," he growled in a raspy voice. "The madness has not made me deaf—yet. But I canna sleep without her. I canna eat without her. I canna exist without her!"

He grabbed the tray of food and hurled it down the winding stairwell. Chest heaving, eyes wild with anguish, he grabbed both jugs of ale from Florie, retreated into the room, and slammed the door behind him.

Ian nodded at all of them. "I told ye he'd not eat a thing."

CAELAN LOWERED himself onto the plaid spread in front of the trio of mirrors and pulled Rachel's little dog into his arms. "I canna believe she left us, Sam," he said in a voice hoarse from bellowing at the powers to return his beloved to him. "She said she loved us."

Sam licked him on the nose, then snuggled back down closer against his chest. The little dog didn't seem to care that he hadn't bathed in days. All the devoted canine understood was that his mistress was gone, and his master was racked with pain.

Caelan stared into the looking glass farthest to the right. Deep in his gut, he sensed if his precious Rachel were to contact him, it would be that mirror in which she would appear. He still couldn't believe she'd disappeared before his very eyes. His glorious wife, full, round, and lovely with his sons in her belly, gone from existence in the breath of a moment. All because his clan would not accept the magick within her. As far as he was concerned, they could all be damned straight into the hottest pits of hell.

His hands closed into fists as he tortured himself with the great hall scene over and over. His dear, sweet lass had been an outcast all her life. Her parents hadn't wanted her. Her ex-husband hadn't wanted her. She'd never belonged anywhere. He and Emrys had seen that while learning more about her.

A sob tore from his chest, and he let the tears flow unashamedly. He had sworn to her she would be welcome in ancient Scotland. Sworn things would be better with his clan. They would be the family she had never known, and they would welcome her with open arms. How could they not? His clan was used to the mystical and unusual because of Emrys.

But he had unknowingly deceived her. How could he have been so wrong about his own people? He had to admit that even he had been shocked at the growing ferocity of her powers, but he knew in his heart Rachel would never bring evil into their midst. And she had proven it by leaving rather than razing the keep to rubble.

"She would never have hurt them, Sam. She would have helped them in ways they never imagined." Caelan rubbed the dog's head as he talked, thankful for the wee companion.

A dull thud at the door jarred his mind back to the present. He pulled his aching head up from the floor and shouted, "Be gone! Leave enough food for the dog and be done with it!"

"For the sake of the bairns ye must pull yourself out of this!" Florie scolded from the other side of the door. "Your lady said she would return to bear them. She said she'd send your sons back to be trained as fine young warriors. Said she had seen it so. How are they to find a father fit to train them if he canna even stand upon his feet or sit upon the laird's dais in the great hall when they return to their home?"

"Get back to the kitchen, Florie! I trusted ye most of all!" Caelan rolled to his feet and staggered to the door, his hands trembling from exhaustion. Shoving the door open, he jabbed an accusing finger at her where she stood, clutching the tray in front of her as though it were a shield.

"I trusted ye to befriend my lady and help her belong," he

accused. "I trusted ye to ease her into life here. Of all here at the keep, Florie, ye have always welcomed everyone and made them comfortable. I knew ye would make my precious Rachel feel as though she belonged. Why would ye not do that for your laird? Why do ye hate me so?"

Caelan fell to his knees, his frustration and sleepless nights taking their toll. He shook his head and stared blindly at the floor while whispering, "Why did she leave me, Florie?"

"I think the lady thought she was doing what was best for ye and the clan." Florie rested her hand on his bowed head. "Ye must fight to stay strong now. For the bairns, ye ken? Remember your sons!" She tugged on his arm, trying to get him to stand.

She went still as Caelan leveled a stony gaze on her and sneered in disgust. "If my clan refuses to accept a witch as my wife, what makes ye think they will accept my three sons who will each be capable of magick as well? Since their mother was so gifted, do ye not understand they will be at least half as strong as she was?"

Caelan knocked away her hand. "If I canna have my entire family, then I shall have none." He retreated deeper into the room, picked up Sam, and gently sat the little dog outside the doorway. He closed and bolted the door, shutting himself inside.

Emrys appeared beside Florie and shook his head. "And so, it begins."

Florie stared at him in confusion. "What do ye mean? *And so, it begins*?"

"Caelan's full descent into madness." Emrys started down the stairwell, Maizy and Sam slowly padding along behind him. "Until Rachel returns to bear the children and chooses to either stay with him or return to the Goddess, he will no longer be sane. I saw it once before with his great grandsire. The entire clan nearly died from it. Hopefully, we will survive it this time as well."

RACHEL MINDLESSLY SLID the silky leaf between her fingertips as she stared across the undulating sea of waving grasses. There were no seasons here. It was never too hot, never too cold, and whether it rained or shined depended on the mood of the Goddess herself.

Today, the sky was the brightest azure blue, with white clouds skimming across the tips of the grasses. As Rachel sat on the stone bench stroking her stomach, she could feel her sons tumbling and rolling and wondered how much longer her womb could contain them.

"Soon, it will be time for ye to return and make your choice, Rachel."

A sense of calm swept through Rachel's entire being, her intuitive signal that she was being graced with a visit from the Goddess Brid herself. She dropped her gaze to her feet or at least to where she thought her feet still were, bowing her head as she folded her hands atop her rounded belly. "I know. I just haven't figured out how I'm going to bring my babies into the world, raise them for a little while, and then send them back into that chaos. And how will I face Caelan again after being gone? I'm not sure he understood why I left."

"All Caelan understands is his pain and his loss. I have watched him closely since ye came to me, and he does not fare well." Brid gently smoothed Rachel's hair away from her face, her cool soothing touch pausing on Rachel's cheek. "The MacKay line holds a special place in my heart, for theirs is a line capable of great passion and love. They are also capable of reincarnating through many lifetimes. There are those who would say they are some of the few mortals whose love could last an eternity—whatever an eternity might be." The Goddess pulled her fiery red tresses over one shoulder as she spoke. She worried with the end of her braid as her deep green eyes gazed off into the distance.

"I never wanted him to suffer," Rachel whispered, her heart breaking at the thought of his misery. "I only wanted what was best for him. For his clan. They were afraid of me. I'll never fit in there." A sense of uneasiness took hold of her and made her shift on the bench.

"Ye may continue to take sanctuary here once your bairns are safely delivered on one condition," the Goddess said. "Ye must be honest with Caelan, and ye must be honest with yourself." Brid allowed her hands to flutter through the flowing gossamer of her gown that swirled around her glorious form. As she meandered about the small clearing, it was as though a pulsating life force emanated from her. The vines and flowers responded, bursting with color and fresh growth.

"I left because—" Rachel started to say.

"Think well and deep before ye finish that sentence, my child," Brid advised, her tone firm but gentle. It was as though time stood still.

Rachel caught her bottom lip between her teeth as the Goddess interrupted the excuse she'd repeated to herself over and over until she'd convinced herself that she'd done the honorable thing and not taken the coward's way out. "I didn't fit in back there," she quietly admitted, the emotions crashing across her like a tidal wave. "And I'm still afraid Caelan will die young and leave me all alone. Medieval Scotland terrifies me. I just want to go back to Kentucky. I miss home. Miss what I'm used to." Rachel dropped her face into her hands and sobbed. "I'm such a freaking coward. I'm so ashamed."

"Shh...now. Dinna cry, my child. Truth is always better. Dry your tears, now. They'll make the bairns get colic." Brid rested one hand on Rachel's head and gently waved at the sky with the other. At this signal from its mistress, the sun went down, the full moon rose, and a soothing evening breeze teased through the leaves in the trees.

"Ye canna return to Kentucky. That part of your life is past." Taking both of Rachel's hands in hers, Brid gently pulled Rachel to her feet. "Walk with me, child. Breathe deeply. Ye must join your heart, mind, and soul in this decision." Brid gently guided Rachel through the clearing, her voice as calming as the evening breeze. "Ye canna return to Kentucky. To do so would upset the balance of time and space because Caelan is of the past, and you are of the future, and your precious wee bairns were created when the two of you bonded in the dream plane—the verra first time ye loved."

Brid's reddish eyebrows drew together over her fiercely green eyes as she gazed up into the brilliant white light of the full moon. "Ye have never fit in or been wanted in all of your life, and yet now, ye have the chance to be loved more than ye have ever been loved in this existence, and ye shy away from it out of fear that once ye embrace it and accept it fully, it will only be ripped away from ye."

The Goddess suddenly gripped Rachel by her shoulders and stood staring down at her, her regal nose mere inches from Rachel's. "Ye are no longer a child, Rachel. Your parents are dead and can no longer torment ye by giving ye your fondest desires, then yanking them away again just to see ye cry and tell ye that ye lost them because ye were not worthy. Ye were treated cruelly. But that is over now. Which would ye rather, lass? One wondrous moment in your life? Or an eternity of safe nothings? Ye must learn to embrace life. When this life is done, ye will be given another. Your soul is immortal and capable of wondrous things."

Her thumb smoothed a tear from Rachel's cheek. Brid frowned; her eyebrows still knotted. "I have said too much. Please forgive me, child."

Suddenly, they stood in a bright, airy room with gauze linens blowing in the moonlit breeze. An inviting bed waited between the many rows of tall windows overlooking the shimmering waters of the silvery lake below. "Rest now, child. Sleep the unburdened sleep of one who finally knows her heart and her fears. When ye awaken ye will find the answer ye seek."

After kissing Rachel lightly on the forehead, the Goddess led her to the bed and helped her ease her unbalanced self into the overstuffed mattress and pillows.

"I realize my fears, Goddess," Rachel whispered, finding herself becoming eerily calm, "but I still don't understand what I need to do. Or if I have the courage. What if—?" Rachel clenched the sheets to her chest, biting her lower lip as her eyes overflowed with more tears.

"Hush now. Not another word." With a light touch to Rachel's forehead, Brid silenced the fretting and gently trailed her lavender scented fingertips down Rachel's face. "Sleep now. Not to dream, but to rest—for ye know your heart, ye know your fears, ye know your past, and ye have shed your tears. When ye awake, ye will make your choice. If I have my way, we will all rejoice."

When the Goddess removed her hands, she smiled at Rachel's even breathing and bent to tuck the sheets closer around her. "Let your mother rest, lads. Three mortal weeks she will sleep, and then ye shall see your father as well. Now be still with ye."

As soon as Brid admonished them, the restless babes in Rachel's womb ceased their incessant wrestling and poking for a better position. Their motions smoothed to what seemed to be a more agreeable, cooperative effort instead of the constant fighting for position.

"Better but ye could give her a bit of rest. The three of ye are going to be history makers. I nay had the heart to tell the lass about that while she's having such a time deciding to return to your father."

Moving away from the bed, Brid idly glanced around the room, darkening it to a soothing, low, blue light with a subtle tip of her head. As she closed the door, she motioned to a passing moon sprite.

"Elera, please see that Rachel's sleep is undisturbed. When she awakens it will be time for the babes to come into the world."

Nodding her silvery head, Elera smiled as the hallway filled with moonbeams. "I shall see to it gladly, my goddess."

CHAPTER 19

Another blast of frigid air howled through the great hall, making the roaring fires in every hearth as useless as sparks on the edges of damp tinder. Members of the clan clustered on the benches beside the long tables gathered their fur mantles and plaids closer around their shoulders while shaking their heads in dismay.

"The keep is cursed," Fergus muttered as he wrapped his chapped hands around a steaming tankard of mulled wine. "When Lady Rachel left us, she not only took away the laird's heart but drained all hope from the Highlands as well." He slowly shook his head. "The MacKay nay deserves this, but we do. We deserve every feckin' bit of suffering that's come to pass."

"Mayhap when she returns and gives the laird his bairns, she'll remove the curse and give life back to the land." Ian heaved more wood on the fire, dodging the popping coals as the damp chunks crackled in the roaring blaze.

"The only way our lady will remove the curse and bring life back to the keep is if she stays." Florie placed a platter of bannocks on the table and knotted her shawl tighter around her shoulders. "'Tis the laird's misery bringing the cold and darkness to this hall. That and the winter solstice being upon us. Ye ken as well as I how brutal it is until the sun returns. When the Lady Rachel blesses us with her presence and brings forth her bairns, we must do our best to convince her to stay. Only then will warmth and light return to MacKay lands."

"Florie is right." Fergus rose from the bench, shrugged his shaggy black mantle higher upon his shoulders, and moved to stand in front of the fire. "Tell the gossips, the servants, and every man, woman, and child of this clan. We must spread the word. Our lady must be made to feel welcome. We failed her, and we failed our laird. Whether from fear or ignorance, it nay matters. We canna fail again."

A dull scraping from the stairwell to the right of the dais drew their attention. Several gasped, but a hush fell upon them as Caelan shuffled into the room. He ignored them and concentrated on putting one foot in front of the other. Any strength and caring he had ever possessed for this clan had left him along with his Rachel.

Weeks of little food had caused his weight to fall away, leaving him bent as an old man. But what did it matter? He nay needed food. He needed his beloved wife. His eyes felt sunken in his face, his reflection in the polished shields reminding him of the old crone living on the edge of the forest at their northern border. His once thick hair had turned thin and lifeless. But again, what did it matter?

He clutched at the ratty plaid around his shoulders, his hand trembling as he cast a disinterested gaze at the shocked faces staring back at him. With a ragged breath, he waved their concerned looks away. They could all burn in Hell as far as he was concerned. And he would join them in those pits. Suffering and torment were with him every waking hour, anyway. At least, if he descended into Hell, it would be a mite warmer. With a shiver, he croaked out an order, "More wood, Ian. Can ye not get the chill from this room?"

"Aye, my laird. I shall fetch more wood and get the chill from this room. I swear it." Ian rushed from the hall.

"Hold fast, my laird. Fergus will put your chair by the fire, and I'll fetch more furs to warm ye." Florie snapped her fingers at Fergus as she ran to the cabinets behind the head table and fetched an armload of furs. As she passed by her man, she whispered, "The MacKay curse of loving one's true soul is killing him. Our laird is dying of a broken heart."

Fergus nodded, hefted the chair off the dais, and placed it as close to the fire as he could safely set it. Going to Caelan's side, he gently took hold of his arm. "Come, old friend. Let us get ye settled."

"Ye spoke against her," Caelan accused, his rage gone. In its place was a cold deadness that never left him. He wondered if, when Rachel left, she had somehow taken his heart and soul with her. He shuffled along, too weak to fight off Fergus's help and make it to the chair on his own. "Ye spoke against her in the hall," he repeated, determined for Fergus to remember the wrongs he had done against them. "I trusted ye, and ye spoke against her."

"Aye, my laird," Fergus quietly admitted. He helped Caelan sit, then knelt in front of him, and bowed his head. "And I am sorrier than ye will ever know. Never should I have spoken against the Lady Rachel. I beg your forgiveness and will take whatever punishment ye deem fitting. I deserve it. My life is yours to do with as ye wish but know that I regret my actions. I was sorely wrong."

"Live with your choices," Caelan rasped. If he had more energy, he would avenge his beloved wife and punish Fergus—punish all of them. But it was too late. He was dead inside. She would never return. No matter what she had promised. And he didn't fault her for it. After all, look how they had treated her. He dropped his face into his hands, needing to sob but unable to because all his tears had been wept. He was as guilty as the clan for making her go. If only he had listened to her fears, listened to her worries, and acted rather than placating her with meaningless words and doing nothing to make things better.

Florie draped a fur around his shoulders and tucked another around his legs. "I've a fine venison stew today. Would ye try a bit of it? Ye've had nothing since yesterday."

"If I must." He stared down at his hands, idly fiddling with his wedding band. It barely stayed on his thin fingers now. Soon, it would slip away and be lost. Like his precious Rachel.

Florie returned with a steaming tankard and wrapped his hands around it as if he were a child learning to use a cup. "It's mainly the broth, my laird, but if ye finish it, I'll bring more with chunks of meat and carrot. Take a couple of sips for me, then I'll leave ye with your thoughts, aye?"

Caelan knew if he didn't take at least a taste of it, Florie would never leave him the hell alone. In order to be rid of her, he forced down a swallow of the rich broth, then shoved the tankard back at her.

"Well done, my laird," she praised like a proud mother. "I'm going to set this right here and fetch ye a crust of bread. When I come back, I want to see that ye've drained it all so's I can fetch ye more, ye ken? Dinna disappoint me, now." She set the mug on the table and wiped at her eyes as she stood beside him, staring down at him, the crust of bread forgotten.

A low humming vibrated through the room. Caelan squinted against it and glanced around, searching for the source of the annoying sound. A shimmering blue light, the tiniest orb of intense energy, burst into the center of the aisle between the rows of tables and steadily brightened.

He grabbed Florie's wrist and sat bolt upright, knocking the furs from his shoulders. "Florie—is it her? Is she truly returning as she said she would?"

"I dinna ken, my laird," Florie whispered. She clutched his arm and helped him to his feet.

As the energy filled the room, it brought a warmth as comforting and welcome as a summer sun. At the center of the circle of light, a form appeared, foggy at first, then it sharpened and focused. It was a very pregnant woman. When the mystical gleam faded, Rachel stood there, slightly bent, one hand holding her swollen belly, and the other pressed against her lower back.

Her dark eyebrows rose almost to her hairline. Concern and shock filled her eyes. "Caelan! Are you dying?" She took a step toward him only to stop, groan deeply, then pant. She grimaced and held her belly with both hands for a long moment, then straightened, pulled in a deep breath, and blew it out. "I need to lie down while you tell me what's wrong with you. Our babies are coming. I need you, Caelan. Tell me you're going to be all right and distract me while I'm in labor."

He stared at her, unable to speak, barely able to breathe.

She grimaced and started her strained huffing all over again. A sheen of sweat broke out across her brow as the pain in her bowels nearly bent her double.

"Rachel...my...my Rachel." He shook himself free of the trance and went to her, almost afraid to touch her, afraid she would disappear again. But he drew on his courage and need to strengthen him as he wrapped an arm around her. Tears streamed down his face, and he didn't care. She was back. She had returned as she had said she would. "Light every torch! Prepare our room. My beloved has returned, and our bairns are coming." Renewed energy pounded through him. The will to live and love gave him the ability to stand at her side.

He kissed her hair, kissed her cheek, and held her close as he helped her move up the stairs. Inwardly, he damned himself for being such a fool and allowing himself to grow so weak. He longed to sweep her up into his arms and carry her to the bedroom, but he knew he didn't have the strength for it. How he wished he'd listened to Florie and Emrys. "Fetch the midwives," he bellowed back over his shoulder. "And whisky! The solar may need extra whisky while I wait for my sons."

"No whisky. You're staying with me and helping me get these babies out."

"With ye?" he repeated. Surely, she had not said what he thought he heard. "The midwives will help ye. They'll not allow me to stay."

"These are our babies, and I want you with me," she growled

while slowly climbing the steps. "If the midwives have a problem with it, I'll be happy to convince them otherwise." She halted their ascent and clenched both his hands, closing her eyes and clamping her mouth shut as another pain hit her. Her nostrils flared with her heavy breathing, and her nails dug into his flesh. "How long has it been since you've bathed?" she groaned. Before he could answer, she wilted against him, nearly knocking them both off balance and sending them back down the steps.

"By Amergin's beard, Caelan!" Emrys shouted as he hurried up behind them. "Dinna let the lass fall! Now ye see why ye should have listened to Florie and meself. Now ye see that old Emrys was nay the fool ye thought." He angled closer, his arms spread wide as though to catch them should they fall. "Come here, lass. Let an old druid show ye a spell ye'll want to learn as soon as ye're able to rise from your birthing bed."

He tapped his ancient, twisted staff on the step, then waved it over their heads in a counterclockwise circle. On the third rotation of the gnarled rod, they stood beside the enormous bed in the laird's chambers.

"Bless him and every druid before him who had anything to do with his training," Rachel breathed as Caelan helped her ease down onto the bed.

As he straightened, she caught hold of his hand. "Now, why do you look like you're ready for the grave? What have you done to yourself? What was Emrys talking about?" She pulled him closer and placed her hands on his cheeks, her thumbs smoothing away the streaks of his tears.

Caelan covered her hands with his. "When ye left, I had no reason to live. I canna believe ye thought I would just move on as though nothing happened." He leaned closer, his clenched jaw aching with his anger. "Damn it, woman! Do ye think I would travel across the planes of time to find the one soul I could truly love, just to forget her, as soon as she tossed me aside? As soon as she decided my love was nay worth the effort? Was nay worth fighting for? That I'd just say, *ah..well, then. Better luck next time*? Is that not what those of your time say?"

Dizziness took hold of him, making him grab the bedpost to keep from tumbling to the floor.

"I never said that, and you know that is not why I left!" Rachel rubbed the sides of her stomach and shoved herself higher among the pillows.

"All I know is that ye left me!" he growled as he sagged down onto the bed beside her. "Ye left me lost and alone." He bit back another growl as he reached out and touched her face. "If ye leave again, run me through with my sword first. I beg ye. Find the kindness to spare me such misery again." He cupped her cheek, then slid his fingers into her hair. "I am nothing without ye, my love. I need ye more than I need the breath in my chest."

Not bothering to knock, Florie charged in with a steaming kettle in one hand and an armload of linens. "The midwives are coming, as are the maids to help with the welcoming of the bairns."

Emrys turned and started toward the door.

"No! Don't you dare leave, Emrys." With her hand knotted in Caelan's léine, Rachel pushed herself even higher in the bed and leaned forward as Florie added to the mountain of pillows behind her. "The only people I want present at the birth of my sons are in this room right now, and Emrys that includes you. Caelan, you're staying whether you want to or not. Florie, I'll need your help." She doubled over and groaned while rocking and huffing.

"Take my hand, lass," Caelan said. "Hold tight. Give me your pain." He sat on the bed beside her, wishing he could endure the agony in her stead.

"Emrys," she said, breathless as Caelan wiped the sweat from her face, "the boys are going to need your help and guidance. I was graced with a vision of what my three young warriors are going to be capable of. They are not only going to be warriors but also quite talented in the mystical arts and at a very young age. Prepare yourself, Emrys. Schooling them is going to keep you and me both busy."

The old druid stared at her, his face filled with shock and indignation. "I canna be present at a birth!"

"The Goddess has ordained it." She stared right back at him, baring her teeth as she panted. "Dare you defy her?" She drew her knees to her chest and closed her eyes. After panting hard and groaning for what, to Caelan, seemed like forever, she sagged back into the pillows and appeared to be struggling to gather her strength.

"Now," she said as she turned her head and fixed Caelan with an angry glare. "There were many reasons I left you, but you know that none of them were because I didn't love you or didn't think your love was worthy." She wet her trembling lips as her eyes filled with tears, then they overflowed and trickled down her cheeks. "Please forgive me for hurting you, for causing you so much pain. I'm the one who has never been worthy of you, and I'm just waiting for you to wake up out of your fantasy and figure it out. Then I know you'll be the one to leave me."

Caelan buried his face in the warm, sweet crook of her neck and held her. "Promise me ye will stay," he said in a rasping whisper. "I beg ye say the words."

"I'll do you one better to ease your mind." She squinted at Emrys and bit her lip while bending double. "Emrys," she groaned as she reached out. "Bring me the ebony crystal from around your neck. Please?"

Touching the jagged black crystal hanging from the leather cord around his neck, Emrys approached the bed slowly, his whiskers twitching upward with a faint smile. He lifted the necklace off over his head and placed it in her hand.

"Give me your hand," she told Caelan, while baring her teeth and groaning again.

Unsure of what she was about to do but praying it was what he thought it was, he held out his left hand, smiling as his wedding band glimmered in the torchlight.

Rachel took the pointed crystal, slashed across the palm of her left hand, then cut Caelan's left hand as well. Grabbing his hand and pressing their wounds together, she locked eyes with him. "As we blend our blood, we bind our souls, never to part, no matter how old. This binding spell cannot be undone, so let it be spoken, so let it be done."

A searing burn started in his left hand, ran up his arm, and surged through his body as though he'd been consumed by a raging inferno, as though he were being doused in flame. He looked to Emrys, narrowing his eyes at the old man's smug look. "Speak, old man. I ken ye are about to burst in the wanting to tell me of your great wisdom."

"Your lovely wife has melded herself to ye with a magick that canna be broken. 'Tis even stronger than your marriage binding. She can no longer leave this plane of existence. She has made her choice, my laird. Ye have a wife forever now. Through all eternity. Most definitely for better or for worse." He stroked his beard, his clear blue eyes sparkling with amusement.

"Why did ye not speak this spell when we exchanged our wedding bands?" Caelan softly asked her.

She closed her eyes and turned her head away from him, once more panting and gasping. Speaking through her pain, she groaned out the words. "I'm sorry. I just couldn't." She curled over her belly and growled louder, panting so hard that Caelan felt himself getting out of breath. "I knew once I said those words, the only thing that could ever separate us was death, and even that will only keep us apart until we find our way back to each other again in the next incarnation." She fell back into the pillows again, her eyes still closed as she struggled to catch her breath. "I wasn't sure I deserved to even hope for your love. I was afraid of so many things."

She reared up, nearly ripping the bedsheets in her fists. "It's time. Florie, get the men over to the window and help me get these babies out." Rachel released Caelan's hand and growled like a cornered beast, her face red with her efforts.

"Nay, lass. I'm here with ye now and here I shall stay." He held her hand with renewed strength, climbing up to kneel beside her and wrap an arm around her shoulders to support her.

"Help me, Caelan! Help me push Faolan out. I swear his head

must be the size of a basketball!" She screamed as she bore down, her face reddening even more.

"Faolan? The wolf? Ye've already named our first son, have ye?" Pride coursed through him at the fine name. He held her upright. "Push, love. I want to meet Faolan."

As the babe's head crowned, she spared him a weary smile. "Faolan. The wolf. For he will be the leader of this small pack and his fierce courage will be known throughout the land once he becomes a man." With one last, long groan, wee Faolan slid into Florie's towel wrapped hands.

Rachel fell back against Caelan's chest, breathing hard with her eyes shut. He wiped her face with the damp cloth Emrys handed him, then gently kissed her forehead as Florie placed wriggling, squalling Faolan on her chest.

"Quickly greet your brave little wolf, for the other two will knock at the doorway soon," Florie advised with a nod.

Rachel lifted her head, smiling as she traced a finger along his velvety cheek. He rootled and squawked in search of her breast. "Not just yet, my son. Your brothers have to come into the world first."

"Come here, my fine lad." Caelan scooped up the babe, held him close, and hummed a nameless tune while rocking the little one against his chest. "I love you, Rachel," he said, almost unable to speak through the tide of emotions.

She wrinkled her face in a grimace of pain. "And I love you. Get ready to meet Ronan." She knotted her hands in the sheets again and drew her knees to her chest.

From the window, where he stood mumbling spells, Emrys called out, "Ronan? The seal? Are ye cursing the lad to a life at sea?"

"It is his destiny," she growled while still breathing hard. "He'll be more at home on the sea than on the land." She groaned loud and long, then pushed. Ronan came out smoothly as though he were as slick as a seal, landing in Florie's waiting towel.

"Be at peace though, Caelan," Rachel said with a squeeze of his hand as he peered down at his second son. "Ronan will have dominion over the sea, and all the creatures in it. That is his gift from the Goddess."

Caelan cast a shocked look at Emrys, then stared back at the tiny babe sucking his fist in Florie's arms. "Dominion over the sea," he repeated in a reverent whisper before returning his attention to Rachel. Panic filled him at the sight of her sagged back into the pillows, exhausted but smiling.

Florie held up his third son. "This wee bairn will bear watching. Crafty, he is! Came right out before giving us time to notice him."

Rachel shoved her damp hair back from her face and smiled at the babe. "Caelan, I'd like to introduce you to Latharn, the fox. This son will by far be the one who will keep us all on our toes because he will be sly and cunning, yet from what I have been able to see, he will also be honest and true."

Caelan took the wee one into his arms, cocking his head to one side while studying the innocent's face. He narrowed his eyes and looked closer, recognizing Latharn's enormous eyes that stared up into his own. "Aye, the fox is a fine name for this wee lad." He turned to Emrys and held out his son while nodding at the old druid. "Look at the cut of his mouth. The line of his nose. Even the way the lad already narrows his eyes as if he's sizing up the room. Who does that remind ye of?"

Chuckling in instant recognition, Emrys held out his arms to take Latharn. "Aye, he is your grandsire made over. Perhaps the old fox has returned to us through his great-grandson."

"Oh, give me the lad, and let me take him to his mother," Florie said. "She'll need to stave their hunger for a wee bit until the wet nurse gets here." She returned Latharn to Rachel's arms where he immediately latched on to her breast.

"Give me Faolan as well," Rachel said. "He was starving before his brothers arrived." She reached for him with her free arm, smiling wearily as Florie settled the firstborn son against her.

"Poor Ronan," Caelan said. "Come here, lad. Dinna fash yourself. Your mother will take ye soon." Caelan held the wriggling bundle close, bouncing as he walked, and gently patted Ronan's wee rump.

After the babe calmed, he settled on the bed beside Rachel and gently rested his chin on her shoulder.

"I canna begin to thank ye for all ye have given me," he hoarsely whispered, his heart about to burst from pure joy.

"Trust me, it doesn't compare with all you've given me." She smiled up at him, her eyes overflowing with happy tears.

EPILOGUE

A loud laugh of pure contentment and joy rumbled free of Caelan and echoed off the surrounding cliffs as he helped Rachel and Florie attempt to keep the rowdy trio of inquisitive babies confined to the heavy plaid spread across the sand.

"Have ye ever seen such fine, lively lads?" Bending to catch Faolan as he rolled off the blanket, Caelan rotated the determined little crawler and headed him back toward his brothers who were making for the other border of the spread facing the sea.

"Ronan will be in the water if ye dinna latch onto him," Emrys said while keeping a finger in his worn leather tome to hold his place. "I told ye the bairns were too young to be this close to the sea!"

Florie blew her hair out of her face as she fished a shell out of Latharn's mouth and threw it far out into the water.

"Watch him." Rachel nodded at Ronan as the wee one glanced back at the group of adults and then furiously started scooting toward the tempting sound of the waves.

"I'll get him." Caelan plopped Latharn down in Emrys' lap, knocking the book from the startled old man's hands.

"No. Let him go down to the water. He needs to be closer. Just watch him." Rachel smiled, her dark hair blowing in the wind as she balanced Faolan on one hip and slowly meandered behind the determined Ronan who crawled with his head down as though ready to plow through anything that might get in his way.

"I canna bear this. The laddie will drown." Florie buried her face in Fergus's chest as Ronan drew closer to the water's edge.

"Rachel will not let her son drown. We agreed to trust her, aye?" Fergus patted Florie, his words belying the look of unease on his face.

Caelan went to Rachel's side, cast a nervous glance at her serene expression, and then turned back to his single-minded son. "Rachel —my love—the water is verra deep here."

"Watch." Rachel smiled and handed Faolan over to Caelan, then squatted down at the sea's edge beside Ronan.

Finally, having reached his goal, the babe sat staring out across the shimmering waves. After a glance at his mother, he extended a pudgy little hand toward the sea, then squealed as though beckoning to the deep.

A sea lion immediately surfaced not too far from shore, as though in answer to the little one's call. Swimming in towards the babe, the creature warily eyed the adults as it made its way closer to the beach.

With a glance at the water beastie and then his mother, Ronan gave Rachel a toothless grin and chortled with delight. Clapping his little hands, he held them out in expectation of the water creature, bouncing in excitement as the seal drew closer.

"Are ye seeing this, Emrys?" Caelan whispered to the druid standing at his side as Ronan reached out and stroked the silkie's nose.

"I am old," Emrys retorted. "Not blind. And did Rachel not tell us Ronan would be so?" The old druid repositioned Latharn to a more comfortable position against his shoulder, warily studying the baby's deep green eyes. "And what tricks have ye to show us, wee fox?"

With a proud grin, Latharn opened one chubby fist to reveal that once again, he had the shell Florie had taken away and thrown into the sea. The brackish water dripped down his tiny arm as he waved it in the air.

Emrys shook his head as he meandered up the beach toward Florie and Fergus, where they sat among the rocks.

"And you, Faolan?" Caelan asked his son in his arms. "Are ye ready to show us a bit of your gifts or are ye going to surprise us some other time?" He chucked the solemn baby under the chin while tipping his head to one side.

Faolan's dark purple eyes stared deeply into his father's gaze. The babe kicked and squirmed to be set down on the ground. He'd never shown the need or desire to be coddled and held, and as he grew older and more agile, his need for independence seemed to grow. He crawled back toward the cliffs, away from the sea, and didn't once glance at any of the adults. Finally reaching the spot he deemed worthy, he spun around from all fours and sat with a slight thump on his round behind.

With a determined scowl at Ronan sitting so perfectly contented nearly within reach of the crashing waves, Faolan extended his wee hand toward his sibling and emitted a low rumbling growl from deep within his tiny chest.

Within the blink of an eye, Ronan was sitting beside Faolan, safely away from the frothing sea. Looking around to discover he'd lost his preferred spot beside the water, and that his friendly sea lion had disappeared back into the deep, Ronan scrunched up his face, turned beat red, and howled in indignation.

Faolan chose that moment to turn toward Latharn and once more held out his chubby little hand. Immediately, Latharn's prized seashell held so dearly in his fist disappeared into thin air only to reappear at Faolan's feet. Faolan frowned down at the shell and squealed as though in anger at the offending object that kept finding its way into Latharn's mouth. As he squealed, the shell disintegrated into a pile of sparkling dust.

Upon seeing his shell so neatly destroyed, Latharn's howls of rage joined Ronan's as he glared across the beach at his brother.

Staring at his sons in open-mouthed disbelief, Caelan pulled Rachel closer. "What have we brought into this world, my love?" he whispered, the words catching in his throat.

With a knowing smile, Rachel patted Caelan's arm. "Wait until you see what their sister will be able to do."

READ ON FOR AN EXCITING
EXCERPT FROM:

Beyond a Highland Whisper
A MacKay Clan Legend
Latharn's Story
Book 2

CHAPTER 1

MacKay Keep
Scotland
1410

"Latharn, are ye sure ye never touched the lass?" His father's scowl burned across the room mere seconds ahead of the words.

The reproach in Laird Caelan MacKay's voice stung Latharn like a physical blow. Tension knotted his muscles and his body stiffened with the bitterness pounding through his veins. Only years of respect for his father held his tongue. How could his sire treat him this way? He wasn't an irresponsible boy anymore. How dare he be treated like a lust-crazed lad!

The great hall of the MacKay Keep spanned the largest part of the castle and housed every important gathering of the clan. Flexing his shoulders, Latharn inhaled a deep breath. From where he stood, the room shrank by the moment. He couldn't believe his father had chosen the monthly clan meeting as a means for resolving this matter. How dare he try to shame Latharn into a confession by confronting him in front of his kinsmen. This ploy had worked well enough when Latharn was a lad. His father had used it often whenever he or his brothers had gotten into mischief. Latharn involuntarily flexed his buttocks in remembrance of punishment received after a confession ousted in just such a manner. However, he wasn't a mischievous boy anymore. This was private; they could handle it between themselves.

Every man, woman, and child strained to hear Latharn's reply. His father's closest warriors leaned forward upon the benches. The servants peeped around the corners of the arches, their serving platters clenched to their chests. Latharn rubbed the back of his neck; his skin tingled from their piercing stares.

His father's face flushed a decided shade of purple. Apparently, he'd delayed his answer long enough. Clipping his words just short of blatant disrespect, Latharn growled through a tight-lipped scowl. "How many times must I swear to ye, Father? I have never laid eyes on the MacKinnett lass. I canna bring her face to mind and I havena planted a child in her womb!"

The hall remained silent. Even the dogs sprawling beneath the tables ceased in their endless scuffling for scraps. The only sound breaking the tense silence was the pop of the wood just thrown upon the fires.

With his hands curled into shaking fists, The MacKay pounded the arm of his chair centered at the head of the great hall. Laird MacKay raised his voice to a throaty growl as he edged forward in his chair. "The MacKinnett clan has always been allied with ours. Their lands join our southernmost borders. Must I tell ye how serious these allegations are to our families? The treaty between our clans has been solid for years. God's beard, son! If ye've dishonored their family, there will be no more peace. This lass is the only daughter of their laird!"

His knuckles whitened on the arms of his chair as he continued his tirade. Laird MacKay tensed on the edge of his seat as though he was about to spring upon his prey. His hair heavily streaked with gray, Laird MacKay's once-golden mane gave him the appearance of a battle-weary lion. Though his body showed subtle signs of an aging

Highlander, his eyes still blazed as his roar echoed throughout the great hall.

"Always, ye've been one to skirt danger, Latharn! I will admit…'twas usually for the greater good. However, you yourself must also agree, there have been times when ye have yanked the tail of the sleeping dragon just to see if it would breathe fire. So far, your quick wit has kept ye safe from whatever troubles ye have stirred. But this time, I must know the absolute truth: did ye lie with The MacKinnett's daughter?"

How many times was he going to ask him? Did he think he was going to change his answer? Anger surged through Latharn's veins. Rage flashed through him like a cruel, biting wind. He crossed his arms as a barrier across his chest and curled his mouth into a challenging sneer. They didn't believe him. No matter what he said, they didn't believe his words. He read it in their eyes. He spat his words as though their bitter taste soured on his tongue. "I swear to ye upon all I hold sacred, I don't even know the lass's name!"

A brooding man the size of a mountain stood at Laird MacKay's side. Stepping forward, he thrust an accusing finger toward Latharn's chest as though aiming a lance for the killing throw. "Since when did not knowing a lass's name keep ye from tumbling her in your bed?" Latharn's brother, Faolan, stalked forward upon the dais, shaking his head at his brother's latest scandal. Faolan was the eldest of the MacKay sons, next in line to be laird. The look on his face plainly told Latharn he deemed his brother guilty on all charges as stated.

Latharn snarled. "Stay out of this, Faolan. Ye may have beat the rest of us out of Mother's womb, but ye're no' the laird, yet." Latharn met his brother's glare, squaring his shoulders as he stalked forward to answer Faolan's challenge.

How dare Faolan pass judgment against him? Latharn didn't deny he'd enjoyed many a maid since he'd grown to be a man. However, that didn't mean he'd ever treated them unkindly or shown them any disrespect. He'd sated them fully and when their time was done, he'd taken care to spare their feelings as best he could. Never once had

Latharn been inclined to give of his heart...nor had he pretended to do so just to lure a pretty maiden to his bed.

"The lady's name is Leanna and you will speak of her with respect." The clear voice rang out through the archway of the hall, causing everyone's heads to turn. Latharn's mother, Rachel, emerged from an offset alcove, her eyes flashing in irritation toward her youngest son. "Her clan says she has named you as the father of her child. If she carries your child, Latharn, you will do right by her."

Latharn winced as thunder rumbled in the distance. Whenever his mother's emotions were in an upheaval, the weather's stability always suffered. Rachel's powers directly connected with the ebb and flow of the forces of nature. Her emotions meshed with the energies coursing through the physical realm. Thunder, while Mother was clearly upset, was never a promising sign.

Latharn's heart sank as he heard the ring of doubt echo in his mother's voice. She had always been his greatest champion. Whenever the rest of the family rushed to deem him guilty when trouble was in their midst, Rachel always kept an open mind until she'd heard his side of the story. If his mother already believed him guilty this time, how would he convince the rest of them he didn't even know this lass existed?

Latharn had emerged as the youngest of the MacKay triplets. His name was Gaelic for "the fox" and it had served him well. Little did his parents know how aptly the title would fit when they had chosen it for the innocent babe. Whenever mischief occurred, the wily young Latharn had always been the first to be accused. But that same charm and cunning that was the source of all the mayhem also bailed him out of any trouble he'd caused. That is until now, until this latest uproar that had the entire family in such a stir.

Casting a furtive glance at his mother, Latharn wondered why he was to blame for the women always chasing him. It wasn't as if he went a-whoring all over the country for just anyone to warm his bed. Since he had reached manhood, there didn't seem to be a lass in the Highlands who could resist him. He didn't know why they always sought him out. He didn't do anything special. He was just nice to them...and they followed him to his bed. In fact, sometimes they didn't follow him. Sometimes, he'd find them waiting for him when he arrived in his chambers. Latharn shifted in place and adjusted his kilt. A lass probably lurked in his private hallways this very minute. It had become somewhat of a problem escaping them.

Latharn had grown restless. Now that he was older, he'd grown weary of their freely given charms. A quick tumble with a lass was once an incomparable elation. Now the euphoria had dimmed. The satisfaction had dulled to basic physical release. Even while lying spent in erotic exhaustion with a sated lass cooing by his side, Latharn knew there had to be more.

Of late, he'd found a night spent in a luscious maiden's arms left his heart troubled, as though a question nagged at the tip of his tongue, and the answer danced just beyond his reach. No matter her beauty, no matter her sweetness, they all left him empty and cold. Loneliness settled over him like a weight crushing on his chest.

There had to be more than the mere physical pleasure of losing himself in a woman's embrace. He knew there was more to be found. The security of his parents' love for each other had strengthened their family as far back as he could remember. He sought that glow of contentment he'd seen in his parents' eyes when their gazes met across a room. No matter how many years had passed between them, the look they shared never changed. He ached for the connection his parents had found. He longed to lose himself in another's eyes and speak volumes without saying a word. It was time he cradled his newborn child in his arms, with his loving wife nestled at his side.

Latharn stifled a shudder; the tension gnawed at his gut. The expressions on their faces told him so much more than words. They'd never believe the things he'd done to avoid the women vying for his embrace. His emptiness ached like a festering wound that refused to heal. He had decided to search for the elusive answer by honing his mystical powers. He'd hoped by refining and perfecting his magical gifts, he might solve the mystery of his untouchable heart.

Of late, he'd been so engrossed in sharpening his goddess-given powers, he'd not even walked with a woman in the gardens for several months. He'd been holed up in the northern tower of the keep. There was no way he fathered the MacKinnett woman's child. By Amergin's beard, it had to have been at least five full moons since he'd been outside the castle skirting walls!

The air of the keep closed in around him; the sweltering heat of too many bodies shoved in one room added to his discomfort. Latharn raked his hands through his hair and tore himself from his tortured musings. His mother glared at him, her foot tapping. Perhaps it was the fire that flashed in her eyes bringing the heat to his skin.

"I know of no Leanna MacKinnett!" he ground out through clenched teeth. Latharn braced himself for his family's damning replies. His gut was already wrenched with the unspoken accusations springing from their eyes.

Raking his own hands through his graying hair, Laird MacKay expelled a heavy sigh. Fixing his gaze on his son with a disappointed glower, he dropped his hands to the arms of his chair. "Their *banabuidhseach* will arrive at any moment. Their clan will not be satisfied with your denials until their seer has had a chance to speak with ye and weigh the truth of your words."

Latharn turned to his mother. There was one more thing he had to say in his defense. He didn't care if the rest of the MacKay clan didn't believe him. His mother would believe his innocence.

"Mother! As many abandoned bairns as I've rescued while on my travels, as many waifs as I've brought home to this clan, do ye honestly think I would be able to deny a child of my own blood, a child I had sired? Do ye truly think I would turn my back on a bairn of my very own?"

Latharn towered over his mother, peering down into her eyes and opening his soul to her senses. She had to believe him. He trusted his mother's intuition to see the truth in his heart. His voice fell to a defeated whisper as he groaned and repeated his earlier words.

"I swear to ye, Mother. I am not the father of the woman's child. I know of no Leanna MacKinnett!"

Rachel's hand fluttered to her throat, and she slowly nodded. "I believe you, Latharn. Moreover, I will do what I can to shield you from their *bana-buidhseach*. I hear this woman's powers are amazing, perhaps even stronger than mine. But I'll do whatever I can to protect you from any evil that may be traveling upon the mists."

With a heaviness in his chest and a catch in his voice, Latharn embraced his mother and whispered, "Your belief in me is all I've ever needed, Mother. Ye know I would never bring dishonor to our family or shame upon our clan."

He brushed his lips across his mother's cheek just as chaos erupted at the archway of the hall.

Her shrill cry echoed through the keep as the MacKinnett *bana-buidhseach* screeched like an enraged crow. "I demand retribution for Clan MacKinnett. That heartless cur has sullied Leanna MacKinnett's good name!"

The bent old woman rocked to and fro at the entrance to the hall, brandishing her gnarled walking stick overhead like a weapon.

Her white hair hung in tangled shocks across her stooped shoulders. Her black eyes glittered in her shriveled face, like a rat's beady eyes from a darkened corner. Her somber robes swept the rush-covered floor with every dragging step. Even the brawniest Highlander in the crowd faded back as she hitched her way to the front of the cavernous room.

Drawing a deep breath, Latharn's muscles tensed as the old crone edged her way toward him. Tangible power emanated from her swirling aura as he studied her twisted form. This seer's energies rivaled those of his time-traveling mother. The battering rush of the crone's malicious emotional onslaught threatened to slam him against the farthest wall.

His mother's powers had been refined through several generations to her in the twenty-first century. However, her aura had never emitted such waves of energy, not even after magnification through the portals of time.

Immense anger emanated from deep within this old woman, reaching out toward Latharn like a deadly claw. The crone's soul overflowed with touchable hatred.

Latharn braced himself as a rising sense of dread curled its icy fingers around his spine. He shuddered, swallowing hard against bitter bile as he noticed something else. The *bana-buidhseach's* aura seethed with an underlying layer of evil his mother could never possess. The witch's pulsating energy roiled with a menacing thread of darkness he'd never seen the likes of before.

Cocking her head to one side, a malicious glint shone in her eyes. Her mouth curled into a grimace as she croaked, "What say ye, MacKay cur? Do ye deny robbing my laird's daughter of her precious maidenhead? Do ye deny ruining her for any other man?"

With a single stamp of her crooked staff upon the floor, enraged lightning responded outside, the flash splintering throughout the room. Everyone in the hall cowered against the walls, shielding their faces from the narrow windows high overhead. The acrid tang of sulfur hung heavy in the air from the burn of the splitting energy.

Theatrics to get her point across. This did not bode well. His hands tensing into clenched fists, Latharn took a deep breath before he spoke. "I fear there has been a grave misunderstanding. I have not been outside the walls of Castle MacKay in the passing of the last five moons."

"Exactly!" she spat, jabbing her bony finger from deep within her ragged sleeve. The *bana-buidhseach* hitched sideways closer to Latharn and shook a threatening fist in his face. "Ye appeared to the lass while she lay in her bed. Your vile essence washed over her silken body by the light of the swollen moon. As your spirit swirled upon the mist of the bittersweet night, ye violated her ripe nest and filled her with your seed."

Eyes flashing with a mother's protective rage, Rachel shoved her way between Latharn and the snarling hag. Resting her hand on Latharn's chest, Rachel stood nose to nose with the crone. "Surely, you don't believe in such an outlandish tale? The girl could not possibly find herself pregnant in the way you just described."

The crone hitched her way even closer to Rachel, her dark eyes narrowed into calculating slits. Hissing her reply, her foul breath nearly colored the air around her as she spat through rotted teeth with every word. "Do ye call me a liar, Lady MacKay? Do ye slur the name of Leanna MacKinnett and the honored MacKinnett clan?"

The hall crackled with the conflicting forces of emotional energy as lightning once again splintered the electrified air. Thunder roared, shaking the walls until debris rained down from the rafters.

Rachel circled the wizened old hag. "I've nothing to say about Leanna MacKinnett or the good name of the MacKinnett clan. I defend my son's honor against your lies. I challenge your slander against an honorable MacKay son!"

With a wave of her hand and a narrowed eye, the hag halted Rachel where she stood. The spell she cast silenced Rachel's voice and paralyzed her body. Sliding around Rachel, she stabbed a gnarled finger into the middle of Latharn's chest. A demonic smile curled across her face as she sidled her body closer. With a flourish of one hand, she withdrew a ball of swirling glass from the folds of her tattered robe. Her cackling voice rose to a maniacal shriek as she lifted the ball for all to see. "Do ye deny lying with every maiden whose head ye happened to turn? Do ye deny withholding your heart from every woman in which ye've ever planted your cock?"

Latharn's voice fell to a low, guttural whisper as dread gripped him in his gut. "Who are ye, woman? What is it ye seek from me?" An icy premonition, fear of what was to come, stole the very breath from his lungs. Latharn knew in the very depths of his soul there had never been a Leanna MacKinnett. This wasn't judgment for ruining some woman or the name of her clan. The stench of something much more sinister hung in the air. It rankled with every breath he took.

With a crazed laugh, the shriveled old woman transformed before his eyes. Her dry, tangled hair lengthened into flowing black tresses. Her sallow, wrinkled skin smoothed into creamy silk. Her bent frame straightened, blossoming into a shapely woman, breasts full, hips round and firm.

Her eyes remained black as the darkest obsidian, and her full red lips curled into a seductive, malicious smile. Her voice became a throaty, honey-laced melody, deadly in its hypnotic tone. "Do ye remember me now, my beautiful Highlander? We were together once, you and I. We were lovers, but now I come here as your judge and jailer. And I have found ye guilty of withholding your heart from the only one who truly deserves your love."

"Deardha?" Latharn recoiled from the seductress bearing down upon him.

As she thrust the deep violet globe into his face, Deardha's voice echoed across the hall. "Aye, Latharn. Ye remember me now? Listen closely to my words. I condemn ye to this eternal prison. I banish ye to this crystal hell. Ye are far too powerful a charmer of magic to be toying with women's hearts. No longer will I allow ye to sow your seed with any poor fool who warms your bed. If ye willna pledge your heart to me, then ye shall wish ye were dead." As Deardha uttered the spell, blinding white energy swirled from the tips of her long pale fingers. The shimmering tendrils flowed and curled, constricting around Latharn's body.

With an enraged scream, Rachel broke free of Deardha's binding spell. Forcing her way between Latharn and the witch, she clawed at Deardha's face.

"Mother, no!" Latharn roared, fighting against the tightening bands of the curse meshed about his body. "Ye must get away from her. Save yourself!" He couldn't breathe. His heartbeat slowed and the room darkened around him. This must be what it felt like to die. Latharn struggled to focus his eyes.

The conflicting forces threw Rachel across the room as Deardha's field of malevolence blasted against the walls. The winds howled and roared as the demonic chaos ripped through the castle. Then all fell silent just as swiftly as the storm had risen and a fog of sorrow settled over the room. Latharn shuddered awake to an icy smoothness pressed against his spine. Finding his arms freed, he flexed his hands, wincing as he rolled his bruised and battered shoulders. Where was he? He lifted his head, staring about in disbelief at the see-through globe enclosed around his body.

Everyone eased their way out from where they'd taken cover: they crawled out from under tables, from behind overturned benches.

Eyes wide with fear, they glanced about the room to see if the attack was over.

Latharn spread his hands on the curved, cold glass. What were they doing? Why did they mill around him like he wasn't there? It was as though he sat among their feet on the floor. What the hell were they doing?

The serving lads rushed to re-light the torches lining the walls. The scattered clansmen and villagers rose from the floor, checking each other for injuries. Tables and benches lay about the room like scattered rushes strewn across the floor. Tapestries and tartans hung in tattered strips, nothing left on the standards but bits of colored shreds.

Laird MacKay shoved his way through the wreckage to his wife. Rachel lay in a crumpled heap beside the hearth, her weakened breath barely moving her chest.

"Mother!" Latharn shouted against the glass. If she was dead, it would be no one's fault but his own. Standing, Latharn stretched to see if Rachel would move.

Laird MacKay cradled her against his chest, pressing his lips to her forehead until she opened her eyes.

Rachel struggled to lift her head, her eyes widening with disbelief as she looked across the room directly toward Latharn. Lifting her hand, her voice cracked with pain as she keened her sorrow to all who remained in the great hall. "My baby!" she sobbed. Waving her trembling hand toward her son, she buried her face in Caelan's chest.

Latharn closed his eyes against the sight of his mother rocking herself against her pain. As her wails grew louder, he covered his ears and roared to drown out the sound.

CHAPTER 2

Washington University
St. Louis, MO
2010

"Professor Buchanan, do I get extra credit for fixing you up with him? You know, the fine piece of man we met? That guy we met at last month's conference?"

Nessa Buchanan peered over the top of her laptop, scowling from behind the pair of reading glasses perched on the end of her nose. "If you were one of my students, Ms. Sullivan, you would've just failed the semester for hooking me up with that so-called fine piece of man."

"Oh, come on, Nessa. He couldn't have been that bad." Trish sank her teeth into the apple she'd been juggling as she sauntered around Nessa's office.

After she tossed her glasses onto the desk, Nessa steepled her fingers beneath her chin.

"Trish, do you remember his lecture on the existence of different realities and their definitions as determined by any one individual's perceptions?"

"Vaguely." Trish nodded as she munched another bite of the apple and thumbed through the exams on Nessa's desk.

"Well, it appears that his perception of all night long is my reality of maybe—and I'm really stressing the maybe part—of about, oh, maybe ten minutes."

Nessa stretched across the desk and slammed her hand down on top of the pile of exams. "And after the questionable ten minutes of all night long, he started snoring!" Snoring didn't begin to describe it. He'd practically rattled the windows out of her apartment.

With a grimace, Trish shuddered and tossed her half-eaten apple into the trash. Wiping her hands on the tight seat of her jeans, Trish shrugged. "Come on, Nessa. Was he really all that bad? He seemed kind of nice at the conference."

"He farts in his sleep." Not looking up, Nessa shoved folders of exams into her backpack in a futile attempt at unearthing her disappearing desk. The guy had been a veritable methane gas factory.

"I see," Trish observed with a sigh. "Well, that settles it since we both know you never fart." Trish groaned out loud, as Nessa handed her another stack of exams that wouldn't fit in her already overstuffed backpack.

"And he sucks his teeth," Nessa continued, holding out two more piles of papers toward Trish.

"Before or after he farts?" Trish asked as she juggled the packets of oversized files.

Nessa grunted. "After he eats." Dragging her backpack over into her chair, she huffed as she kneed it shut and wrestled the straining zipper.

Trish backed away from the desk with a defeated shrug. "Okay! I get the message. No more fixups. I'll just leave you to your fantasies about your nocturnal Highlander."

Nessa stopped grappling with her overstuffed backpack long enough to point her finger at Trish. "I will have you know my dreams of my ancient Scotsman have made me what I am today."

The youngest Ph.D. in Archeology at Washington University, Nessa prided herself on the position she'd attained in her field. She'd worked long and hard to get this far, untold hours of solitude, sweat, and tears. She also knew the reason she'd achieved such a lofty position. Nessa owed it all to the inexplicable dreams she'd had since the summer she turned eighteen.

She'd never forget that horrible summer or the catastrophe of her eighteenth birthday. She'd spent summer vacation mooning over the muscle-bound exchange student staying with her mother's best friend.

Nessa realized now she had grown up an insecure child. And no wonder, the way her thoughtless parents had always maligned her with constant criticism.

"Develop what little mind you've got, Nessa. As plain as you are that's all you're ever going to have." Those words had been their constant mantra for as long as she could remember.

However, her mother had noticed Nessa's infatuation with Victor and had plotted a little birthday surprise. The night of Nessa's party, Victor attended her every move. Everywhere she turned, Victor was there. Nessa was delirious. She was thrilled by his touch. She couldn't believe he really liked her. But at the end of the party, the delightful fantasy shattered when Nessa saw her mother hand Victor a check. Her mother then bestowed a pitying smile upon her and told her, "Happy birthday".

Nessa sobbed herself to sleep that night, the night she'd had the first dream. He had appeared as though in answer to her silent cry of despair, this man, this great, hulking warrior the size of a mountain. Soul-piercing eyes glimmered so green and haunting Nessa felt adrift in a sea of pines. High cheekbones, aquiline nose. She sighed. His features had struck her breathless. He had the reddish blond hair that bespoke of Viking ancestry, the strong Norse genetics forged when the marauding invaders overtook weaker villages and sowed their ancestral seeds. At eighteen years of age, Nessa didn't know much about men. But she knew enough to realize this one was pure perfection.

He'd never spoken to her, not a single time. The first time he'd appeared, he'd stood a few steps away as though he didn't wish to frighten her. His gaze had swept across her body, while the faintest of smiles had pulled at one corner of his mouth. The understanding in his eyes had pushed the loneliness from her heart. He'd reached out to her with the barest touch, brushing the back of his fingers across her arm. The trust had telegraphed like electricity across her skin. At last, she'd found someone who wouldn't humiliate her.

As she'd grown older, his repeated visits had changed and evolved into something much more. The dreams had become a subtle courting, a gentle winning of her heart. He'd found clever ways to draw her close, pursue her with a sensitive glance. Always intuitive, he appeared when she needed him. He never pushed her but never failed to respond whenever her subconscious called out. Her Highlander soothed her with his silent caress. He strengthened her with his touch.

She didn't realize her nocturnal visitor was a true Highlander by birth until one of her history classes touched upon the turbulence of Scotland. She'd always loved his unusual garb but had never placed it until one day when she'd opened to a particular chapter in her history book. His kilted plaid fit snugly about his narrow hips as though it were part of his body. His ancient claymore hung at his side as a silent warning. His hand often rested on the hilt as though he found comfort in its touch.

When he'd taken her hand and guided it over the ancient crest pinned at his shoulder, Nessa had fallen hopelessly in love with the man and all things relating to the Scot.

After that, she had been a soul possessed to find out everything she could about Scotland's past. She'd spent months trying to find the elusive crest, in the hopes of identifying her Highlander's clan. She'd found some that were close, but to her dismay, she'd never located an identical match. That's when she'd decided he was just her fantasy. At least if he was only in her head, it meant he could never leave her. Her Highlander would always be hers.

Even though she'd accepted deep in her heart her Highlander

couldn't be real, Scotland remained the first love of her life. She studied its history with relentless passion, from its bloody past to its determined people, and how it had changed the course of civilization through the ages. The only drawback of her single-minded obsession, and a rather annoying side effect of her dreams, was the fact that any male met during her waking hours didn't quite measure up against her perfect nocturnal Highlander.

Nessa blamed her continued solitude on the fact that apparently, her parents had been right all along. She must be too homely for any man to consider taking home to meet the folks. That is, any man worth having. Any man like the one in her dreams. There were plenty of them out there ready and willing to participate in messing up the sheets. If you weren't too picky and had approximately ten minutes you didn't mind donating to a total waste of time.

"Nessa! You're doing it again!" Trish dropped a stack of books on the floor.

Nessa jumped, jolted from her reverie.

"I mention dream dude and there you go, off into Nessa-land again."

Fixing Trish with a threatening glare, Nessa tucked her reading glasses into the neck of her shirt. "You drop my textbooks like that again, and I'm gonna recommend you for the Research Department! I haven't forgotten how much you just love disappearing into the archives for days—and nights—at a time."

An opened letter on the desk caught her attention and Nessa's irritation with Trish vanished. "You have to see this! Look! Are you up for an extended trip to Scotland?" Scooping up the paper, she pushed it under Trish's nose, then slung the groaning bag over her shoulder. That multi-folded piece of paper held her magic genie. Her wishes were finally granted.

Trish shook her head as she unfolded the paper. "Come on, Nessa. You know I can't afford airfare to Scotland right now. I'm still up to my eyeballs in student loans from getting my master's degree."

Scanning over the well-worn letter, Trish wrinkled her nose as she read. Pinching the page where her reading had stopped, Trish's face grew thoughtful with what she'd just digested. "Where exactly is Durness?"

Excitement bubbled inside Nessa as though she was a can of carbonated cola. All of her studying and long hours of solitude had led her to the land of her dreams. "Northwestern tip of Scotland. The Highlands. It's finally happened, Trish! I finally got the grant!"

Trish's grin spread into an excited smile as she glanced up again from farther down the page. "This is it? You finally got the grant from the University of Glasgow? This is the one you've applied for three years in a row?"

Snatching the letter out of Trish's hands, Nessa waved it in the air. "You got it, my friend. I finally got the grant. I've received the funding to go on an extended archeological study of the Durness sites and the surrounding areas of Balnakiel. All I have to do is register all of my findings with the University of Glasgow. Anything I find will be tagged by their history department for use in further studies. And since you're my assistant, your expenses are just as fully paid as mine."

"Well then, woo hoo!" Trish hooted at the top of her lungs with a jab of her fist in the air. "That's fantastic! You've been trying to get this grant forever. And Scotland...what is it you call it after you've had about half a beer? The land of your heart's desire? Hey! Maybe you'll meet the great-great-grandson of the guy in your dreams and finally have a sex life worth talking about."

Great. She could always count on Trish to put things in perspective. Nessa laughed as she folded the well-worn letter and forced it into the outside pocket of the backpack. "Tell me, Trish. Why is it you can remember things like that but you can never remember what we've named our database files? And is sex all you think about? I think you're the one who needs to find a guy worth taking to bed."

With a wicked wink, Trish patted her shapely rump before she scooped up an armload of folders off the desk. "I'm not the one who has a problem with snoring, farting, ten-minute teeth suckers taking up space between my sheets."

If you enjoyed this story, please consider leaving a review on the site where you purchased your copy, or a reader site such as Goodreads, or BookBub.

Visit my website at maevegreyson.com to sign up for my newsletter and stay up to date on new releases, sales, and all sorts of whatnot. (There are some freebies too!)

I would be nothing without my readers. You make it possible for me to do what I love. Thank you SO much!

Sending you big hugs and hoping you always have a great story to enjoy!

Maeve

ABOUT THE AUTHOR

maevegreyson.com

USA Today Bestselling Author. Multiple RONE Award Winner. Multiple Holt Medallion Finalist.

Maeve Greyson's mantra is this: No one has the power to shatter your dreams unless you give it to them.

She and her husband of over forty years traveled around the world while in the U.S. Air Force. Now they're settled in rural Kentucky where Maeve writes about her courageous Highlanders and the fearless women who tame them. When she's not plotting the perfect snare, she can be found herding cats, grandchildren, and her husband—not necessarily in that order.

ALSO BY MAEVE GREYSON

HIGHLAND HEROES SERIES

The Chieftain - Prequel

The Guardian

The Warrior

The Judge

The Dreamer

The Bard

The Ghost

A Yuletide Yearning

Love's Charity

TIME TO LOVE A HIGHLANDER SERIES

Loving Her Highland Thief

Taming Her Highland Legend

Winning Her Highland Warrior

Capturing Her Highland Keeper

Saving Her Highland Traitor

Loving Her Lonely Highlander

Delighting Her Highland Devil

ONCE UPON A SCOT SERIES

A Scot of Her Own

A Scot to Have and to Hold

A Scot to Love and Protect

HIGHLAND PROTECTOR SERIES

Sadie's Highlander

Joanna's Highlander

Katie's Highlander

HIGHLAND HEARTS SERIES

My Highland Lover

My Highland Bride

My Tempting Highlander

My Seductive Highlander

THE MACKAY CLAN

Beyond A Highland Whisper

The Highlander's Fury

A Highlander In Her Past

OTHER BOOKS BY MAEVE GREYSON

Stone Guardian

Eternity's Mark

Guardian of Midnight Manor

When the Midnight Bell Tolls

THE SISTERHOOD OF INDEPENDENT LADIES

To Steal a Duke

To Steal a Marquess

To Steal an Earl

Printed in the USA
CPSIA information can be obtained
at www.ICGtesting.com
LVHW012233250424
778511LV00030B/869